ONE
STEP
Over the
BORDER

ONE STEP

STEP

Over the

BORDER

A NOVEL

STEPHEN BLY

CENTER
STREET®

NEW YORK   BOSTON   NASHVILLE

Center Street
Hachette Book Group USA
237 Park Avenue
New York, NY 10169

Visit our Web site at www.centerstreet.com.

Center Street is a division of Hachette Book Group USA. The Center Street name and logo are trademarks of Hachette Book Group USA.

Printed in the United States of America

First Edition: June 2007
10 9 8 7 6 5 4 3 2 1

Library of Congress Cataloging-in-Publication Data

Bly, Stephen A., 1944-
    One step over the border / Stephen Bly. — 1st ed.
        p. cm.
    "The tale of a pair of contemporary cowboys on a quest across the Southwest."—Provided by the publisher.
    ISBN-13: 978-1-59995-689-3
    ISBN-10: 1-59995-689-6
    1. Cowboy—Fiction. 2. Ranch life—Fiction. 3. Southwestern States—Fiction. I. Title.

    PS3552.L93O48 2007
    813'.54—dc22   2006024770

Book design by Charles Sutherland

for
Christina Boys
who helped make a good story great

Acknowledgments

It takes a lot of folks' help to get a project like this one published . . . special thanks to my friend Chip MacGregor . . . my editor, Christina Boys . . . my agent, Frank Weimann . . . Cara Highsmith, David Palmer, Lori Quinn, and the whole staff at Hachette Book Group USA, and especially my wife, Janni-Rae, who has always been my "Juanita."

Thanks, Steve

CHAPTER ONE

Central Wyoming, Summer of 1996

The yellow dirt road that stretched before him reminded Laramie Majors of the countryside around his grandparents' place in Oklahoma. Miles beyond the blacktop sat their two-story, white clapboard house with a front porch swing and sweet tea that tasted a bit sinful if you'd just come back from church. As a kid, those trips north lined a route of escape from the tension of home and invited him to a different world. At Grandma's house, no one yelled. No one got hit. And Mamma never cried.

But the parade of gray sagebrush, dull green scrub cedars, and squatty piñon pines on the rimrock reined Laramie back to Wyoming. Yellow grime fogged after his truck like a swarm of South American ants, a creeping disease across the fenders of his silver Chevy pickup.

Dwight Purley had told him to take the shortcut through the south end of the Bighorn Mountains. But Dwight presumed Laramie knew more about Wyoming geography than he actually did. Although the blonde gal with stubby pigtails and logger's biceps at the Sinclair gas station had assured him this was the right way, he now found himself grumbling over her apparent misdirections.

He questioned again if he should have stayed on the pavement out of Casper. This endless dirt road didn't have the feel of a shortcut, and the fuel gauge had dropped near empty. He hadn't seen a ranch, a rig, or an occupied cabin for miles and didn't know which direction to walk to find gas. He considered turning back, but the drive to make it there today pushed him over the next hill. He had promised himself he would not go back to Texas a failure. It was a promise he intended to keep.

Laramie smeared the dirt off the dash and slapped the front of the fuel gauge in hopes that it was stuck, then punched off the CD player. As he crested the hill, he slowed to a stop as two dozen pronghorn antelopes ambled across the road. They turned to gawk at his rude intrusion. He stared back at their blank, clueless expressions, wondering how many times the same look plastered his own face.

The thin blue Wyoming sky unfolded to the west. Hills gave way to rolling sage and brown grass prairie. As he dropped down into a cottonwood draw, he spied a log cabin. Its battered shake roof sported a new satellite dish receiver. Thick gray smoke curled from the chimney. A girl of about ten scampered from the outhouse wearing red striped shorts, cowboy boots, and a Nike T-shirt.

She waved, then disappeared into an unpainted barn.

Laramie waved back. She was the first person he'd seen in almost an hour.

Eight miles further west he reached Highway 20. He turned north and followed the green highway signs and bright hotel billboards that lured him toward Cody. He rolled down the windows, hoping to blow out some dust. And memories.

→══ ══←

Majors parked his pickup under the only shade tree on the level street. He studied the scrap of scribbled brown paper: *Hap Bowman, 2490 Paradise Road, Cody, Wyoming.*

The home looked like a 1960s tract house, only there were no other residences. No landscaping. No parks. No sidewalks. No neighborhood improvement association. Just one dwelling in bad need of paint on stucco with fake brick walls.

The wide, empty street led to nowhere. Laramie fastened the top button on his collar and practiced a crooked smile in the dusty mirror. He knew it was time to cowboy up, to get his small talk in gear. No one discerned how tough it felt for him to meet new people.

A 1992 black Dodge truck was backed into the driveway. Behind it, on eroding blacktop, a wheelless Volkswagen van perched like a miniature diner, propped up by cinder blocks and weeds. A battered canvas awning stretched out the side. A dust devil that had spawned in the vacant lot next to the faded green house seemed reluctant to leave. Laramie watched the dirt swirl a moment as if waiting for an oracle to make a pronouncement.

An aluminum screen door hung crooked, slammed too hard, too often. A half-built front deck stretched out into sunburnt grass, its gray-bleached boards a testament to a long-abandoned building project. The black dog asleep on the porch defied pedigree, but Laramie noticed a huge pink tongue hanging out.

Once again, he studied the penciled note, then surveyed the yard. He detected no horse. No barn. No corral. No run-in shed. Not even a plastic steer head stabbed into a bale of hay. Not one sign that this guy ever practiced roping.

Laramie brushed his gritty fingers through short, curly brown hair and rubbed his clean-shaven chin. He took a deep breath and muttered, "Mr. Dwight Purley, you said I needed to meet this Hap Bowman. You said he could head rope a steer as good as anyone in Wyoming. I will trust you enough to knock on that door. But this scene better improve quick, because it isn't looking real good right now."

When Laramie reached the front step he patted the dog, but the animal showed no interest in him. Afternoon heat reflected off the walls like a radiant electric heater in winter. Laramie longed for the comfort of a glass of Grandma's sweet tea or the throat-clearing rush of an ice cold beer.

He scraped open the busted screen door, hesitating to knock on the peeling white paint of the wooden one when he heard a blast of angry Spanish words, followed by a loud crash and a yelp.

Laramie ground his teeth, then checked the note one more time: *2490.* He eyed his truck and considered a hasty retreat when a man hollered from inside, "Juanita! Put that down."

Even the dog flinched when the lid to a white porcelain commode busted out the front window, scattering glass on the unfinished deck.

The wooden door flung open. A black-mustached man

about Laramie's age sporting a black, beaver felt cowboy hat and several parallel streaks of blood across his cheek emerged.

"Ehhh . . . Hap Bowman?" Laramie stammered. "Dwight Purley sent me to ask you about . . ."

The shorter man grabbed his outstretched hand and yanked him indoors. "Man, am I glad to see you." Then he barreled outside, the door slamming behind him.

The room reeked of garlic and dirty diapers. A divan sprawled backward. A slice of pizza plastered the wall. Majors heard a roar from the yard and peered out the busted window in time to view the Dodge pickup spin out into the street and head south.

The bristles of a broom smacked Laramie's ear. The surprise, more than the impact, staggered him into the trash-covered pine coffee table. He cracked his shin and hopped around the room trying to flee his attacker.

"Who are you?" the dark-haired lady snarled. Her full lips were painted as red as her long fingernails.

"Excuse me, ma'am . . . I didn't mean to intrude . . . I just . . ."

She walloped him in the side, then jabbed his ribs with the broom handle. "Well, you did intrude. Where'd Hap go?"

Laramie hunkered behind a cluttered, mucky end table. "I wish I knew. He's the reason I stopped by. I need to talk to him."

The brown-skinned woman yanked open the gauze curtain. "It figures he'd run out on me." She spun back. "What are you staring at?" She grabbed up a jar of baby food and cocked her arm.

Laramie shielded his face. "Wait, lady. Whoever got you

angry, it's not me. I was told to come talk to a Hap Bowman who lives here."

"He doesn't live here."

"I guess that's my mistake."

"He never lived here. That's the problem."

"Then I'll be leaving. I just wanted to talk to Hap. Sorry for the inconvenience."

"Inconvenience? The jerk ruined my life. Look at me. Look at me! He turned down all of this."

A full, stained yellow T-shirt hung outside her skin-tight jeans. Bright yellow round earrings dangled even with her chin. Smeared mascara darkened her sad eyes. Slumped shoulders belied her feigned defiance.

"I'm sorry for whatever's going on here. But I never met Hap before. I have no explanation for his behavior. I'm a roper and I was told that . . ."

The pureed peaches sailed at his head. Laramie ducked. The glass jar crashed into the black iron table lamp, which tumbled to the soiled green shag carpet.

Laramie retrieved the lamp and shoved it back on the table. "I take it you don't like ropers."

"What he did to me wasn't right." When she tossed her head back, a wave rolled down the massive black curls.

Laramie scooted toward the front door. "I really need to get on down the road."

"That's what they all say." The fake yellow flowers tumbled out, but the orange pottery vase flew across the room and shattered on the wall below a Clint Eastwood movie poster.

Laramie's hand clutched the sticky brass door handle. A baby's cry wafted in from a back room.

"Don't you dare move. I want to talk to you." The

woman scooted down a carpeted hallway and into the next room.

Common sense told Laramie to run, to dive through the glass shards of the broken window if needed. But as he had hundreds of times before, he froze, unable to escape the person who confronted him.

A diaper-clad, cocoa-skinned boy with thick black hair and a round nose rode her hip when she returned. "What did you say your name was?"

"I didn't. But I'm Laramie Majors."

"I'm Juanita and this is Philippe."

"Pleased to meet you both. I presume that's Hap's little boy?"

"Why do you presume that?"

"Well, I, eh . . . sorry, I assumed you two were a couple."

"Do you think I would make love with some scrawny cowboy who treated me that bad?"

"No, I, eh . . ."

"I am not an easy woman. Is that why you are here? Were you told Juanita has no virtue?"

"No, ma'am, I guarantee that was never in my mind. I really must get . . ."

"It wasn't in your mind? Are you saying that I am unattractive?" She threw her shoulders back. "I am not ugly."

"No, ma'am . . . I just . . ."

"Many men want to make love with me. I am not hideous."

"I never implied that you were . . ."

"Do you want to make love with me?"

"Good grief, lady, I don't even know you."

Still toting the infant, she scooped up an open can of soda.

Laramie held up his hands. "Don't throw it. You don't want to mess up your house."

Her glazed eyes appraised the broken front window and the trashed living room. "Yeah, right. It wasn't always like this. But it's not your fault. I'm just mad."

"I can see that." Laramie relaxed when she set the can down.

"Something inside me just snaps when I get angry." She strolled toward him. "But I'm not mad at you."

Laramie's back mashed flat against the door. "I'm grateful for that. Now I need to . . ."

Her voice softened. "You are too skinny, but other than that you are a handsome man."

Laramie's blue shirt collar squeezed too tight. He eased open the front door behind him. "Thanks, ma'am. I hope things start going better for you."

"You must know that under these grubby clothes, I am still a beautiful, sensual Latin woman."

The loud ring yanked their attention toward the kitchen.

"You'd better get that phone, ma'am, and I'll be . . ."

"Here . . . hold Philippe." She shoved the baby into his arms and slalomed through the litter toward the telephone.

Round, brown eyes ogled up at Laramie as he tried to maneuver the six-month-old with a mushy plastic diaper into a comfortable position. He hadn't held a baby more than twice in his life—his cousin's boy, Ronald, at his dedication, and his fourth-grade teacher's one-week-old baby girl when she brought her to school. Panic growled at his stomach.

He rocked Phillipe back and forth. Sweat dribbled down

the back of his neck as Spanish threats boomed from the back room.

"Lady, I have to go," he called. "Come get your baby."

"*Un momento,*" she yelled.

The baby grabbed his ear. Laramie shoved his hand away.

Philippe wailed.

"Now, now . . . shhhh. Everything's okay. You're being raised in the most dysfunctional home in Wyoming, but everything's okay. I know how you feel, little pal . . . I've been there, too, but crying never changed anything."

The baby continued to sob as Laramie hushed him.

There was a hollered, "*¿Viene aquí? ¿Ahora?*" Then silence.

"Juanita, I have to go. Come get your baby. Philippe needs you," Laramie called out.

No reply.

"Juanita?"

Philippe began another round of wails.

"I suppose you want your diaper changed. That's not my department, son. In fact, you've already experienced all of my child-care skills." Laramie hiked toward the kitchen. "Juanita?"

The wooden counter around the sink and the square table were piled with food-hardened dishes. Two metal folding chairs with *Property of Park County Social Club* stenciled on the back completed the furnishings. Next to the open door of an avocado-green refrigerator, a beige wall phone swung back and forth on a long cord that at one time had spiraled.

Laramie paused at the doorway next to the phone and could hear someone still on the line, shouting in Spanish.

In the laundry room, there were dirty clothes piled on the floor and on top of the avocado-green clothes dryer. The back door and screen door swung open in the slight breeze.

A large horsefly buzzed into the pantry as Laramie inventoried the backyard. Brown weeds bunched around an abandoned chain saw. A trackless snowmobile lay on its side next to a dried garland of once-fresh flowers. A faded blue silk banner read: *Congratulations.*

"Juanita?" At the sound of his voice, the baby cried again.

"Shhh . . . just hang in there, little partner. If I wasn't twenty-one, I'd be bawling, too. Your mamma will be right back."

Laramie wandered across the backyard, baby riding his arm. Dry grass crinkled under his boots. He poked his head in the open door of a portable storage shed. "Juanita?" In the shadows of the shed, he spied a heavily chromed and polished Harley-Davidson motorcycle. "Baby, does your mamma ride a Harley?"

Untilled, bare ground stretched for a half-mile behind the house. Laramie circled the entire dwelling but found no one. "Philippe, where did she go?"

Laramie hiked back through the laundry room and kitchen to the living room. The short hallway led to three small bedrooms. In one squatted an unmade, cluttered waterbed. U-Haul cardboard boxes crammed a second room. A window in the third had been darkened with foil and duct tape. Under it was a crib. Beneath the crib, a toy-lined floor.

"Juanita?"

He rapped on the only remaining closed door with his free hand. "Juanita, are you in there?"

He tried the cold aluminum door handle. It wouldn't budge.

He banged again, this time with force. "Juanita!"

The baby wailed.

Majors heard the front door slam and hurried out into the hall. He paused before a hulking, bushy-bearded, tattooed man in black jeans and sleeveless blue denim shirt who tilted the couch back to its rightful position.

"Who are you?" the man roared.

Laramie edged toward the front door. The rancid air of the room now reeked of fresh grease and old sweat. "This is all a big mistake."

The man whipped out a switchblade knife and flipped it open. "Where's Juanita?"

"She, eh, shoved the baby in my hands and took off toward the back of the house. Maybe she's in the bathroom. I'll sit your baby here in this chair and be on my way."

"You ain't goin' nowhere until my Juanita clears this up."

"Look, mister, I never met your wife before today. I just . . ."

"I didn't say she was my wife." The man stalked closer. "You just stopped by to do what to her?"

"I needed to talk to a guy, not Juanita. I was told he was here. But I think I . . . eh, just missed him, and then . . ."

"What guy? Who's been hanging around here?" The big man jabbed the knife in the air. "What was his name?"

"Eh . . . his name . . . I think it was Ha . . . Hamilton. I don't know his full name. A mutual friend mentioned that I should . . ."

"What mutual friend?" the big man growled.

"Dwight . . . eh . . . Dwight Eisenhower," Laramie blurted out.

"Does he work for the road department?"

"No, but I think he did have something to do with the interstate."

"Never heard of him." The man scraped the piece of pizza off the wall with his knife.

"Look, here's what happened. I asked her about, eh, Hamilton, then the telephone rang. Juanita shoved the baby at me, went to answer the phone, and never came back. That's all I know."

"Juanita!" the bearded man bellowed. "Get in here."

"Maybe the phone call was from a neighbor. An emergency of some sort."

"It's a mile to a neighbor's house and they threatened to shoot us if we ever showed up on their property again." The man gazed out the broken window toward the street. "Was the call in English or Spanish?"

"Spanish." Laramie thought about closing his eyes to make the whole scene disappear. But that had never worked when he was a kid and he knew it wouldn't work now.

The man exploded like a jack-in-the-box. "I'm not going to put up with this anymore." He stomped down the hall, then waved his knife at Laramie. "Get down here."

"Why?"

"Because I want to see what's going on in the bathroom. If you even so much as touched her, I'll kill you."

Laramie toted Philippe to the hall.

The big man beat on the door. "Juanita, open up right now."

Laramie figured he could outrun him, provided he didn't have a gun or throw that knife. But he froze again, this time out of fear.

"Did he hurt you, Juanita *mía*?" He jammed the point of the switchblade into the door handle and twisted it. The white door popped open.

Majors spun for the living room when the man disappeared into the bathroom. The scream "Nooooooooooo!" would have rattled windows, if there had been any left. Laramie propped Philippe on the sofa. "Sorry, little man . . ."

"I'll kill you!" The man lumbered down the hall.

Laramie banged open the screen door and hurled himself off the deck.

"Hey," someone to his right called out. "Do you know how to use one of these?"

Hap Bowman stood like a sentry at ease in foot-tall weeds in the front yard. Amazed at the man's calm demeanor, Laramie reached out his hand as Hap tossed him a coiled nylon rope. The big man roared out of the house. The dog on the porch let out a solitary "woof" without raising his head.

As the wild man stormed down the wooden stairs, Hap's rope looped his arms. When he yanked back, the man flew off his feet onto his back. At that moment, Laramie's rope circled the man's legs. Amidst screams about parentage and curses meant to last for generations, the man flailed in tall dead grass and weeds.

Laramie heard a crack, like a bat hitting a baseball. The man collapsed.

"Did he just knock himself out?" Hap asked.

After wading through weeds and trash where the man lay, Laramie scratched the back of his neck. "I think he hit his head on a bowling ball."

Hap meandered over to him. They gawked down at the unconscious man. "That was mighty thoughtful of him, because I didn't know what to do next."

"I'm grateful that you showed up, Bowman, but you were about an hour late. What's going on here? Dwight Purley told me I needed to talk to you about roping together. He said you were cowboy from boot to hat. Then you run out the door and leave me in a situation straight out of the *Jerry Springer Show*."

Hap squatted beside the big man and examined the lump on his head. "It's a long story. I didn't know you were aimin' to stick around and visit with Juanita. I figured you were right behind me, comin' out the door. I waited down at the stop sign, but you never showed. I was beginnin' to think I had the wrong guy. I called Dwight. When he mentioned you bein' tall, skinny, and a tad shy, I figured I'd better come pull you out. Who is this guy, anyway?"

"You don't know him?" Laramie asked.

"Nope. Never seen him."

"He claims to live here. I think he's the father of that baby."

"So, he's the one."

"The baby," Laramie groaned. "I dumped him on the divan when I ran for my life."

Laramie and Hap jogged back to the house. The black dog on the porch opened one eye, then closed it quick.

Philippe stood on the couch chewing a dry, yellow celery stick.

"Where the heck is Juanita?" Hap asked.

"I don't know. She left me holding the baby."

"What do we do now?"

"You check out the bathroom."

"Why?"

Laramie plucked Philippe off the couch. "Because the old boy in the yard spotted something in the bathroom that made him decide to kill me. If you find a body in there, I don't want to know about it."

Hap stepped over a spilled tray of cat litter. "Where's the bathroom?"

Laramie waved at the hall. "You don't know your way around this house?"

"This was the first time I've ever been here."

"You aren't going with this Juanita?"

"We've been talkin' on the phone for three months, but this is the first time we met."

"You made a great first impression. The bathroom is the first door to the left." Laramie bounced the baby and snatched a look out the busted window. "Hurry up. That self-inflicted bowling ball wound won't keep him down forever."

Hap wandered back with two sheets of paper. "She taped a Dear John letter to the toilet seat lid, which seems rather appropriate."

Laramie surveyed the room. "She was leaving all this?"

"It says she's splittin' with a dark, handsome cowboy."

"Who?"

Hap shrugged. "Me, I reckon. That's why she went crazy. I told her there was no way I was takin' her and the baby with me."

Laramie continued to shake his head as he gaped at

the room. "That explains it. A scorned woman." Philippe swatted him in the ear with the dried celery.

"She deceived me, man. During all those phone calls, she neglected to mention that she lived with a guy, had a kid, and had gained umpteen pounds since the picture she mailed me. Worst of all, she lied about having a birthmark in the shape of a horse's head under her right ear."

"What's a birthmark got to do with anything?"

"I told you, it's a long story."

"Hey, is he dead?" The voice from the front yard was female, curious, but not panicked. They found Juanita crouched over the unconscious man. "Did you kill him?"

"Where have you been?" Laramie marched out to the woman and shoved the baby at her.

She straddled Philippe on her hip. "When I heard Francis was on his way home, I knew I had to get out of the house. If he found you here, he would beat on me and the baby again."

"What about me?" Laramie asked. "Weren't you concerned that he would carve me up?"

"Why should I be? I don't even know you." She turned and purred at Hap. "Honey, did you come back for me?"

"I came back for Laramie, my new ropin' partner."

"Well, you're stuck with me now, too," she said. "I'm going with you. When Francis wakes up, he'll kill me, now that you did this to him."

Hap held up his hand. "I told you, I'm not taking you with me. I came up here for a chat. That's all I promised and you know it. We agreed to a 'no strings' visit."

"Do you call ten minutes a visit?"

"A short visit. That's all we needed."

"If you didn't plan on staying longer," she whined, "why did you give this guy my address?"

"Optimistic speculation."

"I'm not staying here. Give me and the baby a ride to my parents," she demanded. "You owe me that much."

"Where do they live?" Laramie asked.

"Greybull."

"Get your stuff, quick, and change the baby's diaper. We'll give you a ride," Laramie offered.

Juanita scampered toward the house toting a celery-wielding Philippe.

"Why did you promise that?" Hap said.

"She has to get out of this situation. That guy's crazy."

"But she chose the situation herself."

"And we complicated it. The least we can do is to get her to her folks."

"Then she's ridin' with you," Hap insisted. "She had this romantic notion that I was comin' up here to rescue her and the baby, then live happily ever after. I don't want her in my truck. No tellin' what she'll do."

"Okay, she rides with me. But we caravan over to Greybull together. Right, partner?"

"Yeah, but we need the ropes. You think he'll stay unconscious?"

While Hap untied Francis, Laramie found the switchblade knife.

"You think that's the only weapon he's packin'?" Hap asked.

"No, but I don't intend to search him." Laramie eyed the front door. "I wish she'd hurry up. Go in there and nudge her along."

Hap threw up his hands. "Not me, partner. I ain't goin'

in that house ever again. And for sure and certain, I won't do any nudgin' with her."

"But she's your Juanita."

"That's the point. She's not my Juanita."

"Get both trucks running," Laramie said. "I'll see what I can tote."

Juanita held the baby wearing a clean diaper, boots, and a T-shirt. Laramie carted a cardboard box and two brown grocery sacks crammed with clothes.

The black dog raised up on his front paws and howled.

As they bolted to the trucks, Francis propped up on his elbow. "Where do you think you're going?" He reached for his black boot and brandished a hunting knife with a ten-inch blade.

"To a better place than you." Hap hefted the sixteen-pound ebony bowling ball with the number 135 engraved next to the holes. He bombed Francis's upraised forehead.

"Did you kill him?" Juanita asked.

"I don't reckon I killed him." Hap trotted to the trucks.

"It's all right with me if you did," she called out.

Hap hopped behind the steering wheel of the black Dodge. With the door still open, he shouted, "Well, it ain't all right with me."

The fifty-mile ride to Greybull took less than an hour.

Philippe slept in his mother's arms as Juanita stared out the window at bleak prairie and irrigated farmland. Laramie gripped the steering wheel tight and focused on the broken yellow line of Highway 14.

The hum of the tires on the asphalt dulled his mind. The air in the cab of the truck pulsed with strong garlic. He rolled down the window. Juanita seemed to slump lower in the seat every mile they traveled.

Laramie mulled over how Juanita might have gotten herself into such a fix. He found it hard to believe that Francis was her best available choice. But then, he had often thought the same thing about his mother.

Litter and dust swirled as they pulled into, then through, Greybull. The Bighorn Mountains towering to the east provided a Wyoming landscape, but the rundown stores and abandoned cars reminded Laramie of many of the dozen or so Texas towns where he grew up. He couldn't help studying every bar they passed, expecting his dad to emerge. When he was young, he had teased his mother about writing a book on the front-door architecture of bars, saloons, and honky-tonks.

He leaned toward the window and gulped the dry summer air.

Juanita pointed to the railroad tracks. "Pull in there."

Laramie found himself cruising through an old abandoned brickyard and following a winding dirt road through the sage. He slowed to a crawl in the foot-deep ruts, glancing at the sleeping baby each time. Gravel gave way to dirt, then two parallel paths in the weeds. Hap's dusty, black Dodge bounced along behind them.

A fortress of top-burnt cottonwood trees shielded three old singlewide trailer houses that curved in a U-shape. Several kids played soccer in the hard-packed dirt yard.

"Are these all your relatives?" Laramie asked.

"Three of them are my brothers. Two are my sister's kids. I can never remember who the other one is."

Laramie parked his truck in the shade next to an International pickup with no hood or engine. "How many live out here?"

"Mamma says there's fifteen now. But it changes all the time."

Hap parked his rig next to Laramie's, then lounged against the front of his truck.

Laramie grabbed the box and sacks of clothes. "Where do you want these?"

Juanita pointed at the center trailer. "On the porch by the blue one."

A small, gray-haired Mexican lady draped in an old, long dress stalked out onto the porch and began to yell in Spanish.

"Who is that?" Laramie called out above the diatribe.

"My mother."

"What is she saying?"

"She's happy that I came home."

The screaming intensified as they neared the blue trailer. Juanita said nothing. When Laramie shoved the box and sacks on the porch, the woman leaned over and spat into each of them, then stormed into the house.

"What was that all about?" Hap called out from his position next to the trucks.

"She's stating the rules," Juanita announced.

"Spitting is part of the rules?" Laramie asked.

"That was for emphasis."

Laramie's voice lowered. "Are you going to be all right?"

Juanita twisted around. She let out a big sigh and shifted the baby to her other hip. "Now do you see why I wanted so bad to go with Hap? But I am better off here than in

Cody when Francis wakes up. I would rather be hit with my mother's words than his fists."

"Take care of that baby. Philippe and I are pals, now," Laramie said.

She glanced down at her grubby tennis shoes. "Are you sure you don't want me to live with you?"

"I'm not the one you need. You can do a whole lot better than me."

Four scrawny white chickens clucked and pecked their way across the yard.

"That's a nice way of saying 'no.'"

"Look after yourself and your baby. Find a job. You'll get some breaks. You were right, Juanita; beneath all that gloom and self-pity, you're a pretty lady."

The two cowboys drove back into Greybull. Hap pulled up in front of the Sportsman Bar & Grill. Laramie parked behind him. Hap wandered back to his truck. "Did you ever eat at Frank's Last Chance Steak House?"

Laramie studied the buildings along the street and watched the doors of each bar. "Nope. Where's it at?"

"About fifteen miles on down Highway 14 toward the Bighorns. Leave your truck and ride with me. I'll fill you in on the deal with Juanita."

Laramie slid out and locked the door. "You think it's okay to leave my truck parked here?"

"Hey, this is Wyoming. You could leave it until February and no one would notice. How long have you known Dwight?"

Laramie flopped down on the passenger's side. "About

two years. I met him at a clinic in Amarillo and worked for him all winter. How about you?"

"I was fifteen when he decided to teach me to rope." Hap eased onto the highway headed east.

Laramie rubbed the back of his neck. "Dwight's a great teacher. He pushes you to the point that . . ."

Hap tapped on the steering wheel. "You almost want to bust his crooked nose . . . but then it . . ."

". . . dawns on you that he's right, and almost in spite of yourself . . ." Laramie boomed.

". . . he's made you a better roper." Hap glanced at Laramie in the rearview mirror. "Geez, we ain't known each other for two hours and we're finishin' each other's sentences."

"I've never known anyone better at sizing up a man than Dwight. That's why I drove up here. If he says we should rope together, it's futile to argue."

"Did Dwight ever take you to the jackpot ropin' in Chugwater?"

"That's the first place we roped together," Laramie said. "He headed; I heeled. We won the money that night and I never argued about his teaching tactics after that."

"No foolin'? Same thing happened to me. I reckon we didn't go over there until I was about sixteen. I headed, and Dwight heeled. I've forgotten a lot of ropin' since then. But I remember that night. We won the average with two 8.2 times."

"This is uncanny," Laramie added. "Dwight and I had two 8.2 times."

"Are you kiddin' me? Maybe Dwight's right. Maybe we are supposed to rope together."

"How much did you and Dwight make that night?"

"My share was $155. I thought I was rollin' in big money. Don't tell me that's what you and Dwight made."

"Nope. We made $475 each."

Hap pushed his hat back. "I'm glad to hear that. This was gettin' weird."

"I went out and bought a video camera so I could analyze my roping. Do you remember what you spent that purse on?"

"Yeah. On a date."

"A $155 date when you were sixteen?"

"It was high school prom night. I rented a limo and ever'thin'."

"She must have been quite a girl."

"I'm sure she was. I just don't remember her very well. She was an exchange student. But she was cute. And I remember her name."

"You remember her name?"

"It was Juanita. They are all named Juanita."

Laramie leaned back and folded his arms. "What is this thing about you and girls named Juanita?"

The walls of the steak house displayed a wide collection of stuffed mounts, racks and heads of most every game animal in Wyoming, plus a few from other continents. The tablecloths were linen, the dishware sturdy, and the floors polished hardwood. With the massive grill in the center of the room, smoke swirled with scents of hot red meat and sweet sauces.

The cowboys finished their medium-rare ribeye steaks and thick-sliced fries, then dissected cherry cheesecake as Hap finished the story about his fascination for girls named Juanita. "I reckon that all seems a tad strange," he offered.

"No, not at all."

"Really?"

"It's not a little strange; it's a big, totally bizarre strange," Laramie chided.

"That's nice. I'm glad you understand so well."

"I don't understand. There's got to be more to it."

"Yeah . . ." Hap pushed his hat back and rubbed his temples. "I suppose there's somethin' that keeps pushin' me. Mamma used to say it's because I'm the middle of five boys. Brad can ride the wild broncs. Terry Wayne's a natural-born farmer. Kenny quarterbacked the football team, an all-around athlete. My youngest brother, Jeb, is a computer whiz at age fourteen."

"So, your distinction is this Juanita obsession?"

"It's an ice-breaker. Most people laugh when they hear about it."

"You do plan to give it up some day, don't you?"

"I ain't goin' to be chasin' Juanitas when I'm thirty, if that's what you mean."

"I guess my only real question is, how does this Juanita obsession of yours affect us roping together?" Laramie pressed.

"Just don't set me up with some buckle bunny that ain't named Juanita. And if we pull into a café with a waitress named Juanita, you got to back off and let me talk things up a while. Other than that, ain't much to it."

"Are we thinking about going down the road this week, this month, or when?" Laramie asked.

"You got some funds set aside?"

"A few hundred. And you?"

Hap stabbed his cherry cheesecake. "I got some. I had thought about workin' for old Tom Beall over in Nevada for a couple months, then crackin' out. But that was before I figured on sharin' expenses. We could go down to Dwight's and work his steers for a week or so, just to see how we rope together."

"Look, Hap, I need to tell you I'm sort of a quiet person. I mean . . . don't expect me to liven up a party or stay up late every night. On more than one occasion, I've been called downright boring. But I like to think of it as being peaceful. I like things quiet and simple."

"Hey, that's exactly the way I like it. Just rope, work a few cows, tell lies with some friends, and enjoy the countryside. Nothin' showy. Nothin' wild. Shoot, I spend a lot of nights just waitin' for the moon to come up." Hap motioned to the waitress. "Say, darlin', could you fill our coffee cups again?"

The waitress, in black jeans and white shirt, swung around by their table with a steaming glass coffee pot. As she swooped down for a quick refill, the spout crashed into the rim of Laramie's cup, tipping it toward him. He sat transfixed as the boiling-hot coffee flooded across the glass tabletop and plunged over the edge into the crotch of his jeans.

"Geeez!" He sprang up and staggered back. His oak captain's chair sprawled across the wooden floor, just as a large lady in green flowered Bermuda shorts stood to leave.

The sliding chair rammed into the back of her bare knees. She tumbled forward onto a table that had not been cleared. A table leg weakened from years of service gave way. The other three legs dominoed with a scream and crash.

Three Japanese men at a table next to her leaped up to help, spilling their drinks and knocking over the candle. The green linen tablecloth flamed as the men staggered back. Thick smoke billowed from plastic flowers now consumed with the blaze.

A cook with a tall white hat propped on his head sprinted out of the kitchen with a fire extinguisher. One quick blast of white foam put out the fire, but the foam kept spraying.

"It won't shut off," the cook yelled as he foamed the Asian tourists.

He kicked open the doors and sprayed his way into the parking lot. A black Labrador, foamed from head to tail, snarled his way into the restaurant, crashing into chairs and tables as he tried to paw the fire retardant out of his eyes.

A lady in sweat pants, who looked about ten months pregnant, crawled up on her chair screaming, "Keep the mad dog away!"

Just then, an old man, with two weeks of white beard, staggered into the dining room from the bar next door. He stared at the screaming woman, pulled up a chair, then shouted, "Oh, good, it's karaoke night."

The original waitress, still standing next to the cowboy's table with coffee pot in hand, grumbled, "Crap . . . I didn't need this."

She glanced down at Hap, the bite of cheesecake still suspended on his fork. "I think I'll pass on that refill, darlin'."

Thirty minutes later, after some order was restored in the restaurant, Laramie and Hap strolled out to the parking lot. Neither said anything until they were back on Highway 14 headed west toward Greybull.

"Does that happen to you often?" Laramie asked. "I'd like to know what I'm signing up for."

"Me? You were the one who jumped up when the coffee hit your Wranglers."

"It was a self-preservation, reflex reaction."

"I don't reckon we'll soon forget it." Hap tugged on his black hat and chewed on a wooden toothpick. "It could have been worse."

Laramie looked over at him. "How in the world could it have been worse?"

"The building could have burned down and that pregnant lady could have gone into labor."

"Well, that was enough excitement for me."

"You got plans where to stay tonight?" Hap asked.

"Hadn't thought about it yet."

"I got an aunt and uncle in Worland. We can bunk with them."

Laramie pushed his hat back. "Are they boring? I would like very much to stay someplace boring."

"Uncle Ralph will talk about his hay crop and whether they had enough moisture. Aunt Shelley may entertain us with some excitin' stories from quiltin' camp."

"Sounds like my kind of people."

Hap tromped on the accelerator and pulled around a

slow-moving cattle truck. "We'll pick up your truck, then head south on Highway 20."

◆━▷ ◁━◆

Laramie stomped around his pickup in the dim streetlight of Greybull, Wyoming. "Look at this! Oh, sure, leave your rig here on the street, you said. Nothing will happen to it. That's what you told me."

Hap pulled off his hat and tousled his black hair. "I reckon it's the first time I've ever seen all four tires slashed."

"Have you noticed that ever since I met you, my life has been out of control!?" Laramie hollered.

"You blamin' this on me?"

Laramie flailed his hands. "I'm just saying, I don't know if I'll be able to live through this partnership. There goes the money I've saved up. Wyoming is a disaster."

"I reckon we can bunk in Greybull tonight. Can't get you new tires until mornin'."

"And leave my truck on the street, looking like some war zone casualty?"

"If you squint your eyes, it kind of has that lowrider effect. It ain't that bad. Just four tires. What happened to the easygoin' . . . kick back . . . stay out of the conflict Laramie?"

"No one should be allowed to abuse women, kids . . . or trucks."

A thin, ponytailed girl wearing a black *Eat Dirt & Die* T-shirt rode up on her bicycle. "Is that your truck?"

"Yeah . . ." Laramie mumbled.

"I saw who did it."

"Who?"

"A big guy on a motorcycle."

Laramie clenched his teeth. "I knew it! There was a Harley in that shed at Juanita's house. Good old Francis must have followed us. He's not going to get away with this. It's payback time."

"Wait a minute, partner. We don't know it was him."

Laramie turned to the girl. "Did he have on a sleeveless denim shirt, with a tattoo on his right arm like a crown of thorns?"

"Yeah, do you know him?" she replied.

Laramie reached down and fingered a slit in his tire. "Not as well as I will."

"He called you some names," she added. "Do you want to hear them?"

"No, thanks. Can't be near as many names as I'm going to call him."

"Cool! Can I listen to you call him names? Maybe I'll learn some new ones."

"Go home, darlin'. It's late." Hap ushered the girl down the sidewalk.

Laramie stomped back to Hap's truck. "Come on."

Hap paused. "I know I'll regret askin' this, but where are we goin'?"

"To 2490 Paradise Road, Cody."

"What do you aim to do?"

"I don't know, but I'll think of it by the time we get there."

Hap slid behind the wheel. "Laramie, you got to think this through. Vengeance ain't a purdy thing."

"No vengeance. But he will get what he deserves. This has to end right now."

"You goin' to shoot him?"

"No."

"Then it might be time to ride away."

"It's not your truck that's sliced up. Why did this happen to me? She was your Juanita."

"I told you she ain't mine. Never was. But I say you need to walk away from it right now. You go over and do somethin' to his bike, or his house, and then he'll come look you up and do somethin' worse than slashin' tires. Back and forth it will go, gettin' worse ever' time, until finally one of you kills the other. So why not just get it over and shoot him now? Either that, or walk away from it. Those are your only two choices."

"Hap, I'm not going to shoot him, but I am going to challenge him. He can't get away with this."

"Don't you think we ought to wait until mornin'?"

"No."

Hap flipped a U and drove out of town. "What if he isn't over there in Cody? What if he's here at Juanita's folks' place lookin' for her? He could have sliced up the entire family."

"That's a happy thought. Go over to her folks' place."

"What if he's there?"

"I'll call him out."

"Now, partner, I ain't questionin' your heart, nor your ability. But he's a big, strong rounder."

"Yeah, but I'm on the side of right."

"That's what Travis and Bowie said at the Alamo."

"If you aren't up to it, let me borrow your truck."

"Oh, no, I'm stickin' with my truck," Hap insisted.

About 11:00 P.M., they pulled through the old brickyard and bounced along the dirt road toward the grove of cottonwoods. No lights shone from the three singlewide trailers.

"You aim to go up and knock on each door?" Hap asked.

"I thought maybe I'd look around for the motorcycle. If it's not here, there's no reason to disturb anyone."

"You need help? Or do you want me to wait in the truck with the engine runnin'?"

"You can help me look," Laramie said. "After all, you are my new partner."

"I was afraid you'd say that."

Cool air drifted from the west as they parked back in the trees. Laramie and Hap meandered toward the mobile homes.

"Do you see a Harley?" Laramie whispered.

"I see an old abandoned 1949 Studebaker, a John Deere two-cylinder tractor without wheels, an Albertson's grocery cart, but no motorcycle. Of course, I know a guy in Sheridan who keeps his motorcycle in his living room. He rolls it into the house ever' night."

"You saying I need to wake everyone up?"

Hap pointed toward the middle trailer. "You don't need to wake up Mamma. She's on the porch with a shotgun."

In the shadows, Laramie spotted the woman's small frame. She looked like a defiant hen standing against the wolves. "Ma'am, we're not burglars," he called out. "We were with Juanita this afternoon. I just need to ask you a couple questions."

"You get two questions, then I pull the trigger."

"Is Francis, the father of Juanita's baby, here at your place?" Laramie asked.

"No."

"Did he come over lookin' for Juanita?" Hap blurted out.

"Yes."

"Did she go with him?" Laramie asked.

They heard her pump a shell into the chamber.

"Wait a minute, ma'am . . ." Hap called out. "We thought you meant two questions each."

"After I chased him off, she took the baby and my pickup and left. I have no idea where she went. If you find her, tell her I want my truck back."

Laramie and Hap trudged back to the idling pickup.

"She got scared and ran to some other safe place," Hap suggested.

"If he was smart, he'd wait at the end of the drive and follow her."

"That's a scary scene. It makes you not want to read the paper in the mornin'. Where are we goin' now?"

"To Cody," Laramie replied.

"Do you ever call it a day and go to sleep?"

"Not until the work's done. Too many times I've backed down just to keep the peace. 'Don't make it worse,' Mamma would say. But it got worse even when I did nothing. Well, no more. This isn't right and I won't retreat."

Little was said on the return trip to Cody. The silence broken only after they circled Juanita's house.

"No one's at home except the pooch on the porch," Hap reported. "And the Harley's gone."

They slipped through the night shadows back to the pickup.

Hap opened the driver's side door. "Do you reckon he's out chasin' her down somewhere?"

"What worries me is that we're going to hear of her murder in the morning. I don't know if I can live with that."

Hap leaned up against the door. "There ain't nothin' we can do. She has to file a complaint against him. What's the plan now?"

"We wait for him."

"You think he'll be back?"

"It's his house."

"Without Juanita and the baby, what is there to come home to?" Hap insisted.

"Then there's nothing for us to worry about."

"I ain't leavin' my truck here. We need one rig with tires. Let's park near the trailer park out at the highway. We can hike back down here." Hap flipped a U in the wide, treeless street and drove north.

"This is a long way to run if we need a quick exit," Laramie said.

"Why will we need to run? You're plannin' on whippin' him, ain't you? If you intend to lose the fight, let me know right now, so I can call an ambulance on standby."

"I don't know what will happen," Laramie admitted.

"On the other hand, if you'd like to just keep on goin', I can head this rig to Greybull or Worland right now."

Laramie motioned toward yard lights. "Pull in next to the blue one with tires on the roof."

After jerking the keys, Hap fumbled around behind the seat. "I expect we'll need a couple ropes."

"I'm not using ropes or a bowling ball this time."

"Well, in that case . . ." Hap yanked out a lever-action carbine. "Think I'll tote my .30-30."

Laramie and Hap prowled south along the street without lights. The breeze from the west hovered between mild and cool.

"What do you plan on doing with the gun?" Laramie asked.

"I'm goin' to try to keep him from killin' you."

"I appreciate that."

"And if that's not a possibility, I can at least put you out of your misery quick."

"That's a real comfort to know."

When they reached the darkened house, they tramped over to the VW perched on cinder blocks. They sat on the cracked, but still warm, asphalt and leaned against an abandoned chest freezer with the door removed. Both men kept their eyes on the street.

"You got a girlfriend, Laramie? I told you about my search for Juanita. What about you?"

"There was a gal at college last year. I thought maybe she was the one."

"You went to college?"

Laramie rubbed on his clenched fist. "Junior college. I was an agriculture major. I thought about going on, but just couldn't get motivated."

"What was her name?"

"Shelby. She's one of those types that's so dadgum beautiful, you're embarrassed to talk to her. But she started talking to me after class . . . then one thing led to another and . . ."

"Wait, wait, wait . . ." Hap interrupted. "We might have a very long night here. There's no reason to skip over one thing leadin' to another. What was the one thing and what did it lead to? Fill in the details, partner."

"We got chummy."

"How chummy?"

"Real chummy," Laramie said.

"Oh, well, that makes a difference. Real chummy as opposed to slightly chummy . . . or unreal chummy."

"The point is, I thought she was the one. Since she majored in elementary education, I even considered ag education."

"And Mr. and Mrs. School Teacher would live happily ever after?"

"Something like that. We had a great time over Thanksgiving and for the next couple of weeks. Then she went home to Baltimore for Christmas break."

"She was from the East Coast? Was she sort of snotty in a good sense with a little upturned nose and bangs that jiggle in time with . . . with the rest of her parts that jiggle?"

"Yeah . . . why did you say that?"

"That's the way all the college girls from the East look," Hap said. "What happened over Christmas break?"

"She didn't come back for spring term. After a week of shock and wonder, I went over to her old dorm and asked around. No one would talk to me."

"Was she pregnant?"

"We weren't that chummy. A friend's roommate worked maintenance at her dorm. He brought me the news that Shelby had gotten married on Christmas Eve."

"She dumped you and married another guy?"

"It seems she was engaged all fall. From what I finally found out, she was worried that maybe she had been in a hurry to get married. She dated me just to make sure she had made the right choice."

Hap whistled. "You kiddin' me?" He plucked up a piece of gravel and chucked it against the VW bus. "I've dated a Juanita or two just like that."

"That's when I decided college wasn't for me. So, to answer your question, no I don't have a girl . . . and I guess I'm not looking too hard for one right now. At least, nothing complicated."

Clouds stacked up against the Bighorn Mountains and blocked the stars in the eastern side of the night sky. Hap rubbed out a cramp in his thigh. He looped his hat over his knee and leaned his head back against the empty freezer. "Laramie, I started this day in Lander. New cologne and a clean shirt. This was going to be huge. Court Juanita . . . find happiness . . . settle down. Now look at me. Sittin' in the dark with a carbine on my lap. Seems I took a wrong turn sometime today and I can't go back."

Laramie watched the dark clouds roll over the stars. When he rubbed his shirt-covered arm, he could feel goosebumps. "You notice that's the way life is? You never get to go back."

"Well, if I could do it over, I'd never have come to Cody. Shoot, I don't think I would have dated that Juanita from Colorado, neither. I learned to stay away from girls more obsessive than I am. If I could go back, I'd spend more time with my dad. He died when I was thirteen. A massive heart attack at forty-two years old. That's way too young. I always figured he had a lot to teach me and we just never got around to it. Kinda sad, ain't it? How about you? If you had a chance to go back . . . where would it be?"

"Are you getting philosophical on me?"

"Just tryin' to stay awake. Don't you have a time you'd like to go back to?"

"New Year's Day, 1985."

"Now, that's specific. What about it?"

"I'd have clobbered my old man with a baseball bat, instead of letting him take it away from me."

Hap traced his finger along the cold, hard walnut carbine buttstock. "Did he get mean when he was drunk?"

Laramie waved his arm to the east. "Did you see that lightning over in the Bighorns?"

"You need to change the subject?" Hap pressed.

When Laramie closed his eyes, he saw the streaks of blood mixed with tears on his mother's face. "Yeah, I'm changing the subject. At least for now. Maybe someday, Hap. Is that fair enough?"

"Partner, I'll listen to anything you want to tell me. But I won't hound you."

"And I'll do the same for you." Laramie cleared his throat. "Do we have a storm headed this way?"

"Looks like it. You should have worn your hat," Hap said.

"I never wear a hat. Except in the arena and that's because they make me."

"You're a cowboy, but you don't wear a hat? What's the deal?"

"Some guys can wear a hat; some can't. I look funny in a hat."

"Who told you that?"

"Molli Peters, when I was twelve."

"Do you mean to tell me what some girl said when you were twelve still controls your life?"

"How old were you when you started looking for your Juanita?" Laramie quizzed.

"Twelve, but it's completely different."

"Oh?"

"Look, that night after I met her, when I was twelve, I prayed. I said, 'Lord, I'm never goin' to ask you for another thing as long as I live. I just want to marry my Juanita someday when I grow up.'"

"So prayer makes your situation different?"

"It's in the Lord's hands."

"Yeah, I guess," Laramie murmured.

Hap raised the carbine and pointed it at the brightest star. "You do believe in God, don't you?"

"I suppose most everyone does. But that doesn't mean I understand his ways."

"What are you thinkin' of?" Hap asked.

"Philippe."

"Juanita's baby?"

"Yeah, Juanita and good old Francis. That little guy hardly has a chance in life. What kind of world is this that he's growin' up in? He's got violence and filth and constant tension. How can he make it?"

"You blame God for that?" Hap asked.

"Not exactly, but I truly don't understand. I have a sister, Diana. She's about three years older. She married Barry right out of high school. He got into computers and made so much money they can't find enough ways of spending it."

"That's a nice problem."

"They've got a big house near Seattle. Diana doesn't need to work. So all she wants is to have kids."

"But they can't?"

Laramie sighed. "Nope. It's not Barry; it's her. She can't bear children. My sis is a saint. She's the sweetest, kindest, smartest lady I know. If I ever find one like my sis, I'll marry her. But for the life of me, I don't get why God above prevents her from having kids . . . and little Philippe is born in a home like this. There's a whole lot of things like that I don't comprehend."

"Here comes a rig," Hap said.

Laramie crouched forward. "Two headlights. It's not a motorcycle."

"Maybe someone's lost." Hap sat cross-legged, carbine across his lap. "I think they're turnin' in here. Duck down."

"Is that a Harley in the back of the pickup?" Laramie whispered.

A red bandanna do-rag around his head, Francis climbed out of the passenger side. He carried a sleeping Philippe.

Juanita bounced out on the driver's side, keys spinning on her fingers. "Honey, do you think we should tape some cardboard over that hole in the front window to keep the bugs out?"

"Just pull the curtains, babe," Francis replied. "I'll repair it tomorrow. You might want to bring in the commode lid, though. I'll put the baby to bed. He's tired. He's had a long day."

"We've all had a long day."

"Did you get it out of your system?" Francis asked.

"Running away? Yeah . . . I think I did. How about you? Did you get your anger out?"

"Nothin' like slicin' tires to relieve stress."

Hap prodded Laramie with the carbine. "Now's your chance. You want the gun?"

Laramie waved him away.

Juanita and Francis paused in front of the busted screen door. Francis leaned down. Juanita threw her arm around him and kissed him on the lips. Then the three, and the black dog, disappeared into the house.

⋆⇒⊨⇐⋆ ⊨⇐⋆

Neither said much on the drive back to Greybull until they hit the thundershowers.

"If it rains hard, they'll wish they had that window fixed," Hap finally offered.

"I sat there most of the night thinking of all the things I was going to do to the guy, but I didn't count on that."

"It's a tough one to figure out."

"It's still a mess. I don't know how they can make it."

"Yeah, but it's not our mess. I hope you learned a lesson from all of this."

"I learned that slashing tires relieves stress."

"You didn't exactly slash them."

"Letting the air out and tossing away the valve cores was the best I could do. I should have carried my pocket-knife," Laramie said.

"You should have let me blast the tires."

"I didn't want to wake up the baby. But I'm glad I let the air out of the Harley, too."

Hap pushed his hat back. "What do you say, cowboy? We make a good team. You ready to rodeo?"

"After today, I'm braced for anything." Laramie rubbed the back of his neck. "Besides, I figure it can only get better from here."

CHAPTER TWO

Matamoros, Mexico, June 2006

For almost twelve hundred miles the Rio Grande separates the state of Texas from Mexico, the country of arduous paths and tumultuous fortunes. But the nearer one gets to the river, the less separates the cultures. Laramie and Hap knew they sat close to the river. In a way, they were no more than one step over the border.

"The only good thing I can say about this Juanita . . . she ain't ugly. She's got pretty eyes." Hap wasn't positive whether the gnawing in his stomach was due to nerves . . . or appetite. He pushed back his black beaver-felt cowboy hat to survey the crowded cantina. Most of the occupants had dark hair and dark brown eyes, all of them smelled like a hard day's work, and almost all were men. It was the kind of place where scars outnumbered tattoos, but just barely. The *A la Luz de la Luna Camara* flashed the first sign across the border offering *"algo de comer"* . . . something to eat.

Laramie rubbed his unshaven chin and peered through the smoky cantina, then lowered his voice. "I agree with you there, but she's rather . . . eh . . . large-boned, don't you think?" He tried, but failed, to slide his glass across the sticky bar.

Juanita's multiringed fingers dwarfed her half-filled glass. Weak elastic strained to keep the scoop-neck scarlet peasant blouse on her shoulders. She leaned close to Hap and pursed her peppermint lips. *"¿Qué dice tu amigo?"*

Laramie nudged Hap with his elbow, then spoke in a low monotone. "I'm glad she doesn't understand English."

Perched between Juanita and Laramie, Hap leaned back on the battered wooden bar stool and studied the woman. "What he said was, 'The Juanita I'm lookin' for don't need to buy two tickets just to fit on the bus to Del Rio.'"

Like a bobcat let out of a cage, Juanita's tight fist slammed into Hap's chin, grin still plastered in place. His hat tumbled off. The back of his head forged against Laramie's forehead like a twelve-pound sledgehammer on a cold anvil.

Both men landed on the worn linoleum floor backside down. Laramie rolled to his hands and knees. Hap got lifted off the grungy barroom floor by two men who made robust Juanita seem petite. Hap struggled to pull his arms free, while Juanita's second blow punctuated his stomach. By sheer strength of will, or blind luck, he turned sideways. Juanita's kick landed on his hip instead of its intended location.

Laramie jumped the shorter of the two men holding Hap. The man spun around so fast that he got tossed like ante into the middle of a Texas Hold 'Em table. Angry shouts and rib-bruising jabs greeted him.

Now held by only one man, Hap ground the heel of his cowboy boot into a sandal-covered foot and jerked loose. With a scratchy CD of Freddy Fender singing "Wasted Days and Wasted Nights" blaring in the background, he dove toward the poker table. A bulky hombre decided to demolish an oak chair into Laramie's stunned expression. The chair missed, but several calloused knuckles looped him to the floor.

Hap ducked a punch from the right. The flying chair splintered across the man behind him. He took two steps for what he thought was the door, but got clotheslined in the neck by big Juanita's fleshy forearm. He gasped, hands on his knees, until someone's roundhouse caught him in the chin and laid him flat on his back again.

The saloon engulfed in a free-for-all, big Juanita took advantage of the inequality of the sexes to clobber one man after another. *"Me los llevo a lo macho,"* she bellowed.

Hap spied Laramie crouched under the poker table. Broken glass sliced through the knees of his split jeans as he inched over to his partner. Angry screams, Spanish curses, and the crack of breaking bones roared in the battleground above them.

"If you're through visiting with this Juanita, I'm ready to go," Laramie hollered.

Hap deflected a flying claw hammer with a broken chair. "I was sorta hopin' to take a leisurely stroll through Matamoros by moonlight."

Both cowboys winced at the sound of breaking glass on the table above their heads.

"It's the same moon as last night," Laramie told him.

Hap tossed the chair remnants out into the room. "I

reckon the stroll can wait, but I never did get my order of buffalo wings."

A battered bar stool crashed into the table leg. Then a wave of beer from a broken pitcher cascaded off the table and splashed over their heads. Laramie rubbed his eyes on Hap's shirttail. "We got to make it to the door without losing life or limb."

A lit cigar dropped to the floor in front of Hap, a yellowed tooth embedded in it. "I ain't payin' for buffalo wings that I didn't get."

"Watch out, Hap. Your Juanita is headed this way."

"I told you, she ain't my Juanita. And it ain't a fair fight with her carryin' a knife."

"Shoot, it's no fair fight when she doesn't have a knife."

Hap slammed his pointed boot into a red-faced man sprawled on the floor who was grabbing his ankles. "Hey, if you want us to go now, that's fine with me. I know how you're shy and don't like crowds and meetin' new folks."

Laramie scurried out on his hands and knees and took a shin to the ear. He slid across the floor.

"The front door's over here." Hap edged through the shuffling feet of the cantina's combatants.

"Hap, no, not that way!" Laramie tottered to his feet and lurched toward his partner.

Ducking a punch, Hap shoved the assailant into a white-haired man in a tattered three-piece suit. The old man broke a maple pool cue over the man's head. Both men staggered to the floor.

"Any door is a good door!" Hap kicked it open and dove inside, dragging Laramie by the collar. The door slammed and locked, and both men wheezed in the darkness.

Mayhem muffled the music on the other side of the door as Hap felt a release from the iron grip of tension around his stomach. While hundreds of Juanitas danced in his mind, he felt the freedom of escape from this one.

"Where are we?" Laramie gagged. "Smells like a . . ."

Hap felt along the grimy wall until he found a light switch and flipped it on. A bare forty-watt bulb hung from a wire and flickered a glow that almost reached the floor. Water from an overflowing toilet flooded across his boots as a rat scampered for higher ground. "Must be the ladies room."

"Ladies room?" Laramie stared in a mirror as murky as water downstream from the herd. He dabbed at blood on his forehead. "Are you sure?"

"Yeah. The men's room ain't this clean."

"I told you the front door was in the other direction."

"You want to go back out there?"

"No, but I don't want to die of suffocation either. Let's see if that window will slide up." Laramie shoved against the side of the two-by-two-foot window. "I bet it hasn't been unfastened in a while."

"Well, it's goin' to open now." Hap stepped up on the rim of the busted john and added his shove to Laramie's push. The entire unit . . . casing, frame, sill, and window . . . tumbled to the hard-packed ground outside the cantina.

Hap scaled the back of the toilet tank for a boost and dove out into the fresh air of the Rio Grande night. His thin, lanky partner followed. Both men lurched to their feet.

"Can we make it to the truck without being ambushed?" Laramie asked.

"I reckon we can meander across the parkin' lot as if we don't know nothin' about no fight inside."

The moonlight glowed just bright enough to reveal their scrapes and bruises.

"Sure, we can tell whoever stops us that we look this way because we got our spurs caught on the bumper of a Peterbilt that dragged us all the way down here from Corpus Christi."

Hap brushed off his black hat. "Wait, we got to go back. I didn't pay my dadgum tab."

"No time to worry about money, partner. Lives are at stake here."

"There ain't nobody ever goin' to say I welched on a debt. I pay ever' bill. You know that about me."

"Mail them a money order."

"Nope. I settle up with cash."

Laramie waved his long arm at the hole in the bathroom wall they just vacated. "Toss it into the ladies room."

"How do I know the owner will get it?"

"How do you know he won't? The door's locked. Besides, he has to feed his rats sooner or later."

Hap dashed back to the hole in the wall and sailed a wadded-up ten-dollar bill and two ones through the opening. "I ain't leavin' them a tip," he muttered.

When morning broke, Laramie poked out his head from a sleeping bag. Hap crouched over a tiny mesquite fire, wearing only jeans and hat.

"You painted up for war?"

"Mercurochrome. Stops the bleedin'. Not easy to find these days, but nothin' works better."

Laramie pulled his long legs out and reached for his socks and boots. "I didn't remember you getting cut that much."

"Thin skin is a family tradition."

"I always thought that was a figure of speech."

"In my family, it's a painful reality." Hap hung the long-sleeved black denim shirt on his back as if it were sunburned. He took great care with each snap.

A live oak tree and the horse trailer blocked their view of the highway. It gave the camp a private feel. What grass had grown in the powdery yellowish dirt had long since turned brown. Even though the sun perched on the eastern horizon, a wispy, faded gray three-quarter moon stenciled the pale blue western sky.

Hap ambled over to the horses tied to the trailer. He shoved a flake of hay in each of their feed buckets, then stroked the black gelding. "Good mornin', Luke. You ready to get a taste of Texas? Bet you'd like to stretch your legs and chase a cow this mornin'. So would I, partner. You didn't plan on livin' in tight quarters this long."

Hap pondered how things turn out different from what a man plans. He had deliberated for years coming down to Texas and solving this thing with Juanita. But now he faced the undeniable fact that he didn't have a real handle on how to find her. Laramie had often said it was all an excuse to avoid any relationship. Though those were cutting words, Hap decided maybe he was right.

He asked for Luke's right front hoof, then held it and studied the frog and shoe, trying to concentrate on equine care as his mind locked on his quest to find the childhood

Juanita. He couldn't explain why it ate at his soul or how it pushed him through every day's activity. At times he felt trapped in a Broadway play beginning its nineteenth season. The same old lines, the same old scenes.

He put down the hoof and tapped Luke's right rear leg.

Yet, he couldn't release the dream. His heart still jumped when he recalled her voice. And when he got lost in the memory of that day, he gained a certain vitality, a feeling of being fully alive . . . that he didn't experience any other time. Others told him it was puppy love. They said it would soon pass. After almost two decades, they had all been proven wrong.

He inspected Luke's left rear hoof. The black horse winced when he ran his calloused fingers over the frog area.

He glanced back at Laramie and watched his partner pull on a green Carhartt Henley shirt. Hap marveled that he would trek down to south Texas with him on what amounted to a lark, and knew Laramie's loyalty piled up a debt almost impossible to repay.

"You want me to start the eggs?" Laramie called out.

"Yeah, go ahead. Lukey's got a bruised foot. How did he do that in the trailer?"

"You goin' to slap a rubber boot on him?"

Hap studied the horse's hoof. "Yeah, for a few days anyway." He glanced over at Laramie's blaze-faced bay. "You want me to check Tully's feet?"

"Don't let him kick you."

Hap rubbed the horse's neck. "Well, Mr. Tully. I don't worry about you. Horses kick. And bite. And buck. Nothin' can change that." He hefted Tully's right front hoof and muttered. "But people can change. Anyway, I surely hope so."

Both men dressed and huddled next to the fire, blue tin cups of bitter coffee in their hands.

Somewhere under melted yellow cheese and chunky red salsa, a half-dozen scrambled eggs lined their blue tin plates. Using a rolled-up corn tortilla for a scoop, Hap crammed a spicy bite into his mouth. "I believe my tongue is hot enough to boil water."

"They do make good salsa down here." Laramie swished his coffee around in his mouth before he swallowed it. "But this is a long drive from Wyoming just to find it."

When Hap sucked in a breath of air, it felt cool all the way to his tonsils. "I know what you're thinkin' about our brief stay in Mexico last night. But she's got to be somewhere. I have to give this a try."

Laramie used his tortilla like a washrag and wiped his plate clean. "It was nineteen years ago."

"Some things a man don't forget."

"A man? You were twelve years old when you visited with that cute Mexican girl for two hours while your daddy fixed their car in Wyoming."

"You know it's been eatin' at me ever since. You knew that from the first day we met. I explained it in the steak house east of Greybull."

"I know I'm the only one who would put up with your idiot obsession."

"You're right about that, partner. But it's a drive . . . a goal . . . a life purpose . . . not an obsession. It's more like a dream. Without dreams, a man dries up inside."

"Hap, you're thirty-one years old and you refuse to date anyone not named Juanita. It's a full-blown obsession."

The cool westward wind drifted over them, pregnant with heat to be birthed later in the morning. A distant rooster sounded startled to crow so late. Bacon grease congealed in a black skillet parked in the dirt between them.

"Laramie, I'm tryin' harder this summer to understand than I ever have. I know one thing: this is my last season of searchin'. I got to give it my best shot. That's the only way I'll be able to walk away from it."

"If last night's any indication, we won't live another week. Sometimes it's like walking the floor with an addict. I try to keep you upright and moving until this 'drug' works out of your system."

"I sorta figure that last night was progress."

"Progress?" Laramie waved his boot like a pointer stick. "You don't have a clue whether she lives in the U.S. or Mexico, or whether it's in Texas, New Mexico, or Colorado. She could have moved to Cody, Wyoming, by now. Think of that for irony."

"We checked out Cody ten years ago."

"You've got to narrow it down some, Hap. It's like looking for some particular penguin in Antarctica. We're going to find Juanitas all over, but how can we tell the right one? So far the only site we've crossed off the list was that rundown cantina in Matamoros."

Hap studied the tanned creases around Laramie's eyes. He kept thinking of the old rodeo phrase, "It ain't the years, boys . . . it's the miles." His voice lowered. "I eliminated some others last night. I was layin' there in my aches and pains tryin' to think it all through and it dawned on me. My Juanita is the kind of gal to make somethin' of herself. We were lookin' in the wrong place last night."

Laramie shook his boot out. Something dropped to

the sand, dug a quick hole, and buried itself. "What was that?"

"A beetle, I guess. Now, listen up. This is huge. I decided there will be no more searchin' out cantinas, saloons or casinos. I'm just sure my Juanita's teachin' at a school, nursin' at a hospital, or runnin' the soup kitchen at the gospel mission. We need to be lookin' on the good side of town. That's the kind of woman she is."

Treeless brown prairie grass stretched north of them. Laramie gazed at the horizon as if expecting a fox to jump up. "The Rio Grande's eighteen hundred miles long. That's not what I'd call narrow."

Hap stood up slowly, unlocking his back as if it were a pair of vise grips. "We ought to go search a hospital. Maybe they'd rent us a cheap room for the night. That would do us the most good."

Laramie wiggled his toes, then shoved his foot into his boot. "Hap, I promised you I'd ride the river with you. And you know I keep every promise. But that doesn't mean I comprehend all of this."

Hap scratched his unshaven chin. "Look, if it's any consolation, I don't understand me either. Sometimes this drive feels like a disease. But I aim to get cured. And the antidote is somewhere between here and the headwaters of the Rio Grande near Creede, Colorado. I guarantee, partner, this is the last summer you and me have to put up with this."

Laramie filled both tin cups with steaming coffee. "You know why I put up with this? One reason: I know for fact, you'd do the same thing for me."

"If you had an idiot obsession? That's tough to imagine."

"Well, it's not tough for me to imagine. I got some fears

all scrambled up inside. They don't drive me toward something, but away from lots of things. Maybe it's a good thing to always be focused on your quest. It keeps me from looking over my shoulder. But right now, a cash-paying job would be a helpful thing. Our funds shriveled up with your transmission repair and new water pump."

"If we get to the Midway Café in McAllen at 8:00 A.M., E. A. Greene promised us some work."

Laramie took a slow, deep breath and exhaled into the steamy cup. "Does this mean we're finally bidding a fond farewell to Brownsville?"

Hap felt the blue tin cup warm the calluses on his fingers. "Not until we finish our coffee."

Like a jet trail hugging the ground, dust plumed from E. A. Greene's red Dodge dually and long gooseneck stock trailer. Laramie and Hap cut through the silt fog like an F-14 through wispy clouds as they followed him to the entrance of the Hidalgo County Land and Cattle, Ranch 21.

Laramie rolled down the window when they pulled over the cattle guard and through the large open gate. A dozen outbuildings littered the ten-acre site with no apparent order. All had dulled, flaking white paint. Hard-packed, reddish dirt separated the buildings. The windblown terrain looked broom swept.

"We've entered indoor rodeos in a smaller arena than that old barn," Laramie said.

Hap parked the truck and horse trailer next to an empty stock tank and broken windmill. Three rail corrals cross-checked the pasture. Stacks of bone-dry tumbleweeds lined the east side of the fence. "Lots of holdin' corrals, that's for sure. But no water. Ain't that strange?"

"The big house is a little run down, but the bunkhouse seems okay. Usually it's the other way around. I don't see a soul, though. It's got an air of being deserted. Reminds me of that job we took in Dubois."

"The one that went belly-up while we were out on gather and no one bothered to come tell us? Yeah, I'm getting an uneasy feeling about this job."

Hap climbed out of the truck and stretched his arms. "E.A. said the crew headed out with the herd two weeks ago. We took too much time gettin' here. That busted transmission almost cost us a job. Nice of him to put us on anyway. I bet it would have felt different if we had been here with the crew."

"I've never worked a ranch that didn't smell like manure." Laramie unfolded his long legs, locking them into place like a card table. "I don't think this place has housed anyone since the war."

"Which war?"

"World War II." Laramie peered into the horse trailer. "We might want to get paid in advance for this job."

Hap felt his neck stiffen. "We don't get paid until we do the work. We ain't changin' that code now, partner."

"So this guy, E. A. Greene, was a friend of your daddy, right?"

"I don't think he knew Daddy. He's a pal of my uncle Mike, my mom's only brother. You heard him. The pay's good for some day work. Two weeks and we can go back to searchin' for my Juanita."

Though Greene stood in at five-eight, he loomed tall from the back bumper of his pickup. A polished bear claw clasped his braided leather string tie. The collar of his flower print western shirt was unbuttoned and dirty. "Here's the plan, boys. I've got a bunch of kids and rookies up there with the herd trying to play cowboy and move them to the summer range. It's for sure and certain that they're goin' to lose some along the way. That's why I'm payin' you top wages. I want you to bring up the rear and round up the ones they missed or left behind. Seasoned hands like you two shouldn't have any trouble. There are corrals and loading ramps every eight to ten miles. Pen them there and make sure there's water in the stock tank. I'll be back with this rig, then trailer the strays up with the main herd. I'm guessin' you'll have fifty head or more before you reach the Sargosa Valley range." He stopped to swat two flies that buzzed at his neck. "If I had experienced hands like you to begin with, I wouldn't need this follow-up."

"When do we get paid?" Laramie pressed.

"Normally at the end of the two weeks, but I can pay you a week at a time, if you want."

"Yeah, that's what we want," Laramie added.

"You said you'd provide the chuck?" Hap asked.

"That's right." E.A. dug in his pocket, pulled out a short, brass key, and handed it to Hap. "Each corral has a chuck box. I'm loadin' 'em up as I head west. You just help yourself to what you need and leave it locked for the next crew."

Laramie gazed across the empty brown prairie. A hamburger wrapper scurried like a windblown rabbit until it impaled on a squatty prickly pear cactus. "They all shorthorns?"

"It's a mixed lot, boys."

Hap drew his worn brown boot across the hard dirt. "All branded Bar-HC?"

"I haven't had time to brand them new ones I brought up from Mexico. Most of them have a running H with some curlicues on each side. You know how them Mexican brands are."

"Draw us out a picture of your brands, then sign and date the paper," Laramie said.

"You reckon he needs to do all that?" Hap challenged.

"Yeah, I do."

Greene scribbled something on the back of an oily brown sack, then shoved it at Laramie. He was back in the truck and had roared off before Hap got his chaps fastened.

One foot on the bumper, Laramie buckled up his spurs. "You know, that's as little instruction as we ever got. How well do you know this guy?"

"My uncle Mike was with him in Vietnam. I don't need any more credentials than that." Hap licked his lips and could taste the alkali dirt. "Besides, roundin' up fifty head don't sound all that tough."

"Do you know anything about Mexican brands?"

"I ain't never cowboyed south of Colorado until now. You know that." Hap snapped his chap strap behind his knee. When the wind gusted, he screwed his hat down.

"That's why I insisted on this." Laramie tucked the folded brand sheet into his pocket as he led Tully away from the trailer.

"Kind of desolate out here, ain't it?"

"Yeah, I expected us to ride out among the bluebonnets on some historic Texas ranch."

"This isn't much different than searching for strays

south of Wamsutter, Wyoming." Hap buttoned up his black leather vest. "I reckon cattle is cattle."

Bedrolls tied to the cantles and cinches pulled tight, Laramie and Hap swung up in their saddles with a smoothness learned from years of practice—plus a wince or two, a result of the night before.

South Texas now sweltered July hot. Sweat dribbled down their bandanna-wrapped necks. Squatty prickly pear cactus marked the parched prairie. Lumps of brown grass looked like mountaintops poking through the dust clouds. Wild islands of tangled brush thick enough to inspire Uncle Remus to spin a story filled the landscape. It hadn't rained for seventeen days.

The duo found the tramped dirt trail of E. A. Greene's eight hundred head. Without assigning tasks, Laramie skirted the northern edge of the herd's track. Hap rode the southern boundary. Both cowboys studied the windswept tracks, trying to spot where a cow or calf had strayed away from the others. They rode in sixty-foot circles, hoping to cut across a track or sign of herd defection.

Hap stood in the stirrups, stretched his legs, then plopped back down on the hot, slick leather saddle seat. He always had a hard time explaining to the carbound how good a saddle felt. The guy who worked at Boeing collapsed in his La-Z-Boy recliner every night, but Hap relaxed best in his saddle. He figured it was the rhythm of horse and cowboy . . . the sway . . . the fresh air . . . not counting the lousy food, the icy November rains, and the stink of burning cowhide. He knew it meant nursing a calf all night in the bathtub and then watching the wolves devour it six weeks later. But he had chosen this life, and he knew he wouldn't trade it for something so confining as a fast food franchise. He also realized it had been a long time since he had any other choice.

They wound their way through the brush-choked barranca, a narrow, steep gulch no more than thirty-feet wide and a half-mile long. Hap emerged with a brindle yearling who trotted ahead of him, bleating about the rude intrusion.

"I've got rounded small cloven tracks within bigger ones that veer off toward the brushy oasis. I'll check it out," Laramie hollered. Soon the wet pair, cow and calf, scooted ahead of him.

With a dry breeze at their backs, Laramie and Hap plodded the horses at a slow enough pace not to tire the cattle, following the contour as it mimicked the river. Only the screech of a red-tailed hawk circling the prairie with mouse-filled talons broke the silence. The steady clomp of Luke's hooves provided the percussion for the hawk's shrill violin. The sun hung halfway to noon when they pushed the little gather into the shade of a live oak tree.

"You should get yourself a sombrero," Hap teased. "It will get hot this afternoon. This ain't Wyomin'."

Ignoring the suggestion as he had for ten years of working cattle together, Laramie wiped his forehead with his bandanna. He pulled out the brand list and studied it. "Do you think we're doing this right?"

"We got four steers, three cows, two calves, and that young brown-and-white bull that's been followin' behind us for a couple miles. They all have one of those brands on it. Sounds right to me."

"The bull hasn't come close enough for us to read the brand, so I think we can let him trail along for a while."

"Laramie, did you ever wish you got married when you were younger?"

"Geez, where did that come from?"

"You mentioned the bull . . . that reminded me of Greybull, Wyoming . . . and Juanita. She had a kid. What was his name?"

"Philippe."

"How old would he be now?"

"Eleven, twelve, I guess."

"He must be playin' Little League. You or me could be sittin' in the stands at a Little League game in Rock Springs yellin' for our boy when he came up with two outs and the bases loaded in the ninth inning."

"I think they only play seven innings in Little League."

"Make 'em throw you a strike, Philippe!" Hap hollered.

Laramie stared at his partner. "You had too much sun?"

"I guess I was ponderin' how much of my life I've wasted on this Juanita thing. I'm goin' to be in my forties before I ever watch my kid's Little League game."

"Is this going anywhere?" Laramie demanded.

"Don't you ever think about things like that?"

"No."

"Don't you want to have kids?"

"I don't think so. Are we going to round up some cows or just talk all day?"

Hap watched Laramie ride north. It wasn't the first time his partner had iced up over the subject of family. He reckoned if he hung around long enough, Laramie would open up on the issue. But not today. Hap turned Luke south and trotted him to the edges of the trail.

When the tracks swung north of a brush-filled ravine, Laramie signaled Hap to shouting distance. "We got a cow down there. She's dropping smaller and smaller sign. It hasn't crusted over yet."

"Ain't this a wonderful business?" Hap shouted back. "We get to spend our day studyin' cow manure."

"And to think, my mamma wanted me to be a lawyer," Laramie called back.

"From what I can tell, this ain't all that much different."

"One of us ought to push the bunch up around to the head of this ravine. The other can plow the brush and try to jump it out."

Hap stood in the stirrups to survey the rugged tangle of brush and rocks. "I reckon I know who will do what."

"You got the best cow pony, even if he is wearing one boot. Tully won't cut brush unless he sees your horse do it first."

"Luke's so smart, maybe I could just send him down by himself."

"Holler up, if you need help."

"Yeah. I'll just call you on your cell phone."

"You laughed at me when I suggested we get cell phones," Laramie said.

"It's sorta like trainin' wheels on a bicycle. If you know what you're doin', you don't need 'em." Hap turned Luke to the right and laid just enough spur to switch gaits. There was a gradual slope to the descent, but the trail choked down quick until the dead brush combed hair furrows in the black gelding's shoulders.

Brindle clumps of cow hair clung to fresh-broken brush as Hap picked his way through the ravine. "Lukey, we got one down here somewhere. But I'm not sure we can flush her out. I can't see more than three feet in this tangle."

The further he descended, the taller the brush. By the time he reached dry sand at the bottom, the sun was blocked. He rode in the shadows with no air movement. Steam rose off the ground like cold water poured on a hot rock.

Luke's ears twitched as he stared at the north wall. Back in the brush, Hap spied a cow bedded down.

"Hey-yah!" he yelled. The cow raised her rear legs, then her tail. She relieved herself, then trotted farther up the gully.

Hap studied where the cow had lain and noticed a small cave carved into the limestone cliff. Dead brush formed a tunnel too short for Hap to ride, so he dismounted to investigate what looked like ribbons and flowers perched at the cave's mouth.

He tied his horse to a mesquite limb and crawled on his hands and knees, avoiding the pile just dropped by the cow. "It looks like a shrine or a marker, boy," he called out as if Luke had an opinion on the matter.

When he reached the opening, he deliberated on each object. At the front, three green glass jars held the remnants of once-alive flowers. Dry, brown petals carpeted the floor in front of the jars. An ornate plastic cross was wedged into the limestone with a battered and crucified plastic Jesus attached. At the back of the cave, a dust-covered picture frame of turquoised copper filigree rested like a silent witness to a sad, haunting story.

He plucked up the framed picture and held it out in the

variegated light of the brushy ravine. He blew on the glass. Dust fogged his eyes and mouth. He coughed and squinted as he wiped the glass with the elbow of his black shirt.

The words engraved in the brass plate: *Nuestra Miranda.*

"Darlin', I don't know your story, but you were way too young to die down here."

A brown-faced girl with black hair in a starched white dress smiled at him. On the back of the picture was written, *Niña bonita de Rufugio Álvarez Estrada y Francisca Dominga Estrada.*

Hap yanked out his red bandanna, wiped the photograph clean, then did the same for the vases. He pulled off his hat, wondering why a child's shrine would be hidden in such a lonely place.

"Well, darlin', I wish I had a flower to stick back in them vases. They look abandoned. But you got to understand, with this dry wind a real flower don't last more than a few days."

He tugged off his turquoise and black horsehair hatband, then laced it around the photograph like a necklace for the little girl.

He swatted a buzzing horsefly, then wiped his eye.

He couldn't figure why he would become melancholy over a stranger or tear up like his mamma watching her soap opera on television.

He crawled back to where the brush thinned enough to stand. He remounted and plodded west, until he sighted the cow's rump.

"There she is, Lukey. Let's run her at the brush at the end of the barranca. She can open it up and we'll ride through without losin' any more blood."

As the trail ascended, the ravine walls tapered off on both sides, and he sensed they would soon be back up on the prairie. "Don't give her time to even think about turnin' around," he coaxed his black horse.

The dense undergrowth at the top of the grade grew no higher than a three-rail fence. He spied Laramie, sprawled with his hand back on Tully's rump, waiting for him to exit.

Hap spurred his black gelding to a gallop. The trail widened and the panicked cow stampeded straight ahead. But the cow spun left at the last moment and stumbled to a stop just short of the brush wall.

Without any knee commands, Luke dodged after the cow with just a quick turn, leaving only an unsaddled Hap to charge the brush. Propelled over the horse's neck, he dropped the reins and felt his hat tumble off as he flew through the four-foot brush wall at the end of the ravine.

His right hand slapped a prickly pear cactus as he tried to stop the tumble. When he reeled to his feet, shaking his thorn-pricked hand, Laramie leaned over and drawled, "Say, mister, you didn't happen to see a horseback Wyoming cowboy pushing a cow out of that barranca, did you?"

The shorthorn brindle cow blundered around the end of the brush and trotted over to the other cows, while Luke snorted out of the ravine and refused to look at Hap.

"Glad to see your horse knows what he's doing," Laramie hooted.

Hap yanked a cactus needle from his hand. "If he knew anything at all, he would have fetched my dadgum hat."

⊶⊜ ⊜⊷

* * *

The red sun poised above the western horizon suspended for a last wink at the world before it plunged into night. Laramie and Hap drove the little herd into a brush corral. While Laramie tended the horses, Hap built a trench fire and warmed up a big can of beans and fried processed meat they had found in the larder.

The second coffee can contained Girl Scout thin mint cookies and a swarm of tiny white bugs. "I think we'll pass on the cookies, but we might read the 1994 September issue of *Western Horseman*."

"Hap, do you get the feeling all this food is left over from Y2K or something? I don't think we've ever worked for this cheap of an outfit."

"Yeah, the powdered milk came straight from government surplus. It says so on the box. If these meals get any worse, we can just eat mud pies and save time."

The boiled coffee was thin, but plenty hot. They didn't talk much until they had scraped their tin plates clean. Hap waited for the perfect moment, when the tin cup coffee was drinkable, but not cold. "I'm glad we only signed on for two weeks. I got ripped up in the cantina and torn up flying out of the barranca—at this rate, I won't have a square inch of skin left in two weeks."

Laramie plopped on the dirt and eased back against his saddle. "I can't even remember what a soft chair feels like. So, you found a grave at the bottom of the ravine?"

"Not a grave, a shrine. A purdy young girl. Such a shame. She's got a grievin' mamma and daddy someplace."

"Some things are just too sad to ponder." Laramie tapped his pocketknife on the rectangular tin container. "You want that last bite of canned meat?"

"I didn't want the first bite of canned meat. I'm hopin'
the grub gets better."

Laramie snorted. "If we had that cell phone, we could
call out for Chinese."

"It's hard to tell 'em where to deliver, when we don't
know where we are."

Laramie sat up. "Hey, I got an idea. Let's turn these
bovines in to Greene tomorrow, draw our pay, and head
on down the road. Too many strange things, Hap. And he
didn't fill those larders. That food is old."

"You know I ain't never quit a job."

"Yeah, you're right." Laramie sighed. "Neither have I,
but there's been a few of them I never should have taken in
the first place."

For the next three days, neither the work nor the menu
changed.

On the third evening, Hap made his stand. "I ain't eatin'
that stuff again. Do you remember that cook at the Circle
YP? What was his name?"

"Elmo Polly."

"Yeah, you, me, Blackie, and Thumper went out with
the wagon and had to eat his cookin' for twenty-one days.
I lost eighteen pounds."

Laramie stabbed a canned peach and sucked it into his
mouth like a raw oyster. Truck headlights bounced down
the dirt road toward them. "Here comes Greene. Looks
like you can complain to the boss."

"I was hopin' it was a pizza delivery guy."

E. A. Greene glanced at the cattle milling in the brush

corral. "I knew you boys could do it. I'm a fine judge of cowboy skills. You're as good a hand as your uncle Jake."

"It's my uncle Mike that knows you," Hap corrected. "And he's an accountant, not a cowboy."

"Speaking of accounts," Laramie pressed. "We need some of our pay."

"What are you going to spend it on?" Greene pressed.

"Groceries," Hap said. "All that stuff in the larder came over on a covered wagon."

"Them kids with the main herd must have scarfed the fresh stuff. But I have a solution for that. Scoot over here." He motioned them to the back of his truck. E.A. pulled off his black-rimmed glasses and they hung tethered around his neck. "You boys want free fine meals and make a hundred-dollar bonus tonight?"

"Tonight?" Laramie groaned. "We had a tough, hot day. We planned to shoot some pool, watch TV, and soak in the sauna."

"That's a little trail humor," Hap explained. "It means we're tuckered out. It's been a long day. What kind of work do you have at night?"

"Here's the deal . . . now I ain't sayin' anyone rustled my cattle, but them dang kids with the herd let fifty head or so disappear. I'm guessing they crossed the river about four miles up the road."

"Across the Rio Grande?" Hap asked.

"I can't officially claim someone stole them, if I didn't see it happen. The Mexican government will report the cattle crossed over on their own. There's no extradition of cows. If I find some over there with my brand on it, they will sell them back to me, at a tidy profit."

Laramie rubbed his thin, chapped lips. "That sounds

like quite a rip-off. But a border is a border. Not much we can do about that, right?"

"There is only one way to handle this. I need you to ride with me over the river and convince that fifty head of cattle to wander back into Texas before daylight. On their own, of course. But with the right argument, bovines can be reasonable. If I don't, the ol' boys on the other side will round them up by tomorrow and pen them in the corrals at Camargo, waitin' for a buyer."

Hap patted the side of Greene's pickup, then tried to rub the stiffness out of his temples. "You want us to find your cattle in the dark?"

"He wants us to go to Mexico and steal cattle," Laramie huffed.

"It ain't stealin' if the cows belong to you in the first place. Boys, if this was the border between Texas and Oklahoma, you'd just ride across, make a gather, and bring your branded cattle home."

Laramie folded his hands behind his head and narrowed his eyes. "Mexico is a foreign country."

"At times, so is Oklahoma," Greene said. "Don't worry. I'm ridin' with you. That other crew doesn't have the horse sense to run cattle across the river, much less gather at night. I'd rather you get the bonus than them."

"You payin' in advance?" Laramie asked.

"You need the money tonight?"

"No," Hap mumbled.

"Yes," Laramie corrected. "We might find something in Mexico we want to buy."

"He might be right about that." Hap dragged his boot heel across the dry yellow dirt. "Laramie's a little worried we'll wind up in a Mexican jail."

"Trust me, boys. This is just the custom along the border. They run a few head over the river, and we go get 'em and bring 'em back."

Laramie frowned. "I don't like the idea of sneaking across the border like that."

"I hoped you might like a little Mexican food. Angelina and Pete Lopez fix a fine meal. We'll have us a feast. Then about midnight, we'll bring my cows back across. Their daughter plays a nice acoustic guitar."

"What's the daughter's name?" Hap asked.

"Can't remember. One of those common Mexican names. She's a music teacher. Must be about thirty by now."

"Can you see the river from her folks' backyard?"

"They had a place right next to the river, but it flooded out about ten, fifteen years ago. Don't know if you can see the river now or not. What about it, boys? Let's go get ourselves some genuine Mexican *comida* then bring my cows home."

Hap rubbed his stomach. "Sounds mighty good, don't it, partner?"

"I'll ride over for supper," Laramie said. "But I want to study the situation before I start bringing cows across the Rio Grande."

The three men swam the horses across the river right after dark. The lukewarm muddy water left a gritty feel to their jeans and socks. They waited until they reached the cantina to pull their boots back on.

The two-story adobe building was a good one hundred feet wide, but only twenty-five feet deep. Within a half-hour they sprawled on a patio behind the Lopez café. Grapevines entwined the latticework awning, blocking the sun by day and the stars by night. The light breeze felt warm, like a propane burner set real low. Jeans still wet, they ate by candlelight and listened to guitar music dance out the open back door. The rest of the customers were crammed inside.

"Where did E.A. go?" Laramie asked. "I didn't much appreciate his horse cutting in front of Tully. I got soaked from toes to nose."

Hap motioned to the room above the café. "Said he had some phone calls to make. But he did give us some pay tonight."

Laramie rolled up a huge Monterey tortilla, then scooped the chunky fire-drenched salsa and shoved it into his mouth. "That guitar player is quite a lady." He choked out each word while grabbing for the water.

"She has a certain Spanish beauty." Hap stabbed the pulled pork with his fork as if it were still alive. "And she is a teacher."

"Not only that, she is *treinta y uno*."

"But she's never been to Wyomin' and her name is Teresa." Hap dismissed the guitar player with the wave of an iodine-tainted hand.

"Yeah, I could tell that was a setback for you."

"But you got to admit this is better chow than that canned meat."

"The food's good, but I've never been very good at reading brands after dark. How are we goin' to tell E.A.'s cows from someone else's?"

"You've got the brand chart he drew out." Hap chomped into a yellow pepper, and tears rolled down his cheeks. "I reckon . . ." he puffed, ". . . that's all . . . we . . . need. That and a fifty-pound block of ice."

⊷⇌   ⇌⊷

In the glow of the cloud-shrouded moon, they discerned the silhouettes of shorthorn cattle from the ridge. When the moon popped between the clouds they could even see its distant reflection off the Rio Grande.

"This isn't working, Mr. Greene," Laramie reported. "We can see the cows, but can't read the brand until they turn their rear ends to the moonlight. Maybe we should wait until daylight."

"Boys, boys, boys. You got yourself worked up for nothin'. We don't need the identical fifty head. Any fifty will do. It all balances out that way."

Laramie sat straight up in the saddle. "We didn't ride over here to find someone else's cows."

Greene flipped his hands as if swatting wasps. "Now, Laramie, if you had a neighbor take five oranges off your tree, you might hike over to his house and look in the fruit bowl. If he's got ten oranges there, you'd only take five. That's fair. But you wouldn't worry about whether they are the same five oranges."

Hap brushed down his black mustache with his fingertips. "You lost me comparin' oranges to cows and international borders with backyards."

"Trust me. This is my territory. I know what I'm doing. It's the way things are done down here."

Laramie leaned back on Tully's rump. "Just because it's the way things are done, don't mean we'll do it. We'll cross back over to Texas and keep pushin' your strays. You can do whatever you want here in Mexico."

"I never figured you two for quitters."

"We ain't quitters," Hap barked, "and we ain't quittin' this job."

"Hap!" Laramie challenged.

"I'm goin' to ride up and start cuttin' my cows," Greene said, "while you two hash this out."

Laramie and Hap rode over to a squatty mesquite tree, the only shadowy form without four legs and a tail.

"Hap, what do you think you are doing? This guy wants us to steal cows."

"They stole some of his cows. He wants them back."

"It isn't retrieving lost cattle when you go across an international border. It's a felony in a foreign country."

"We agreed to the job."

Laramie's voice rose higher. "We agreed to come look at the job."

"I can't quit, Laramie."

"Why? This isn't a time to be bound by some stoic cowboy pride."

"It's a lot deeper than that. I don't want to talk about it."

"Well, you'd better talk, partner, because in about ninety seconds I'm riding back to Texas with or without you."

Hap knew Laramie deserved an explanation, but fought to stay calm enough to talk. "Give me a minute, here." He rode close enough to Laramie that their chaps touched. "Uncle Mike plays a special place in Mamma's life. The day Daddy died, I was with her. But she was beside herself. She loved that man as if he was life itself. I was only a kid, but I was just sure she was going to grab a gun and kill herself, just so she could be with him in heaven.

"Laramie, I've never been so scared in my life. Then Uncle Mike came over. He was big brother. He held her and rocked her and talked to her about times when they were kids. He stayed with us until Daddy was buried and to this day Mamma says he saved her life. He's always been her hero. He got two Silver Stars and a Purple Heart in Nam. Uncle Mike said we should work for his ol' army pal, E. A. Greene. I can't go home and look her in the eye and tell her I let down Uncle Mike's pal. I can't do it, Laramie. You go on. But I have to stay."

"Hap, you never told me any of that."

"It's been eighteen years since Daddy died and I can't talk about it without tears in my eyes. I apologize for that, partner."

"So what are we going to do, Hap?"

"You go on back to Texas."

"We're partners."

Hap felt loyalty versus legality tugging at his soul. Both men looked up as E. A. Greene rode toward them.

"I've been thinking how I like you bein' men of principle. But I need a little help. I'll cut them out and I'll move them across the river somehow. Can you just help me trail them down to the river? That's all. You can even cross over to Texas first. Now, is that a fair deal? And I'll still give you the bonus."

Hap glanced at Laramie, who nodded at him.

"We'll push them down to the river, and we might help you with any bearing your brand. But we'll not swim another man's cattle over to Texas," Hap said.

Like fog that melts at noon, the wispy clouds disappeared, leaving just enough moonlight to count heads. The treeless, sageless Mexican desert rolled out in front of them. Even in the night, patches of alkali could be seen. Heavy sulfur smell filled the air, like right before lightning strikes. But the clouds had blown west. A million stars clicked on and off like switches in a humongous computer chip.

"E.A., you got yourself sixty-one head cut out. I thought you said you only lost fifty," Laramie probed.

"Fifty was an approximate number. Besides, I might have missed a few of the brands myself. I figured we'd sort them out at the river. That's the place to make the final count."

Hap rode over to Laramie. "I know what you're thinkin', partner. At least, let's drive them to the river. Do it for my uncle Mike."

"I don't know your uncle Mike, Hap. But I'll do it for your mamma. She's a saint."

Laramie and Hap rode out to the flanks. E. A. Greene rode drag. Hap hummed a soft version of "Goodbye Ol' Paint" as his mind raced. He reached down and patted his horse's neck. "Luke, I'm not sure how we got into this. We set out to work for a friend of Uncle Mike's. Look for some lost cows. Eat a good meal. And now we're cuttin' out another man's brand. I hope you don't think poorly of me for it."

Hap stretched out his arms and yawned. He longed for a hot shower and a soft bed. Even a meager bedroll on hard ground sounded better by the minute.

After an hour of steady plodding, Greene signaled them

to join him at the back of the herd. "Thanks, boys. Can you just waltz these bovines up to that rise and hold them? With all the fencing going on along here, that's the only place along the border that I can get them across. It's hard to spot at night. I'll signal you from the river with my flashlight. You start them toward the beam. When we get them to the river, we'll use the flashlight to sort brands, and I'll push them over myself if you want to quit then."

"We don't quit," Laramie insisted. "But we don't steal, either."

It only took a moment for E. A. Greene to ride out of sight. Laramie and Hap moseyed sixty-one head of short-horns toward the distant Rio Grande. The sluggish cattle bunched together, so the boys rode side by side to push them along.

"Laramie, I've been deliberatin'. I think you're right. No matter what brand is on their hide, this feels like rustlin' cattle to me."

"Did you ever rustle cattle before?"

"Not that I know of. I've pushed a lot of bovines that belonged to other people, but I reckon they all knew what I was doin'. But one of the first lessons my daddy taught me: Don't quit until the work's all done. What lesson did you learn from your daddy?"

"Don't become a drunk," Laramie mumbled.

They peered through the shadows and plodded the cows along. The breeze cooled them enough to stop sweating, but was not so nippy as to rub their arms. Besides the shuffling of bovine hooves on desert sand, the song of myriad crickets rolled up from the Rio Grande. Even those noises died down as they reached the last rolling rise, before a gradual descent to the river.

Laramie shoved a canteen at his partner.

Hap unscrewed the cap. "One thing about it, these Rio Grande nights are pleasant. Kind of a light gulf draft driftin' up the river. Makes a cowboy want to sleep on top of the bedroll thankin' the good Lord for that meadow up above full of twinklin' stars."

"Do you see Greene's signal light?"

"Nope. This is peaceful, so far." Hap sighed. "Let's just swim back over and build us a fire to dry out our jeans. One thing I like about this cow business are the quiet, remote places. Gives a man the opportunity to sort out his life and review the choices . . . good and bad. I like to remember old pals from bygone days. And I try to recall the lessons my mamma taught me with her sweet smile and the Good Book in her lap."

"You've been thinking about all that?"

"Shoot, yeah, Laramie. That's what soft summer nights do to me. They flood me with melancholy, in a good sort of way. I reckon that's the way it is with all cowpunchers. What are you thinkin' about this evenin'?"

"Ants."

"What? You wastin' a fine evenin' like this meditatin' on ants?"

"I want to know . . . do those little suckers work hard because they're smart, or because they're dumb?"

"I don't exactly get your drift, Laramie."

"Ants do what they're programmed to do and they do it well. But they don't stop and scratch their little heads and say, 'This just isn't right.' No ant contemplates his own destiny or how he fits into the grand scheme of history and the universe. They follow their genetic code even to their own demise."

"Is this biological discussion leadin' somewhere?"

Laramie circled his arm to the north. "It's leading to the Rio Grande."

Hap rubbed a cramp out of his shoulder. "You figure we're just following our genetic cowboy code? You think we're headed to our own demise?" Hap patted his scabbard. "You reckon we ought to pull the carbines out?"

"That makes it seem like we know what we're doing. I think we'd better stick to the dumb, innocent routine." Laramie nodded toward the river. "That must be Greene's flashlight."

"It was either that or a cigarette lighter, but we haven't see a livin' soul since we left that cantina. It must have been Greene."

Grass-filled during the day, the cows moved slowly, as if looking for bedding ground. Laramie and Hap picked up the pace. The smooth saddle leather fit them like their old Wranglers. Even the jingle of their spurs fell silent in respect for the night's quiet.

Within a few minutes they reached the dirt roadway that paralleled the river and boundaried the banks of the Rio Grande.

"Do you see Greene anywhere?" Laramie asked.

"No, but I felt a twinge in my genetic code."

At the first gunshot, they dove at their scabbards. But when the headlights of three pickups triangulated their position, they threw up their hands instead.

"Hold it, compadres, we ain't lookin' for a fight," Hap called out.

Four carbine-toting Mexican men hiked into the headlights from the east, three more from the west.

A hatless man in a three-piece suit without a tie laid

his gun over his shoulder. "Stealing cattle is against the law, no matter what side of the border you're on." The spokesman's English was good, with a hint of accent.

"Yes sir, we'll agree with that." Hap tried to make out the man's face. "We had a few shorthorns stray across the river. We wanted to take them home so they wouldn't eat your pasture."

"These are Mexican cows," the stocky man insisted.

"We can see that now that you have the car lights on," Laramie said.

"Señors, we shoot cattle rustlers over here," a thin, carbine-toting man with a New York Yankees baseball cap announced.

"We're new to south Texas," Laramie explained. "We were told that any cattle that strayed across the border should be gathered up and brought home. Don't you ride over to Texas and bring your cows back? We thought it worked both ways."

"I don't steal another man's cattle," the man in the suit replied.

A long discussion in Spanish ensued. Hap surveyed the river for a sign of Greene. He lowered his hands slowly, then walked his fingers closer to the scabbard of his Winchester.

The man in the suit waved his gun like a professor making a point to the freshman class. "We have two options. Either we shoot you as rustlers or we take you to town and throw you in jail."

Laramie rubbed his beard. "Hap, does it surprise you that the boss is nowhere to be seen?"

"Hope he's got a good Mexican attorney."

"You working for someone else?" the hatless man asked.

"Yes, sir. We were tryin' to track his cattle across the river and thought these belonged to him," Hap insisted. "Laramie, show him the list of brands we were sent to fetch."

Laramie reached in his damp shirt pocket, but the wet note tore as he yanked it out.

The man in the suit pointed to the cattle that had already begun to bed down. "Señors, that is my family brand."

Laramie tossed the remnants of the note to the dirt. "We were a little confused in the dark."

"Get off the horses," the man in the suit commanded.

Laramie dug his boots deeper into the stirrups. "I don't believe that would be a smart move."

"We can shoot you off," the man barked.

"Yes, sir. But, as we see it, we ain't committed a crime," Hap said.

"You were stealing my cattle."

"Is this property still your ranch?" Laramie asked.

"Yes, of course."

"Then we haven't stole anything. The cattle are still on your property."

"We were just cuttin' across your place to get back to Texas," Hap explained. "And this bunch of cows jumped up and trotted in front of us. I'm sure they would have turned back at the river and we would be on our way home. We didn't see any *No Trespassing* signs."

"That's absurd. No one would believe that," the man said.

"You better hope no one believes it," Laramie said. "You've got six men here to watch you kill us. You'll have to keep them happy and quiet the rest of their lives. We don't show up at our regular place tomorrow, a search will begin. Folks know we're over here to gather strays. So the police, maybe the FBI, will start poking around. The twenty-four-hour news station will set up camp and make a circus out of it. One day, one of your vaqueros might get peeved with the meager pay you give him. At that point they will extort you or you'll have to shoot them all."

"They wouldn't do that."

"Did you ever see the kind of cash those cable channels offer for an exclusive story?" Hap said.

"In that case, we'll turn you over to the policía."

"Say, do any of you know Mr. E. A. Greene?" Laramie said. "He can explain this better than we can."

"*¿Trabajan para el* Señor Greene?" a stocky, hatless man in the shadows grumbled.

"Yep," Hap replied. "He hired us to gather up his strays."

The suited man raised his gun, "Shoot them both. Emmett Greene is a crook."

Hap kept his hands raised. "He owns Hidalgo County Land and Cattle."

"He doesn't own an inch of ground on either side of the Rio Grande."

"But we were followin' his big herd, pickin' up the stragglers," Hap said.

"Those belong to the Hidalgo County Land and Cattle. But that's owned by Miller and Robles. They have spreads on both sides of the river. Greene steals strays before they have a chance to comb the brush. He loads them up and hauls them straight to a back-street slaughterhouse on Sixteenth Street in San Antonio."

"Seems like you know a lot of details about him," Laramie remarked.

"Two of my men worked for Greene. They got arrested and spent time in jail, but Greene escaped prosecution. He always has an alibi. He hires cowboys to do his stealing, but heads for some public location during the actual crime. If you get caught, he doesn't have to pay you. Now, get down," the suited man commanded again, "We're taking you to jail."

Laramie kicked at the man's hand when he reached for his boot. "No, sir, I told you, we're not getting off our horses."

"May the saints have mercy on your mortal souls," the man shouted. "If you don't get down right now, I will shoot you for resisting arrest."

Laramie locked his knees against his horse's flank.

Hap backed his horse toward Laramie. "So much for the 'band of brothers' during the war. I wish I had listened to you, partner."

"*Un momento . . .*" the stocky, hatless man called out. "*Mira eso.*" He pointed at the left, rear hoof of Hap's horse. "*Tiene una bota de caucho. Son las mismas huellas que habían en la barranca, cerca del relicario de mi sobrina.*"

"What did he say?" Hap asked.

"He said you have one rubber boot like the tracks near his niece's shrine in the barranca."

"Little Miranda Estrada?" Hap said.

The stocky man with long-sleeved white shirt buttoned at the collar stepped up to Hap's stirrup. "She was my sister's daughter."

Hap yanked off his hat. "I'm truly sorry about the girl.

She was a very purdy young lady and I'm sure her family grieves for her."

"Where is your *cinta*?" the man asked. "Your hatband."

"We were roundin' up strays a few days ago down in that barranca. I stumbled across the memorial your family made for her. I dusted off the picture, but didn't have any flowers to leave, so I pulled off my hatband. It's black and turquoise horsehair. I braided it myself. Took the hair right out of ol' Lukey's mane. I thought it looked nice."

The man's voice cracked. "You are the one who did that? My sister thought an angel had stopped to visit the site."

"How did she die?" Hap asked.

The man wiped the corner of his eyes on his shirtsleeve. "Miranda liked to ride a black stallion. For some reason, the horse panicked and stampeded toward the arroyo. She stayed in the saddle and tried to turn him. But the stallion didn't stop until he crashed into the barranca. By the time my brother-in-law got there, both my niece and the horse were dead."

"I'm truly sorry." Hap shoved his hat back on.

The ranch owner lowered his carbine.

"That was a kind thing to do. I won't shoot you, but I am taking you to jail. This rustling has to stop right now."

"Mister," Hap said, "if you eliminate me and Laramie, will you abolish your rustling problem?"

"Not with Greene on the prowl."

"That's what I'm thinkin'. I reckon you're smart enough to figure out once we cross that border, we aren't comin' back. But what if we send him over to you? What have you got to lose? We aren't much of a threat anymore, and there's a chance we can deliver E. A. Greene to you."

The stocky man cleared his throat, then stared down

at his battered boots. "I would like to tell my sister that a cowboy . . . not a cow thief . . . visited the shrine."

The boss stared hard at them for a long moment. "Get out of here . . ." he growled at last. "If you show up on this side of the river, we will shoot you. And if you don't deliver Greene in the next twenty-four hours, we might come over and shoot you anyway."

The mesquite tree next to the brush corral offered slight shade as Laramie and Hap lounged against its trunk.

"We ain't exactly takin' south Texas by storm," Hap observed.

Laramie watched two ants crawl across the toe of his boot. "We're alive. After last night, I consider that real progress. You know why I stayed? I thought, *If I leave Hap in Mexico and he gets killed stealing cattle, I'm going to have to be the one to go to Wyoming and tell his mamma.* So I reckon neither one of us has the nerve to disappoint that sweet lady."

"Well, our safety might only be a temporary condition. You think those Mexicans might come over and track us down?"

"If they have more cattle stolen, and we don't deliver Greene, they'll regret the decision to turn us loose. Sort of makes me wish we were riding for a ranch up in the Wind River range."

"You reckon that dust cloud comin' this way is Mr. E. A. Greene?" Hap eased himself into the saddle, then tugged his hat a little lower in the front.

Laramie yanked the cinch tight around Tully's stomach.

He swung up as easily as most men drop into a recliner in front of the TV. "Are you ready for this, partner?"

"Oh, yeah."

The dually towing the long gooseneck stock trailer pulled up to the brush corrals. E. A. Greene bounded out of the cab. "Boys, am I glad to see you. I ran into some vaqueros last night and led them downstream to give you safe passage back here." He stared out at the empty brush corrals. "Were you able to sort them out and push my cows across?"

"We took care of things for you," Hap said.

"You did?" Greene rubbed his hands together. "This calls for an extra bonus . . . two hundred dollars apiece. Did you lose any?"

"Not one of your cows was lost," Laramie reported.

"I knew you boys were ranahans the minute I saw you at the café. They aren't in the corrals up here, so where are they?"

"We figured if those vaqueros got to missin' any head, they would swim over and look in these corrals," Hap said.

"Good thinkin', boys. You made my day." He yanked out a worn tooled-leather wallet and shoved two one-hundred-dollar bills at each of them.

Hap tucked his money in his shirt pocket. "Get out your saddle horse, E.A.; let's go retrieve your goods."

Greene opened the long stock trailer and led out his horse. "One of you grab my keys. The kind of riffraff that crosses the border here ain't against stealin' my truck."

Hap swung down. When he pulled himself out of the cab of the truck he toted keys and a small white cardboard box. He handed the keys to Greene and flashed the box at Laramie. "Looks like you had a fine Chinese supper up in

San Antonio. Is this the takeout place on Sixteenth Street?" Hap asked. "I hear they serve a fine Mu Shu Pork."

"Yep, it's across from the meat locker. Everything they serve is tasty," Greene said. "You boys should try it next time you're up that way."

Hap led the way. Greene followed. Laramie rode drag.

The level, sandy ground was bordered by thick brush that kept them from seeing the Rio Grande. The trail through the green-leafed thicket zigzagged so much they almost lost sight of one another.

Hap peered back to see a pleased look on Greene's face, an unlit cigar clamped between his teeth. Hap mused that most folks plodded along like that, chewing on life's cigar, happy and content, without any idea what's around the corner.

"Are you sure you got them penned in? I don't remember any corrals down by the river," Greene called out.

"We hired young Mr. Fernando Valenzuela Ortega to watch them," Hap replied. "Isn't that a fine name for a thirteen-year-old?"

"You got a thirteen-year-old Mexican kid watching my sixty head?"

"Your goods are right where we left them," Laramie assured. "Think about it: If the Mexicans cross over and stumble upon them, no one can blame you . . . or us."

"You boys think of everything."

"We like to be thorough, E.A.," Hap said.

When they crossed the last rise, the brush ended. They dropped down the wide, flat riverbank. E. A. Greene stood in the stirrups and surveyed the river. "I don't see my cows."

"We got ever'thin' that belongs to you right over there."

Hap trotted the trio toward a young boy in a blue Los Angeles Dodgers shirt.

Greene yanked the cigar out of his mouth and shoved it back in his denim shirt pocket. "Where are my cows?"

"Come on, have a little faith in your top ranahans." Laramie winked at Hap. They eased coiled ropes into their left hands.

"I did just like you asked."

"You did fine work, son." Laramie unsnapped his shirt pocket and handed him a folded ten-dollar bill.

"What's goin' on here?" Greene demanded.

"There's your goods." Hap nodded at the sand.

"Five oranges?" Greene blustered. "Where are my cows?"

"You don't own any cows. You never owned any cows," Hap said. "But you did compare cows to oranges."

"What are you talking about? I happen to own . . ."

"You don't own Hidalgo County Land and Cattle, that's for sure. We rode on up and visited with Señor Robles at the break of day. Seems like someone has been rustlin' his cattle."

Greene slammed his heels into his horse. The buckskin bolted forward. Hap's rope slipped over the man's shoulders. When the rope's other end was dallied around the saddle horn, E. A. Greene hit the ground hard.

He fought to regain his footing. When he stomped toward his horse, Laramie's rope slipped under his step and laced his boots together. With both ropes dallied, the boys backed up the horses until Greene swung in the air, stretched out like a pig on a barbecue spit.

Curses streamed from the dangling man's lips.

"I have never seen a man strung up like that before," Fernando hollered.

"It's a rodeo event we've been doin' since we met," Hap replied. "This version's called Rope-A-Crook."

"Is that all there is to it? You just rope them like in team roping?"

"After he's stretched out there, one of us is supposed to run down the rope and stuff a bandanna in his mouth," Hap said.

"Can I do that?" the boy asked.

Laramie pulled out his bandanna and handed it to Fernando. He sprinted to the fountain of curses and plugged up its source.

"I did it!" The boy ran back to Laramie. "What do you do now? Do you turn him loose?"

"Nope." Hap studied Greene's empty saddle. "We need some piggin' string, but the leathers on his saddle will work. We'll secure his feet and arms with a couple of wraps and a hooey."

"Just like tie-down roping?" Fernando asked.

Laramie laughed. "Yep. It's a timed event. They might even have it at the finals in Las Vegas one of these years. They've got an endless supply of crooks there."

With E.A. tied hand and foot, they bound him to the saddle, then led his horse down to the river.

Fernando sprinted beside them. "Are you going to drown him?"

Hap scratched the back of his neck. "I hope not, but we think this pony might enjoy a little swim."

Laramie led the horse about ten feet into the water, then dropped the reins over the saddle horn. He leaned over, slapped the horse in the rear, and yelled, "Heyahh!"

The buckskin bolted to the middle of the river, but stopped when the water lapped his stomach.

Hap swung down out of the saddle and scooped up some pebbles by the water's edge. He pelted the horse, who inched out into deeper water.

"You want the horse to swim over to Mexico?" the boy asked.

"That horse is free to go any direction he wants. If he ends up in Mexico, that's his decision," Laramie replied.

"I'm thinking he wants to stand in the middle of the Rio Grande all day," Fernando replied. "Did you know that I am very good at baseball? I was even named after the great Los Angeles Dodger pitcher Fernando Valenzuela. I am very good at pitching. Would you like to see?"

Hap surveyed the riverbank. "You have a baseball?"

Fernando sprinted over to the five oranges and hurried back. He laid four on the sand next to the water and stared at the distant horse as if looking for a sign from the catcher. "I am going to throw my fastball," he announced.

"That seems like a good choice," Hap said.

Taking a full windup, Fernando leaned back, rolled his eyes up to the light blue south Texas sky, then fired the orange out into the river. The medium-sized citrus rocketed toward its mark and slammed into the horse's right hip. The buckskin leaped forward into the deep water and swam toward the Mexican shore.

"That's great, Fernando. I'm impressed," Laramie said.

"I have a good curveball, too, but my slider needs work. You want to see my curveball?"

"Maybe your mamma would like to have those four oranges," Hap suggested.

"Yes, she would. Would you like to come meet my mother and my sister?"

Hap glanced over at Laramie and back at the boy. "What's your sister's name?"

"Selina. She is five years old."

"Thanks for the invite, but we need to retrieve our truck and get on down the road."

"Do you live around here? Perhaps sometime, you could come watch me play baseball."

"Thanks, Fernando, but we live in Wyoming. We're just down here sort of looking for someone," Laramie said.

"Who are you looking for? I know everyone who lives in this area."

"It's kind of difficult to explain," Hap said.

Laramie ran his fingers through his short, curly hair. "My partner here is searching for a gal named Juanita. Do you know anyone named Juanita?"

The boy's brown eyes widened. "I know dozens of girls named Juanita. My mother's named Juanita."

Hap rode over to the boy. "Do you know a gal named Juanita with a birthmark under her right ear that sort of looks like a horse's head?"

"Oh, yes. I know her."

Hap sat straight up and felt the hairs on the back of his neck bristle. "Are you kiddin' me, son?"

"No, that sounds like Juanita Elaina Cortez."

"Juanita Elaina Cortez, that's a nice name," Hap said. "How old is she?"

"She is old. Your age, I think."

"We're on the right trail, partner," Laramie said. "How many pounds does she weigh?"

Fernando glanced at Laramie, then at Hap, and back to Laramie. "How many pounds?"

Laramie circled his hands. "Is she heavy?"

"On the top or on the bottom?"

"Around the waist," Hap insisted.

"She is thin there."

Hap pulled off his black hat and wiped dirt and sweat off his forehead. It dawned on him that if he actually found his Juanita, he wasn't sure what would happen next. That was a dilemma he had never had to face. "Where is she?"

"I think she is in Zapata, about forty miles west from here. She used to be a neighbor of my grandmother's."

Fernando strolled beside them, oranges in hand, as they rode back out of the riverbed. What breeze had existed along the river had now died down.

"Where can we find this Juanita?" Hap quizzed.

Fernando shrugged. "At the jail, of course."

"She's in jail?" Laramie said.

"Oh, no." Fernando grinned. "She works at the jail. She teaches them English and cooks."

Hap shoved back his black hat. "A teacher? A cook? My age?"

"And a birthmark under her ear," Laramie added. "Hap, it can't be that simple."

"Destiny can be simple," Hap replied.

"Destiny?" Fernando called out. "I thought you were searching for a girl named Juanita."

CHAPTER THREE

In Laramie's mind, all midsize towns looked identical after dark. Geographical distinctions faded with the setting of the hot summer sun. Each town had one particular street where the rainbow of bright lights summoned customers. It could be Broadway, or Lincoln Avenue, or Twenty-first Street . . . they all appeared the same. When Laramie and Hap followed the flashing red and green lights into the parking lot of Jose's Git-N-Go, he assumed it was just another fast food night.

"This ain't my idea of a fine supper." Hap glared at the microwave window where a foot-long green chili burrito twirled a pirouette in slow motion.

"We did get overtime money for waiting for that last load at the feedlot. But I'm surprised all the decent cafés close before midnight." Laramie juggled a large bag of barbecued potato chips and two frozen cheeseburgers while he tried to swipe away the dirt caked to the front of his jeans. "I don't think a decent place would let us in until we cleaned up, anyway. Did you rip open the end of that burrito bag?"

Hap's black T-shirt hung sweat heavy. A denim shirt layered it, unbuttoned and untucked. "You naggin' me about how to nuke a frozen burrito?"

Laramie studied the poster of a polar bear with shades, who slurped an iced blue drink. "Just a reminder . . . if you don't let the air out, it could blow up."

Hap stomped off some of the dust on his pointed-toe boots. "I'm so tired of lookin' at the rear ends of cattle that an explodin' burrito might be an interestin' diversion."

"Working at the feedlot did get your mind off the disappointment of Fernando's Juanita."

"I don't remember a thing about her, except she wasn't the one."

Laramie's white teeth beamed out from a dirty-faced grin. "Now don't tell me you forgot about . . ."

Hap held up his hand. "I told you, an explodin' burrito ain't the worst thing that can happen in life."

A sudden blast staggered Hap into the paper products rack. He came up kicking Styrofoam cups and clutching a fifty-pack of fluorescent-colored straws. Angry words screamed out in a southeast Asian dialect bounced between the walls of the small store. Laramie pulled himself off a cardboard Budweiser girl who sported shorts meant to make Daisy Duke look modest.

The second shotgun blast from outside the minimart didn't vibrate like the first. When Hap retrieved his black hat from the rack of cake doughnuts, the quiet ding of a bell seemed out of place.

Laramie glanced over at the unscathed microwave. "Your burrito's ready."

Both cowboys scurried to the front door in time to witness a petite Asian woman in black jeans and a Hawaiian blouse brandishing a pump shotgun. Only a few neon lights remained to mark the route of a would-be thief. Other than a distant train whistle the street was silent and empty.

"Are you all right, ma'am?" Hap asked.

She spun around, then lowered the weapon. Gold-framed glasses perched on the end of her tiny nose. "It happened again." Deep wrinkles around her eyes tightened.

Hap stepped up beside her. "Did you get robbed?"

"He tried. I think it was the same man as last month. He's out on bail awaiting trial. I am sick and tired of this."

Laramie studied the hole that had been an eight-by-six-foot plate-glass window. "What can we do to help you?"

The lady tiptoed through the broken glass to the front door. "You want to buy a minimart, so I can retire? I'm too old to put up with this. I need to phone the police."

The summer night air smelled like a combination of a snack bar at the ballpark and the floor of a movie theater.

Hap peered through the dark shadows of the empty Laredo street. "What'd he look like?"

"Like a man in a ski mask. Were you serious about the offer to help?"

Hap glanced over at his partner. Laramie nodded and said, "I was taught to always help a lady in distress."

"Did your father teach you that?" she asked.

"My mother. She is in distress most of the time."

The woman held out her hand to Laramie. "My name is Sam."

"Is that short for Samantha?"

"It's short for Vingh Duc Sam." The lady with short salt-and-pepper hair took a long, deep breath, then dialed 911.

Laramie and Hap had restacked the antifreeze, scraped up the Little Debbies, and swept most of the broken glass on the inside of the store when the police finished their reports.

Sam clutched her arms. "I expected this cleanup to take all night. I phoned my daughter earlier to come over and help when she gets off work. You boys are like angels from heaven."

"Hap is often mistaken for an angel," Laramie chided. "It must be the cheap mustache. What did the police tell you?" He fought a rising emotion and questioned why the woman had to run a minimart alone after dark. In his mind, every woman ought to have a safe place at night. Especially those married to drunks.

Sam kicked at a piece of broken glass with her Nike tennis shoe. "They think they'll be able to track him down. I remembered the license plate number on his getaway vehicle. 'Wyoming, 2-4570.'"

"Wyomin'?" Hap's chin dropped. "That's my license number."

They raced out to the gas pumps. Hap punched his fist into the lip of a plastic trash can. "He stole my dadgum truck, Laramie. That two-bit thief stole my truck!"

It was after 1:00 A.M. by the time the police filed the stolen-vehicle report. Laramie and Hap nailed plywood over the broken window.

"I ain't never had someone steal my rig before. Have you, Laramie?"

"Quincy Bob stole the Circle A crummie one time when you were up in Alberta. But he was too soused to have a clue what he was doing. I had to walk fourteen miles back to the ranch. They found the crummie two days later parked in front of the White Horse Inn, with Quincy Bob asleep on the balcony."

"The White Horse Inn's been closed for twenty-five years."

"I told you old Bob was soused."

Hap hoisted the plywood up with his shoulder and drove in another nail. "My daddy had his two-ton hay truck stolen one time when I was about ten. They took it right out of the shed. They got as far as Belfry before it ran out of gas. Daddy's ever'day spurs was in the jockey box. He stewed more about losin' them than the truck. A wrecker from Bridger called us. Said he had the truck in his yard and retrieval cost $167. Daddy pondered it a while, and then we went up to fetch it. He did it for the spurs."

Laramie pulled nails from his mouth and shoved them into his shirt pocket as he climbed down the six-foot aluminum ladder. He watched as narrow headlights of a small convertible bounced into the parking lot. It was a crisp powder blue like the late-afternoon sky over the Bear Tooth Mountains in summer. The music from the stereo died when the car door opened. "Now, there's a pretty one for you." The pain in his right shoulder melted away and he scratched his cheek to hide a boyish grin.

"It's one of them little Mazdas. It's got two bucket seats and no backseat. I hear they're fun to drive in the mountains. I reckon the mileage is good, but it would be kind of cramped with the top up."

"I wasn't talking about the car, Hap."

A very tall, slender lady, with straight black hair pulled back behind her ears, swung out of the convertible. She wore white crepe-sole oxfords, a short-sleeved white dress down to her knees, and opaque white hose, but she strolled the parking lot like a lissome model on a designer's runway.

Laramie's voice lowered. "There's one fine-looking nurse . . . sort of a young, olive-skinned Audrey Hepburn." He searched for lines that he'd practiced for years. He'd always told himself that someday a lady would appear who might erase his bad memories. As he tried to exhale slowly, he realized he wouldn't mind if she erased everything on the face of the planet except the two of them.

"Hi, I'm Annamarie Buchett. You must be the cowboys mother hired to help clean up."

Hap pulled off his hat. "Sam is your mother?"

"Yes, is she inside?"

Laramie shook his head. "She sure is beautiful."

Annamarie narrowed her eyes. "My mother?"

"Eh . . . no . . . I . . ." He stammered as if his *witty but friendly* file had been deleted.

"My partner, Laramie, was admirin' your . . ."

"Your sports car," Laramie gasped. "She sure is a beauty." Images of some movie with Hugh Grant and Julia Roberts came to mind, but he couldn't remember any of the suave lines.

"Thank you, Laramie. You have good taste . . ." she turned and grinned at Hap. " . . . in sports cars."

He tipped his hat. "My name is Hap, Miss Annamarie."

She shook his hand. "Laramie and Hap? I don't suppose those are the names your mothers gave you."

"Hap was my dad's idea."

"And Annamarie was my father's."

"Say," Hap added. "Is Buchett a French name?"

"My mother's father was French. That makes me one-quarter French, one-quarter Vietamese, and one-half stubborn Texan. Buchett is a good, east Texas pioneer name."

"You don't say," Laramie murmured. "Mighty pretty . . ."

"My car?"

Laramie cleared his throat. "Yes, ma'am." He watched her disappear into the store, hoping, somehow, she favored shy, pathetic bumblers.

⊷⊜   ⊜⊶

With all the boards in place, they toted the tools and ladders around to the shed in the back. Hap snapped the padlock. "I ain't never seen you tongue-tied like that."

"I spent most of my early years too scared to talk. This is different. Real different. It all became clear to me in an instant."

"What became clear?"

"For weeks I've been trying to figure out why in the world I am down here in Laredo, Texas."

They hiked back around to the front of the store and watched as an ambulance, lights flashing, but no sirens, raced down the street. "We're searchin' for my Juanita," Hap reminded him.

"Yeah, but that doesn't explain why I'm here. Now, I know. It's divine providence that I meet Annamarie."

"Are you claimin' the Lord led you here? What about Koni in Gillette? Or Martie in Lander? Or Sara in Cody? Or the Cainette twins in Encampment that you were too shy to even speak to twice? You said they were all divine providence, too."

"Hap, Annamarie has a classic beauty. She could pose for one of those Greek statues."

"Statues? You ain't just ponderin' her . . . sports car?"

"I was talking about her face. And her eyes. Have you ever seen eyes like that? They make a man feel alive and important and . . . and . . ."

"Yeah . . . right. Laramie, she's just a diversion. We've got to clean up out front. Then we've got to figure out somethin' about my truck, how to get back to the motel, how to go pick up our pay at the feedlot. Where are you goin'?"

"To get diverted," Laramie said.

Laramie leaned his backside against the counter close to where Annamarie sat, legs drooped over the edge. She rocked back and forth and chewed on a long round stick of pepper-spiced beef jerky. A one-sided phone conversation filtered out from the office in back where Sam had retreated with a stack of forms and receipts.

"Anyway, that's the short version of my life story . . . and Hap's . . . and what we're doing in south Texas." He fought to keep focused on her eyes and wished he had his dark glasses on to filter his enthusiasm. "Thanks for listening. I appreciate your graciousness after my brain freeze in the parking lot."

"I enjoyed the visit. Mother is the only one I have time to talk to much anymore. It's nice to hear someone else's voice."

"I want to hear more about you. You just got started when I interrupted."

"Now, that will take a while. But you heard the most important parts. The more I talk about it, the more complicated it sounds." Her cheeks dimpled with her smile.

"I don't have many plans for the next few decades, other than Hap's idiot obsession, and I'm a good listener."

"You'll need to be. My motives get so confusing, I can't even figure them out. Would you believe this is the best talk I've had in three years?"

Hap ambled into the minimart, hat pushed back, broom over his shoulder. "Don't bother comin' out to help me, partner. I got the parking lot swept up."

"Annamarie and I got busy visiting. Sorry about cutting out on you."

"We were comparing college courses." Annamarie's teeth were straight and bright, like an ad for whitening gel.

"College? What's there to talk about? He was an ag major in junior college."

"I had to take organic chemistry," Laramie announced. "Same as nursing majors like Annamarie."

"Well, us weldin' majors had to study the density of metal. At the moment my dense brain feels like an exploded burrito. If you're through with intellectual pursuits, I reckon it's time to head back to the motel. I've got to phone my insurance company and figure somethin' out about my truck."

Annamarie reached over and clutched Hap's elbow with her long, thin, ringless fingers. "I think what you are doing is terribly romantic."

Hap stared at her hand. A grin crept across his face. "You do?"

"Looking for your Juanita and all. Laramie told me all about it."

"Some days it seems foolish."

She broke the jerky in half and handed a piece to Laramie. "In a way, it reminds me of something my husband did when he was young."

Hap glanced over at his partner.

"Annamarie's husband got killed in Iraq." Laramie bit off a bite of jerky that burned his lower lip.

Hap yanked off his black, beaver felt cowboy hat and held it over his heart. "Was he in the service, ma'am?"

"No, he worked for a Texas-based drilling company. He went over to help get their oil wells up and running. It wasn't war-related. Not directly, anyway. The derrick collapsed. Stress tests on the steel used are not the same all over the world and this one just gave out."

"I'm sure the pain is just as severe." Laramie detected that when she talked about her husband, her eyes didn't look as sad as they did numb. It was as if the grief had already wearied her.

"Nate volunteered to go over and work because he wanted to do something that mattered. Drilling's what he knew how to do. I think he would have worked for free."

"When did it happen?" Hap asked.

"Three years ago. But what I wanted to say, the summer Nate turned sixteen, he worked on a long letter to the girl he would someday marry. He explained what was important to him and how he envisioned his future. It was a twenty-page typed letter. When we were in our senior year at Southern Methodist he proposed to me. He said, 'Before you answer yes or no, you need to take this letter home and read it.'"

Hap rubbed his forehead. "So, what did you think?"

"I cried and cried. I got to see his sixteen-year-old heart. When a man is twenty-three, he's covered up most of that vulnerability. I knew when I read the letter, he was the one for me."

"You think I should have written a letter to Juanita when I was twelve and saved it all these years?"

"No, but don't lose the fervor of that twelve-year-old heart."

⟶▭   ▭⟵

With the restrooms scrubbed, the coffee machines cleaned, and the gas pumps read, Sam shut down Jose's Git-N-Go and locked the front door. "I would sell the store, but who would buy a place that has been robbed twice in the last two months? Annamarie, you give Laramie and Hap a ride home. It's the least we can do, since they refused any money."

The three watched Sam drive her white Volvo out of the dark parking lot and turn right on the quiet Laredo street. They strolled to the parked Mazda.

"Oh, dear . . ." Annamarie sighed. "My convertible is a little small. I'll take two trips."

"It's the middle of the night and you've worked all day. Hap and me will scrunch in here somehow."

Hap studied the two small pale blue leather bucket seats. "There's only so much scrunchin' a man can do."

With his hat screwed down tight, Hap sprawled across the concealed rag top and the chrome luggage rack, his boots hanging down between Laramie and Annamarie just above the gearshift lever.

"Are you sure you're okay up there?" she asked.

"It's kind of like sittin' on a rank bronc at a rodeo. You ain't sure you're goin' to live through it, but if you do, you'll have quite a story to tell. But I'd prefer you don't hit speed bumps goin' fifty miles per hour. Other than that, I'm okay."

The one-story, single-family houses lined the street behind scraggly lawns and cracked sidewalks. Distant red lights slowed and stopped phantom traffic. A rubber and asphalt aroma still radiated from the daylight-warmed blacktop. The only sounds were the Bridgestone tires rolling along and the conversation in the front seat.

"It was foolish to buy such a small car," she said. "I'm only comfortable with the top down. I traded in my Subaru and Nate's Ford truck and bought this about three months after he died. I guess it sort of symbolized my feeling at the time. I needed something fun . . . but I wanted to be alone."

Laramie's struggles with his past paled as he considered Annamarie's. "I like the car. It makes you look good . . . I mean, it's a nice match. You and the convertible. Did it accomplish its goals?"

"Driving fast with the wind in my face is just about my

only joy. I don't think there's been one or two other guys who've ridden with me. I guess it has done that much."

Laramie fought back the urge to ask who the other guys were that rode with her and whether she was dating anyone. "I never owned a convertible, but the breeze is sort like the time I raced Tully along the Oregon beach."

"Tully is your horse?"

"Yeah, he's a pain and a pal. But it's hard to imagine a day without him."

Annamarie roared through a dip in the street. Laramie glanced back to see Hap clutch his hat and the luggage rack.

"Sorry," she called back. "I forgot you were there."

"That's all right," Hap called out. "Bein' a quiet and shy fella, I'm often overlooked."

"You've been too quiet back there, cowboy," Annamarie replied.

"I've been prayin' a lot."

"Praying?"

"That I'd live to see daylight. Besides, I ain't a big fan of eatin' bugs." Hap glanced around. "Whoa . . . there's a black Dodge truck down there."

She yanked a hard right. Laramie reached back and held on to Hap's boot as she sped down the side street. An exterior supplemental chrome fuel tank was tucked in the bed and the rig displayed Texas license plates.

"Sorry about that," Hap said as Annamarie zoomed back to the main street. "I had to take a look."

She did come to a complete pause at the stop sign, but spun her tires as she zipped around the corner. "Tomorrow, I'm off at four. I'll drive you two around and we'll search Laredo for your truck."

"That's great," Laramie said. "Other than the feedlot and the minimart, we don't know anything about this town. But we hate to interfere with your life."

She laid her hand on Laramie's arm. "Trust me, you are not interfering with my life."

Annamarie slammed on the brakes when the light changed. Hap slid forward between her and Laramie, catching his hand on the windshield.

"I don't mean to show ingratitude, but I don't reckon I can ride up here many nights," Hap said. "I'm sure my insurance company will rent me a truck. Why don't we drive it tomorrow night? I reckon Laramie's right. We surely could use a guide."

⊷═⊳   ⊲═⊶

Hap parked behind the blue Mazda convertible in the driveway of the sprawling ranch house. When he turned the engine off, the motor continued to sputter. "I'm gettin' new insurance." With a loud explosion and a puff of smoke, the engine died.

"Well, they did provide a rig. I think the quality of the rental is reflected in the coverage you have."

"This ain't funny. How can a 1995 Ford Fiesta with 120,000 miles and busted air-conditioner be a replacement vehicle for a two-year-old Dodge pickup?"

"I bet it gets good mileage." Laramie scrunched down so his head didn't rub against the top of the cab, then slowly pulled himself out. "This isn't so bad, Hap. Just depends on your comparison."

"What are you comparin' it to?"

The passenger door closed with a bang and a rattle.

Laramie leaned down and stuck his head through the open window. "How about the back row on that commuter airplane we took between Greeley and Rapid City?"

Hap tilted his head sideways and tried to slide on his hat. "A coffin would have been roomier than that plane."

"You see, this is feelin' spacious already. Plenty of room for four."

"What do you mean, four?"

Laramie stood up and leaned against the side of the car. "Annamarie is bringing Sara."

"Who's Sara?"

"Her roommate."

"This is the first time I heard of this. I thought she lived here with her mamma."

"She has her own apartment in the basement. Sara lives with her. You don't mind a little female company, do you?"

"Laramie, you know I ain't lookin' for a girl named Sara."

"This isn't a date. We're just searching for your truck. Four sets of eyes might be better than three. Annamarie didn't think it was polite to leave Sara all alone tonight."

Hap kept an eye on the front door of the house. "What's this Sara like?"

"Annamarie said she's outgoing and friendly."

"Laramie, I ain't feelin' real sociable tonight."

"I'll talk; you drive. The ladies can sit in the backseat, if you want."

"I'm not that unsociable. You and Annamarie take the backseat. Sara can sit up front with me, providin' she ain't too talkative."

"I doubt she says much. I'll go get the girls."

Ten minutes later Annamarie and Laramie hunkered down in the backseat of the mostly white Ford subcompact, while Hap chomped on a wooden toothpick and glared in the rearview mirror.

Sara stuck her head out the open window on the passenger's side and barked.

"What kind of dog is she?" Hap asked.

Annamarie reached up and scratched Sara's ear. "A boxer."

"I thought boxers were big."

"She's a runt. That's why I love her. The day I heard of Nate's death, I went out running. I had to do something before the grief consumed me. I jogged about five miles and decided I'd keep running and never stop."

"Like Forrest Gump?" Laramie probed.

"I suppose. I thought maybe I'd collapse along the road and be lucky enough to have a semi flatten me. But instead, Sara showed up and decided to run with me. No matter how I tried to lose her, she trotted right along. So I gave up punishing myself and went home. I posted flyers and tried to find her owner. She's a house dog. I know someone missed her. But no one claimed her, so I moved her down here and we've been roommates ever since."

Laramie studied the brindle dog's head hanging out the window. "She likes to go for a ride."

"She probably thinks we're going to Dairy Queen. She likes the hotdogs there."

⋆⇒   ⇐⋆

At 9:00 P.M., they scooted into a booth by the window of the Caliente Café and ordered three number 12s with extra salsa on the side. Hap sat across from Laramie and Annamarie.

Sara waited in the car.

With a new toy from Dairy Queen.

High, padded red vinyl seatbacks in the booth gave them a sense of privacy. A six-pack of various hot sauces and a stack of paper napkins perched on the table below a window overlooking a street filled with lowriders and mind-thumping bass notes.

"I guess this was sort of stupid, tryin' to find my truck by drivin' all over town," Hap said. "I just feel like I have to be doin' somethin'."

"Sara enjoyed it," Laramie remarked.

One glare from Hap silenced him.

Annamarie spun the ice in her Coke with her long finger. "And I got to hear some wonderful stories. So, how did you decide that Fernando's Juanita Elaina Cortez in Zapata was not the right Juanita?"

"The wide gap in her front teeth, plus the birthmark under her ear turned out to be a tattoo of Mickey Mouse," Hap reported.

"I thought you turned her down because she cussed like a rookie bull rider and told you her mother had a better mustache than you." Laramie dumped red Tabasco into the salsa.

"That, too." Hap stabbed four tortilla chips into the bowl, then popped them into his mouth.

"What now, guys? You said the work was done at the feedlot. Where do you go from here?" Annamarie asked.

"Can't go anywhere without my truck," Hap said. "I ain't goin' to haul a horse trailer behind a dadgum Ford

Fiesta. I reckon we'll stay around here a while. One of the cattle buyers offered us a few days' work."

Laramie eased his arm to the back of the booth and slipped it around Annamarie's shoulder. He felt more like sixteen than thirty-one. "Do you know a man by the name of Pete Struckmann?"

The stiff, open collar on her white, long-sleeved blouse covered most of her long neck, except for a small silver heart that dangled from a delicate silver chain. "He owns a car dealership, radio station, plus some other businesses. He's on the board of directors of St. Mary's Hospital. He seems like a nice man . . . you know, in a rich sort of way."

Laramie felt muscles that had been taut for months, perhaps years, begin to relax. "Struckmann bought four hundred head of steers at the feedlot. According to him, he purchased himself a nice spread and wants to go into the cattle business. He said the ranch he bought has been tied up in an estate contestation for five years. The bank he purchased it from assured him the fence was in great shape, but he's not real confident in their assessment. He's going to corral his cows by the stock tanks until we check it out and repair the fence. It might take us a few days."

When Annamarie glanced at Laramie's arm, he pulled it back.

"That sounds so nice and peaceful. On horseback, out in the hills . . . a time to relax." She tugged Laramie's arm back around her shoulder. "What size is this ranch?"

"Over twenty thousand acres. Bigger than a five-mile square."

"My, it really does sound serene. No emergencies. No

panic. No danger." Her hazel eyes took on a greenish hue as she leaned back against his arm.

Laramie felt as if an electroshock had restarted his heart, rekindling the memory of how good the attentions of a classy lady can make a man feel. "Do you ride?"

"I used to ride twice a week without fail. I have a friend that runs a stable down at Noche Negra. But since I started working overtime in the emergency room, I'm too exhausted to do things like that."

The sound of dishes crashing to the floor spun their attention toward the kitchen door. A teenage boy in white jeans scurried to clean up the mess.

"You're invited to come along, if you like . . . you know, providing you have the time," Laramie offered.

Hap pushed his hat back. "Annamarie don't want to ride fence with us. Shoot, I don't even want to ride fence with us. It's hot, sweaty, dull, boring, routine work. We probably won't see another soul for three or four days."

"That sounds wonderful, I'll do it. I've got so many days off piled up, the hospital administrator has been begging me to use them up. I'll make some phone calls and line it up tonight. Do you have a horse and tack I can borrow? I could get one from my friend in Noche Negra, but I don't imagine she could be here tomorrow morning."

Laramie's grin seemed to be hanging from his earlobes.

Annamarie paused. "Was that a serious offer?"

"Oh, yeah." he gave her a squeeze.

Daylight flooded in from the east and the air drifting from the river felt almost coastal. From the edge of the dirt road, the range rolled brown and treeless. To the south, the ground leveled out into irrigated farms. Beyond the horizon sprawled a town and further away, the Rio Grande.

The predawn thunderstorm barely sprinkled the soil, but the raindrops cleaned the air and gave it a fresh, misty taste. Luke and Tully sensed a day on the range and shuffled their hooves as they stood tied to the trailer.

Hap tugged the rubber boot off Luke's left rear hoof. "What in the world are we doin', takin' a beautiful, sophisticated lady like Annamarie Buchett with us ridin' fence?"

Laramie watched the road toward town. "She needs a change of pace, Hap . . . some downtime. She doesn't really have anyone to ride with."

Hap eased Luke's hoof back to the ground, then pushed his hat back. "So, we're doin' this for her?"

"Of course."

"I thought for a while it was just for you. You've been actin' as blissful as a bull in springtime. But, if it's for Annamarie's sake, of course we got to do it."

Laramie hiked closer to his partner. "She's a nice lady, Hap. A real nice lady."

Hap smoothed the white, red, and blue Navajo saddle blanket on Luke's back. "And she's tall. With classic long legs. And narrow waist. And good proportions elsewhere. But I reckon that don't enter into this at all."

"Partner, you know the feeling when you're going down a road you never traveled and you think something exciting's up around the next bend or just over the next hill? An urge pushes you to keep going, to see where it leads. Well, I got to see where this leads."

Hap set his saddle down easy on the Navajo blanket.

When he turned, his eyes locked on Laramie's. "Seein' where it leads? Now, that, partner, is somethin' I know about." He studied the sky. "It looks like a good day to ride."

"Yep. And today, I am glad I'm me."

The blue Mazda Miata pulled up near the trees next to them, the black soft top up. The first one out of the car had black hair, old jeans, and a beat-up straw cowboy hat. The other had short, pointed ears and a flea collar and yelped at Hap.

Laramie led the way, then Annamarie on the paint mare with Sara straddled awkwardly in her lap. Hap held the lead rope for the pack mule. All three had bedrolls lashed to the backs of their saddles.

They rode west, parallel to the dirt road. Laramie divided his time between surveying fence and stealing glances at Annamarie. Her eyes were covered with orange-framed sunglasses. Matching orange earrings dangled from her ears. Her long-sleeved white blouse danced with orange and yellow embroidered daisies.

Laramie admired the way she rode . . . straight, chin up, reins low, toes barely tucked in the stirrups. The sunglasses hid her eyes and hints of what was going on in her mind. So did Laramie's. At that moment, he was glad they did.

Throughout the morning, several pickups raced down the unpaved road rolling dirt clouds their way. The air tasted dry, acrid. Even when the wind drifted away from them, they rode in the aroma of sweat and old leather.

About 10:00 A.M., Laramie dismounted in the shade of three mesquite trees.

"If the entire fence is like this first part, it won't take all that long." Annamarie waited as Hap lifted Sara to the ground.

Laramie loosed Tully's cinch and dropped the reins to the dirt. "Fences seldom break down next to the road."

Annamarie stretched her long legs and rubbed her backside. "Why do you think that is?"

"It's one of life's mysteries." Hap checked the load on the pack mule. "Fences bust where it's most inaccessible." He pulled off his black hat and wiped his face and hair with his bandanna. "They bust on rocky ground, edges of cliffs, or in the middle of a cactus patch. It's a cinch you'll have to tote a full roll of wire on your back for a mile uphill. It's as if they have a mind of their own and an evil, unrelenting hatred for cowboys."

"Boy, you're a pessimistic cuss today." Laramie drove a staple into the fencepost to pin down a dangling strand of barbed wire.

Hap squatted to scratch Sara's ears. "I'm still fumed about losin' my truck."

Annamarie gazed across the road at a distant green field. "What are you guys going to do after you get Hap's truck back and finish this job?"

"Head toward Del Rio, I reckon." Sara jumped up and licked Hap's cheek.

"Chasing Juanitas?"

Laramie pulled the canteen off the saddle horn and ambled over to her. "I promised Hap we'd scout the Rio Grande from Brownsville to Creede, Colorado. If we don't find his Juanita, he has to give up the hunt and live a normal life."

"Yeah, but I don't have a clue what normal is."

Annamarie tugged off her sunglasses and dangled them from a black nylon braided strap around her neck. The bright sunlight illuminated her hazel eyes with foxy tints. "Neither do I."

Laramie pushed his sunglasses to the top of his head. "How about you, Annamarie? Do you aim to be an emergency-room nurse in Laredo the rest of your life?"

"Not really. I moved down here three years ago when my husband was killed. I thought the two widows could take care of each other. It was the right thing to do at the time."

"Your mamma is a widow, too?" Hap poured water into the palm of his hand and held it out for Sara.

"Daddy died from cancer about five years after he got back from Vietnam."

"Was it caused by Agent Orange?" Laramie asked.

"That's what we think, but back then no one would tell us."

Hap took a swig from the canteen. "That's tough losin' your daddy and your husband." He handed the canteen to Annamarie.

"I'm trying not to lose my mother as well. I struggle to talk her into selling the store." She wiped the mouth of the canteen on the sleeve of her blouse and took a swig.

"What would she do if she sold the minimart?" Laramie quizzed.

"Maybe move to Santa Ana, California. Her brothers own a catering business. She could work for them or just retire."

"If your mamma moves," Laramie took the canteen she handed him, "where does that put you?"

"I'll be in a hospital somewhere. It's who I am. I like being a nurse, but I wouldn't mind slowing the pace some. Mother says I was born to wear white, crepe-soled shoes."

"You look good on horseback, too."

Hap grinned. "Shoot, she'd look good anywhere, doin' anything."

Annamarie rubbed her long, thin nose, then grinned. "You guys have no idea how great those compliments sound."

✦══◦   ◦══✦

They worked the southern fence line, then turned north along the western boundary by midafternoon. The sky hued a thin blue, weakened by the constant heat rising off the ground. No breeze. The air tasted stale, used . . . like that above a dance floor after the crowd has gone home. As far as they could see, there wasn't another person or animal on the prairie.

Most of the repairs could be handled by one man. Where two were needed, Annamarie dismounted to walk Sara and stretch out her stiffness. The boxer constantly tugged at the leash as she ran to investigate one bush after another.

Hap set the wire puller. "You don't think Sara would get along out here on her own? You don't have to cradle her all day."

Laramie spliced in a short section of wire. "Don't go telling someone else how to raise their dog."

"I've been thinking about it." Annamarie squatted and

stroked the panting dog's head. "It does seem a little weird to bring Sara out here, then force her to ride in my lap. But she's such a house dog. She even acts nervous in Mother's fenced backyard. She's never had this kind of freedom. I don't know how she'd do and I'm a little scared to find out."

"That's exactly what Big Jim Mayes said."

"Hap, that is not a fair comparison."

"What isn't fair?" she pressed.

"We rode with Big Jim one year in Nevada. After that he up and got married. Now that surprised us, since Big Jim was . . . well, he didn't seem like the marryin' type. Anyway, this short little gal from Korea who didn't know any English showed up in town. They got the mayor to do the service and he took her out to the ranch. No one saw her again for months. He never let her off the place."

"Oh, my," Annamarie said.

"I saw Big Jim in at the feed store one day and I said, 'You need to let that new wife of yours out the door. Don't you think she can get along on her own?' He said somethin' to the effect that she has never had that kind of freedom. He didn't know how she'd do and he was a little scared to find out."

"So, what happened?"

"He let Kimmie out from under his thumb . . . and sure enough, she ran off."

"Oh, dear, I had hoped for a better answer."

"But she came back the next day and didn't run away again. They have four kids now, so I reckon things worked themselves out."

⋆⇒○   ○⇐⋆

The rest of the afternoon, Sara dashed ahead of the horses. But she never let Annamarie out of sight as she explored every clump of grass, rock, and mesquite.

Laramie and Hap mounted up after driving wire staples into a railroad tie post. Annamarie led her horse.

"You give up ridin'?" Hap asked.

"My heart wants to ride, but other body parts need a break," she admitted.

A little after 6:00 P.M., they crested a rise and spotted a row of four stunted poplar trees along a dry sandy creek-bed.

"Looks like camp." Laramie stepped down and took Annamarie's reins. "I'll tend to the horses. Hap will unpack the mule and set up camp."

"What can I do? So far, I've just walked the dog and sat on the saddle. I haven't been much help."

"That's not true. Having you along made it a good day," Laramie said.

"How's that?"

"Well, for me and Hap good days are measured by two factors. How much work did we get done? How fast did the time fly? We covered over one-third of the fence line . . . that's quite a bit. And having you to visit with made the hours hum. So, it's been a great day."

"I take it you don't often work a crew with a woman along?"

Laramie slipped the bit out of the paint mare's mouth. "Other than the boss's wife cooking chuck from time to time, we've never had a gal on the crew."

"That ain't entirely true." Hap eased the cook sack to the ground. "We did take along that red-haired girl you befriended in Douglas."

"I wouldn't call her a member of the crew," Laramie sputtered.

"What would you call her?" Annamarie asked.

Laramie scowled at Hap. "A hitchhiker."

Annamarie rolled up her long sleeves. "Can Sara and I gather some firewood down there?" She pointed to a brush-lined draw that dropped off to the east.

"Oh, no," Hap protested. "Firewood is my detail. As soon as I get the mule unpacked, I'll head down there myself."

"No, you won't," she insisted. "Those aren't just bushes. That's the ladies room."

"Eh, yes, ma'am. Like we said, we ain't used to a gal on the crew."

Luke seemed at home grazing on tall dry grass alongside the paint mare and the mule. But Tully, as usual, preferred to eat by himself, and Laramie picketed him on the other side of camp. The rise of the prairie to the south cut off the line of sight of farms and town. The place had a feel of total isolation.

Laramie dug through his saddlebag while Hap blew on the fire.

"What are you lookin' for?" Hap asked.

"I wish I'd remembered to bring some clean shirts." Laramie tossed down the saddlebags.

Thick smoke made Hap's eyes tear up and he wiped them on his shirt. "I reckon you'd like a shave, haircut, and your nose hair trimmed, too. Have you got a date tonight?"

"I just want to look my best."

Hap shoved a couple more dry sticks in the fire. "You ain't known her any time at all."

"Are you jealous?" Laramie poured water into his hands and splashed his face. "You know, partner, there are times that I'm glad you have your Juanita to chase. It cuts down the competition."

"And there are times I start considerin' the stupidity of it all. A gal like Annamarie can make a man change his plans. You got good taste, partner."

"Isn't she something? Polite. Smart. A beautiful nurse who can ride."

"But don't it seem a little foolish of her to ride off with a couple of rounders who she barely knows? I mean, we could be a couple of perverts who drift around the country kidnappin' beautiful women. Makes you question her wisdom."

Laramie's grin was soft and easy, like a man with a cool, crisp slice of sweet watermelon. "She's a good judge of character."

Hap brushed back his mustache. "But can she cook?"

"Does it matter?"

Hap studied the limber, olive-skinned woman as she sauntered with the boxer toward them. "Oooweee. No, sir. It don't matter at all."

"Look at what Sara found down there." She held up a bright green object. "It's one of those neon colored jelly thong sandals that just came out last May. I almost bought myself a pair."

Laramie peered around. "Then someone's been down here since May."

"Doesn't this land seem too rugged to be wearing light sandals?" she asked.

Hap fingered the thong. "I figure the invasion of flip-flops is a terrorist plot to weaken the morals of American women. Maybe this is where they cross the border into the States."

Annamarie burst out laughing, then slapped her hand over her mouth. "He was joking, wasn't he?"

"Don't get him started talking politics," Laramie cautioned. "It's not a pretty sight."

She grabbed the flip-flop. "Maybe a coyote dragged it back here from the road and just gave up on eating it." Annamarie held it up to her foot. "I wish I'd found two of them."

⊷⊜   ⊜⊶

The ground heat lessened with the coming of darkness. When the fire flickered out, the three reclined in the shadows as the sky turned from blanched blue, to charcoal gray, to black. Smoke still hung in the air, but the bugs seemed to retire.

Annamarie huddled between Laramie and Hap, an arm's length apart.

Laramie picked his teeth with a stiff weed straw. "Well, the beans were fairly tasteless, but the Twinkies stayed fresh. It was nice of your mamma to send them along."

"Mother believes Twinkies will solve any problem."

Hap brushed crumbs off his thick, black mustache. "She might be right."

"Do you have a list or journal of all the Juanitas you've known?" Annamarie asked.

Hap chuckled. "Nope. But me havin' such a photographic memory, I can remember ever' one."

"Okay, which is your favorite? You must have found some you liked better than others."

"Are you sure these stories ain't borin' you?"

"No, this has been a hoot. I usually run on pure caffeine and adrenaline. It's one crisis after another. I love helping people, but it's one hundred percent stress the whole time. Now, here I am, out in the wilds on a warm summer night and I feel no stress at all."

"Well, my favorite is Juanita DeCampos. A couple of years ago, I got this packet in the mail. A pal in Colorado we call Two Lip got to blabbin' . . ."

"Why did you call him Tulip?"

"T-w-o L-i-p . . . I reckon it had to do with his looks. Anyway, he talked up my hunt for Juanita and I get a brown manila envelope in the mail from a girl named Juanita DeCampos. She had heard about the Juanita search and wanted to apply."

"Apply?"

"She had some professional photos and a six-page dossier all about herself."

"Wow, she was serious. Did you like what you saw and read?"

"Laramie claims she's the most perfect Juanita he ever met."

"Oh, yeah . . ." Laramie added. "I mean to tell you this gal was a winner. Smart, cute, talented, aggressive, polite, hard-working. I told Hap she only had one flaw that I could see."

Annamarie pulled the rubber band from her ponytail and swished her hair loose. "Wow, one-flaw girls are difficult to find."

"Yes, ma'am, they are." Laramie stared at her through the shadows, trying to imagine her one flaw.

"So, what was it?" she pressed. "What was the defect?"

"Her age. She was thirteen years old," Hap said.

"Yes," Laramie hooted, "but she said that people often mistake her for seventeen or eighteen."

"She was a cutie," Hap replied.

"I suppose you broke her heart."

"I tried to convince her to wait a few years, that she could do a whole lot better than me." Hap caressed the sleeping dog. "Sara's tuckered out. All that freedom drained her." He unrolled his sleeping bag and tugged off his boots. "The two of you can keep guard. I'm goin' to sleep."

"What threat shall we look for?" Annamarie said.

Hap yawned. "International terrorists sneakin' into the country totin' hand-held nuclear weapons or lead buckets brim full of biological plagues."

"Oh, my, anything else?"

"Guard the grub box."

"I can't imagine someone wanting to steal that."

"Twinkie theft is a real problem in rural America."

Laramie didn't glance at his watch, but he figured he and Annamarie visited for at least a couple of hours. As darkness thickened around them like a comfortable blanket, their voices softened and they scooted closer together.

Hip touched hip when they finally whispered, "good night."

Hap tended a small fire as daylight eased into their make-shift camp. Sara rested on his knee. He stroked the dog's wide head as he studied Annamarie's face, the only part of her that wasn't covered by the sleeping bag.

"You ogling my woman?" Laramie sat up on top his bedroll.

"Your woman, huh? I considered askin' her if she'd be willin' to have her name and nationality changed."

"I called it first. She's mine, partner."

"Now, Laramie, you're always beggin' me to end this . . . what do you call it . . . 'idiot obsession' with girls named Juanita. Maybe this is the right time."

Laramie combed his short, curly brown hair with his fingertips. "I want to officially ask you to forgive me for calling it an idiot obsession. I think it's an appropriate fixation, one you should not release, at least, not for a while."

"That's very kind of you, a real comfort in my time of distress. But Annamarie does make a cowboy believe in the benefits of cloning."

Laramie beat his boots against the tree trunk and shook them out. A large fluorescent green bug the size of a praying mantis flew out of one of them. "She's a heart thumper, isn't she?"

"I like her, if that's what you're askin'. And I ain't just talkin' about the fact she is a fine-lookin' lady from head to toe . . . and I do mean from . . ."

Annamarie propped herself up on her elbow. "Before this conversation gets more embarrassing, I'll head down to the ladies room."

⊶⊜   ⊜⊶

The sun stalled straight up, producing one of those hot days that pins a man to the face of the earth. Every movement proved a chore. Hap parked Luke and the mule by a tiny stream and waited for the others to catch up.

"What do you make of this?" He pointed to a one-by-two-foot flat metal box.

Annamarie rode closer. "Looks like a little solar panel."

Hap pulled his sweaty bandanna from around his neck and wiped his forehead. "What do they need electricity for?"

"Maybe they electrify the fence?" she asked.

Laramie rode up. "No, you need different wire and you string it with insulators. This is too big a place for a hot wire." He dismounted and hiked down the fence at the creekbed. "These are the only metal fenceposts we've seen. Hey, there are recessed hinges in here. I think this is a gate."

"A gate to what?" she asked.

Laramie studied the prairie on both sides of the pasture. "It doesn't lead to anything. Maybe the previous folks owned both sides of the fence. They could drive the cows through here."

Hap swung his leg over Luke's head, but remained in the saddle. "I never saw a transfer gate at the bottom of a creekbed before."

"Is it wide enough to drive a pickup through?" Annamarie asked.

Laramie stepped it off. "Nope."

Sara splashed into the tiny creek. Laramie stooped down to scratch her ears.

"Are you sure it's an electric gate?" Annamarie asked.

Hap dug through his saddlebag. "There's one way to find out. I need my backup truck keys."

"I'm not following this," Annamarie said.

Hap held up the keys. "See this little black unit? It's a garage door opener for my mom's garage. Sometimes when she's on a trip, I go over and mind the place for her, so I have this opener on my spare keys."

"Are you saying it's the same frequency as this one?" she asked.

He pressed the button. "Nope. But we got a pal named Porty Hammond who used to be a caretaker on the Harrison Ford ranch over near Jackson."

"*The* Harrison Ford?"

"I didn't know there was more than one. That place has electronic security gates runnin' out the kazoo. Porty told me how to reset an opener to open any remote door." Hap pulled out his pocketknife and flipped open the back. "He said you just short out these two points and hold it there until they pick up the new frequency." He snapped the case back together, then pressed the button.

The five-foot electronic gate yawned open toward them.

Sara yipped and raced in a large circle.

Annamarie clapped. "It works. But you ruined your key. Now you can't open your truck."

"No, this is my mom's garage door opener, not my truck lock. Of course, I can't reset it until I go home."

"I'm very impressed that you got it open," she said. "But we still don't know why it's out here."

"Some folks just have too much money," Hap muttered as he punched the gate closed and swung back up into the saddle.

The air felt dry, caustic against their sweat-drenched clothes. Annamarie rolled her lime-checkered shirtsleeves above her elbows and tried to straighten her wind-tangled hair. She dismounted, hunkered down in the shallow stream, splashed water on her face, then dried with a bright, lime bandanna. "Do you think this water gets any deeper upstream?"

Laramie gazed at the meandering flow. "Probably not this time of year."

"Do you mind if I ride on up the creek?" Annamarie asked. "If I found a wash as deep as a tub, I'd like to soak."

"Would you feel safer if one of us rode along with you?" Hap said.

"I'd feel safer if you two promised to stay down here and fix the fence." Annamarie mounted the paint mare. "Come on, Sara."

The boxer lifted her head from the sandbar, then glanced over at Hap. "Go on, darlin', Mamma wants you."

The dog splashed through the water and over to Annamarie.

Laramie rubbed the back of his neck. "Stay near the creek and fire that concealed revolver if you need us."

"Are you packin' a gun?" Hap asked. "I didn't see one and I looked you all over."

"All over?" she quizzed.

"I didn't mean all over . . . I meant . . ."

"Hey," Laramie grumbled. "If anyone is going to look her over, it's me."

High, wispy clouds drifted in, raising the humidity. Laramie and Hap found the fence in good repair and spent most of their time in the saddle. Around noon, they discovered a roofless rock house that marked the corner of the range.

"Must have been a line shack before the wire." Laramie stood in the stirrups and glanced south.

"You worried about her?"

"No, I'm not worried. Are you worried?"

"Nah . . . what do you think she's doin'?"

"I don't want to think about it."

"Neither do I. In fact," Hap drawled, "I've been 'not thinkin' about it' for the past two hours."

At the distant report of a gunshot, both men spun their horses around. By the time they reached the stream, they had their carbines pulled from the scabbards. Laramie splashed across the shallow creek and turned east. Hap, still leading the pack mule, plowed through thick brush on the north side.

When they broke out of the thickets, they found Annamarie on horseback. Sara barked at a distance.

"Are you all right?" Laramie hollered.

"Yes, but I have something to show you. After my soak, Sara chased a skunk. She found a nice spring."

"Struckmann said there were good springs on the place."

"It's the irrigation system that's impressive."

"Someone used to farm back here?" Laramie asked.

"They still do."

"Someone's livin' here?" Hap probed.

"I don't think they live here, they just farm," Annamarie reported. "Come, look at this."

The arroyo dipped deep enough that they could no longer observe the rolling range in any direction. Thick cottonwoods blocked their view to the east. As they approached the trees, Annamarie pointed to a holding pond. "Someone dammed up the spring to form that."

"Did it to water the cows, I reckon," Hap said.

"Perhaps, but the water is now taken by ditches to irrigate the crop."

Laramie stood in the stirrups. "What crop?"

They circled the trees to a panorama of neatly rowed plants.

Hap whistled and pulled off his hat to slap off the sweat. "Must be three or four acres of weed."

Laramie surveyed the field. "It's marijuana, all right. We ran across some over in Oregon when we rounded up those wild horses near Mitchell. Some kind of cult had a place down near the river. They claimed it was for religious purposes."

"But they were amateurs compared to this." Hap rubbed his matted hair. "That's the cleanest-lookin' crop I've ever seen. Even my mamma's garden isn't this manicured. Straight rows, no weeds, healthy plants. Someone knows what they're doin'. I wonder if there is such a thing as professional marijuana growers?"

Sara quit barking at a brush pile and trotted over to Hap, who swung down from his saddle. He crouched next to one of the two-foot-high plants. The boxer leaned her head against him. "I wonder when it's time to harvest? These leaves look mature enough. Could be a million street dollars' worth of this stuff. They claimed that patch in Oregon would bring in four hundred thousand once it was processed and sold to dopers."

They tied up their horses near the pond and hiked to a small shed.

Laramie peered inside. "Just shovels, rakes, and hoes."

Hap and Sara hiked south. "They are irrigatin' those last dozen rows. There's water standin' in them."

Laramie surveyed the creekbed to the west. "Which means someone might come to check on things. One of us needs to ride out now, cut straight across, and get to the road before dark. Hap, maybe you ought to head out and phone the sheriff."

Hap glanced at Laramie, then Annamarie. "Yeah, someone needs to go. You know that your Tully is faster than ol' Luke. I reckon you ought to be the one to go."

Laramie frowned. "I want to see what happens when the irrigators show up. You go."

"I ain't the one. Luke's had a sore frog and you know it. He needs some rest."

Annamarie snickered. "I feel like one of those little balls in a Foosball game, getting battered from one side to the next. I'll take Laramie's horse and ride back myself."

"We can't let you do that," Laramie insisted. "I'll go with you."

"You?" Hap choked. "You begged to stay here and see the action."

"I'm going by myself," Annamarie insisted. "I trust both of you, but I need to obey my daddy."

"Two cowboys, ever . . . one cowboy, never?" Laramie offered.

"Yes. And besides, I know a gal who's a dispatcher at

the sheriff's office. I'll phone her. Her name happens to be Juanita."

"Juanita?" Hap echoed.

"She's the sweetest lady you'll ever meet. Her husband is pastor of Iglesia Baptista in Agua Frio. She's about my mother's age."

Both cowboys napped as the afternoon stretched on. The shade of the tall cottonwoods made a peaceful, comfortable afternoon even though no air moved. The buzz of an occasional horsefly and the panting of a tired boxer provided the only sounds.

The sun sank low as Hap spread canned fruit cocktail on a slice of white bread.

"Kinda feels like we wasted the afternoon," Laramie offered. "We didn't get a lick of fence repaired."

"I expect she's made it to town by now, as long as she didn't take a tumble."

"Or run into the marijuana growers coming this way. We shouldn't have sent her alone."

"I think we ran around that mountain before," Hap mumbled.

Sara jumped and let fly with a solitary yelp.

They grabbed their carbines.

"Do you hear somethin'?" Hap asked.

"Dirt bikes, maybe. Sounds like small motors revved up."

"A few miles to the west. Could these marijuana farmers be riding motorcycles?"

"Maybe . . . they can't pack much in and out, but they

could escape in a hurry with that electric gate. If they get
out into the field, we could sneak around to the creek and
cut off their retreat. Meanwhile, we can let them work as
long as they want. That gives Annamarie more time to
bring in the sheriff."

The rumble got louder. Hap rubbed Sara's head. "Easy,
darlin'," he whispered. "No need to bark."

Two black four-wheelers burst out of the brush and slid
to a stop near the pond.

"Would you look at that," Laramie whispered.

"They ain't who we're lookin' for. They look like teenagers."

Two girls, one with a short blonde ponytail and the other
with a long black braid hanging down her back, climbed
off the ATVs. Both wore shorts, halter tops, flip-flops, and
dark glasses.

"What are they doin' back here?" Hap said.

The blonde hiked to the tool shed and emerged with two
sets of coveralls and tennis shoes.

Laramie crawled closer to Hap. "Do you believe this?"

"What are two dadgum teenage girls doin' messed with
a marijuana patch?"

"Maybe someone hooked them for a summer job and
they think they're growing carrots."

Hap held up his hand. "Looks like they're arguin' over
somethin'."

"Maybe they saw our tracks."

"Oh, crap."

"What?"

"They spied some dog poop. They got to see horse
prints, too." Hap glanced down at Sara. Her tongue hung

out as she panted and watched the two girls. "How do they know it ain't a raccoon?"

The dark-haired one tugged on coveralls, then tossed off the flip-flops. She leaned against the four-wheeler tire and slipped on the tennis shoes.

"Let's wait until they're out in the field, then sneak around between them and the ATVs," Laramie whispered.

The blonde pulled off a neon-green jelly flip-flop, then tossed it in the air toward the shed. Sara let out a yip and raced, bobtail wagging, toward the object two hundred feet away.

Both girls dove for the ATVs. The black-haired one brandished a black semiautomatic .45 in front of her. She fired two rounds at the sprinting boxer.

Hap threw his .30-30 to his shoulder and squeezed off a round that splattered rock ten feet in front of the girls. The armed girl fired two shots in Hap's direction, then both girls jumped on the four-wheelers and roared back to the brush.

Laramie and Hap raced for the horses.

"I don't think sweet, innocent teenagers is a fitting description. Why did you reveal our position?" Laramie shouted.

"I couldn't let them shoot Sara," Hap replied.

The duo leaped to the saddles and turned the horses.

"We can't catch four-wheelers," Laramie hollered.

"No, but they're goin' to follow the creek and brush out. We know where the gate is. If we cut across the range, we might be able to stay up with them."

Hap led the way. Laramie thundered behind on the paint mare. Sara dashed after them, but soon dropped out of sight in the hoof-thundering dust. They rode with their carbines across their saddles, the treeless brown grass stretching before them on the empty prairie. On the rises they could see the distant ribbon of brush that marked the creekbed. After a half-hour of hard riding, they reached the fence line and the closed, solar-powered gate.

Evening shadows dimmed their vision as Hap stood in the stirrups. "Do you hear those engines whine? I think we beat them."

"Let's block the gate and stop them right here. Maybe they'll veer off into the fence," Laramie said.

"You think they'll take the bluff?"

"Two teenagers in bathing suit tops? Sure they will," Laramie said. "Seeing the carbines close up will convince them."

The four-wheelers crashed out of the brush at full speed and raced at the gate . . . and Laramie and Hap.

The first shot from the semiautomatic smashed river rock in front of Hap's horse. They didn't wait for the second shot.

Laramie galloped north, Hap south.

The automatic gate opened and the girls fired a couple more rounds as they bounced and splashed the ATVs into the adjoining range. The gate closed. They spun to a stop on the adjoining hill to look back.

Laramie and Hap circled the horses and galloped after them.

"Open the dadgum gate," Laramie yelled.

Hap retrieved the spare truck key from his pocket and punched the button on the garage door opener. As soon as the girls spied the gate swinging open, they roared off over the hill.

When Laramie and Hap reached the dirt road, a few of the brightest stars hung in the south Texas sky. They sweltered under the oppressive heat. A few farm lights blinked on the southern horizon.

"You think they made it out?" Hap asked.

"Considering they knew where they were going and we didn't, I suppose they're in town by now." Laramie slid out of the saddle and tied Tully to the fencepost. "We might as well hike down the road and see if we can spot them. The horses need a rest, anyway. They're sweatier than we are."

"And we need to give Sara a chance to catch up. I don't remember seein' her after the electric gate."

Both men climbed through the barbed-wire fence toting carbines.

"The road sign leading back here said this was a dead end. If that's true, they had to come toward us. Maybe they left some tire tracks or something for the sheriff to follow."

When they crested the third rise in the road, Hap pointed at a pickup and trailer taillights. "Maybe they left the whole outfit."

Laramie led down to the culvert that divided the dirt road from the fence. "I can't figure why they're still here," he murmured. "Stay low. If anyone is up there, the night shadows can hide us."

They crept close enough to hear a diesel truck idle and catch the movement of the girls as they pushed one of the ATVs up the embankment to the road.

"This sucks. We should have left your four-wheeler out there where it broke down. We could have been back to town by now," the black-haired girl fumed.

"Oh, sure, that would have been cool. It's registered in my dad's name."

"Those two old cowboys could have caught up with us," the dark-haired one griped.

"But they didn't. Let's load this picker and get out of here."

With the machine down in the culvert, both girls leaned their backsides into the ATV's rack and shoved.

"I'm going to shoot Rivera. They had an opener to the gate. He set them up to chase us off. Now that the crop's about ready to harvest, he's trying to move in and take it all. I told you we couldn't trust him."

"Don't shoot him before he pays us. We've been working our butts off out here. Push harder."

"Me? You're the one that needs to push harder," the blonde one huffed. "We aren't going to lose this deal now. We grew the best crop they've ever seen. Besides, I've got to get that start-up money back into my college fund by September 15."

The four-wheeler sprang up on the level gravel roadway.

The dark-haired one steered the rig around to line up with the ramps. "Rivera will pay. We know too much."

They rolled it up in the trailer, then shoved the tailgate in place.

Hap leaned toward Laramie and whispered. "Is that duct tape on the right taillight? I think that's my dadgum truck!"

The girls marched toward the rig.

"We have to stop them before they drive off," Laramie replied.

Hap jammed his hand in his pocket and plucked out his spare set of keys. Ignoring the garage door opener, he pressed the round button on his remote key lock.

"Oh, crap," the blonde fumed. "You locked the keys in the rig."

The dark-haired girl beat on the driver's side door. "I can't believe this. I did not lock the doors."

The blonde stomped around in front of the headlights. "Oh, sure. You have fouled up things all summer."

"Me? It was your ATV that broke down."

"And you were the one to bring Rivera into this. We didn't need him."

"Like, where were we going to sell this grass? Not out behind the gym."

"Okay, oh brilliant one, what are we going to do now? I told you we didn't need a truck, even if it was a free loaner. We should have just driven the four-wheelers like we have all summer."

"Find a big rock and bust a window."

When the girls stepped to the driver's side with a grapefruit-sized rock, Hap fired two quick shots over their heads.

"Hands on the hood of the truck, girls, right now!"

They dropped the rocks, but didn't move.

"Hands on the hood," Laramie yelled.

"It's those cowboys," the blonde snarled.

"Get over there or we'll shoot," Hap warned.

"You won't shoot us," the dark-haired one insisted. "There's no money in it for you."

The bullet from Laramie's gun shattered the side-view

mirror next to the girls. They both slammed hands on the hood.

"I can't believe you shot my truck," Hap groaned.

"It worked. Frisk them."

"Who, me?"

"They shot at us with semiauto .45s. We need to disarm them."

Laramie kept them covered while Hap crept up behind them. "Are either one of you named Juanita?"

"Go to . . ." the blonde growled.

"Nice girls, huh?" Hap interrupted. "The dark-haired one had a gun in the back of her jeans, but I can't find anything on the other one."

"Rivera sent you, didn't he?" the blonde snarled.

"Tell it to the sheriff."

"You're going to turn us in?"

"We're doin' you a favor."

"Go ahead, do it. We'll tell them we were out for a ride, stumbled across some marijuana growers, and you tried to rape us. Who do you think a jury will believe, you two drifter cowboys or innocent teenage girls?"

"You think Rivera will testify on your behalf?" the dark-haired one added.

Laramie noticed distant car headlights racing toward them. "That story won't wash, little darlin's . . . you've got a gate opener in your pocket. We have another witness to the discovery of the pot field, who is right now contacting the county sheriff. Besides that, this truck was stolen from a minimart two nights ago."

"No wonder Rivera gave it to us." The dark-haired one kicked at a tire. "He set us up to be caught."

A car pulled up behind the trailer with blinding head-lights.

"Who is that?" the blonde called out.

"Looks like Rivera to me," Laramie said.

"I'm going to get you, Rivera . . ." the blonde yelled. "It will make *Kill Bill* look like a kid's movie. That pot field belongs to us and you don't get one dollar out of our idea. We planted it. We farmed it. We put in the gate. It is ours, you son of . . ."

"Who in the world is Rivera?" A lady's voice floated out of the shadows.

"Annamarie, did you bring a deputy?" Laramie called.

A uniformed law officer stepped out into the headlights. "You catch these girls growing a little weed?"

Laramie stepped back. "No, sir, we caught them grow-ing a lot of weed."

With the girls in custody and statements given, Annamarie hiked with Laramie and Hap back down the headlight-illuminated road toward the horses. "And where's my Sara?"

"Sara!" Hap gasped.

"Don't tell me you . . ." Annamarie studied the dark prai-rie. "Oh, here she is!" She hunkered down as the boxer scampered up. "What have you got in your mouth?"

Laramie reached down and tugged at the object. "Looks like she found your other bright-neon-green jelly flip-flop."

All the windows were replaced in the minimart when Laramie and Hap entered Jose's Git-N-Go two days later.

Sam swirled toward them in a bright red Hawaiian floral print dress and an exuberant smile. "Boys, have you heard the news?"

"We haven't heard much of anything since they arrested those girls. We had to finish that fencing job," Hap reported.

"I sold the store."

"Good for you," Laramie said.

"Mr. Peter Struckmann bought it. He's going to tear it down and build a car lot here. Says it's an excellent location for his lower-priced used cars. The deal should clear in a month, but he'll lease it from me and run the store until then."

"Does that mean you take a little vacation?" Laramie asked.

"Yes, I'm going to visit my brothers in California. Did Annamarie talk to you today?"

Laramie leaned against the counter. "Just for a minute. She said things were hectic and we'd talk tonight. Said to meet here."

"Good. Do you boys want a burrito or cheeseburger? My treat. I'm in a very happy mood."

Laramie peeked out into the parking lot. "Thanks, Sam, but we treated ourselves to a steak tonight at the El Grande Vaca. We'd been eating out of cans for three days."

Annamarie drove up in her Mazda Miata. When Laramie met her at the door, she slipped her hand in his. He held it tight, relishing that feel of belonging that brought an armistice to his mind and spirit. "Your mama told us the news."

"It was your contact with Mr. Struckmann that set it up."

"I hear she's headed to California."

"Yes, tomorrow." Annamarie tugged him down the potato chip aisle.

Laramie gazed into her hazel eyes. "That soon?"

She clutched his other hand in hers. "I searched the net for some of those last minute ticket deals and found a couple bargains between San Antonio and L.A."

"A couple? Are you going with her?"

"Yes. I need the break, too."

Laramie loosed his grip. "I sort of suspected that was coming."

"Do you know what's coming next?" Annamarie refused to release his hands.

"Eh, no, I don't think so."

"Neither do I. That's why I'm taking Mom to Santa Ana. Laramie, my husband's death hit me hard. I was so in love with him and content. Ever since that day, I've struggled between anger and bitterness."

"Angry at who?"

"At the oil company. At my husband for going over there. With the president for the war in Iraq. With God for allowing both my father and my husband to die. I worked day and night in the emergency room to keep my mind occupied. There wasn't time to think about myself. I know I was able to help others and for that I'm grateful. But do you know what the best help was?"

"What?"

"You and Hap for the past four or five days. You helped me to laugh, to enjoy the present moment . . . and to dream about a future again. I needed that."

"And now you're taking off?"

"Yes. I need some space to think . . . about you."

"Me and Hap?"

She squeezed his fingers. "No, just you. I like the way your hands feel. I like the way we can sit and talk for hours. I even like it that you're taller than me!"

"I like all those things, too. But what does all this mean?"

"I need to set the past aside now . . . and plan for the future. I don't know what that means for you and me, but for the first time in years, I have something fun to think about."

"How long are you going to be gone?"

"Mother has to return in three weeks to sign the papers. I might be home before that. Laramie, do you know what your future holds?"

"I don't know anything beyond chasing Hap's Juanita."

"Would you think that through? When I come back to Texas, I want to talk about my future . . . and your future . . . and our future."

"But we won't be here in Laredo. We're headed to Del Rio. My aunt's sister-in-law lives there and we sorta promised we'd help her with a roof job."

"You guys do roofing, too?"

"Not really. She claims there's a Juanita in her church that makes the Zorro chick look like a fencepost. Hap feels the call to Del Rio."

"I'll come there to see you."

"For sure?"

"Guaranteed. I have to come pick up my dog."

"Sara's going to be in Del Rio?"

"Yes, Hap agreed to take care of her while I'm in California."

"He did? He didn't tell me anything about it."

Annamarie led Laramie to the counter where Hap and Sam debated the merits of Texas-made salsa. "Hap, I'm going to California with my mother for a couple of weeks. Would you take care of Sara for me while I'm gone?"

"Yes, ma'am . . . eh, your dog? You want us to keep a house dog?"

"I want you to teach her some responsible freedom. Then I'll come pick her up in Del Rio."

Hap turned back to Sam. "Have you noticed them two sportin' the same silly grin?"

"I see Annamarie with life in her eyes. For three years, when she comes home, her eyes look dead. She is very plain-looking with dead eyes, trust me. But now, she looks alive, animated. She might even be considered somewhat attractive. What kind of man is this tall, skinny cowboy?" She pointed at Laramie.

Hap rocked back on his heels. "He's an honest man, true to his word. He's the one man on earth I'd entrust with my life. Kind of quiet at times, sometimes extremely shy . . . but everyone likes him. He don't sleep good at night and sometimes spends hours sittin' in the dark, tossin' poker cards in the trash can, and he never chews his peaches, but swallows 'em whole. Let's see, what else?"

"If these two insist on embarrassing us, let's go get a blue Icee." Annamarie tugged Laramie toward the soft-drink machines.

Out of her mom's sight, she hugged Laramie's neck, then pressed her lips against his. "You will wait for me to come back from California, won't you?"

He wrapped his arms around her thin waist.

"Oh, I'll wait. I'm just debating whether or not I'm ever going to turn you loose."

"I like the way you tease, cowboy."

Laramie pulled her closer, felt her warm, soft arms around his neck. He closed his eyes when their lips touched again. The chronic gnawing in the pit of his stomach disappeared.

CHAPTER FOUR

The two-lane, paved road north of town turned to gravel about a mile from the arena. The rolling brown foothills flattened to wide open pasture. For most of the year, the wooden bleachers perched like ancient ruins on some long-deserted plain. But this was rodeo week. Pastures converted to parking lots. A three-day camper city appeared out of nowhere. Concession booths and horse trailers circled the grounds.

Inside the loose dirt arena, most eyes focused on two mounted cowboys.

Rope coiled in his left hand, loop in his right, Hap backed his black horse into the roping box at the west end of the arena. While Luke's hooves pawed dirt, he studied angus-cross steer number 341.

The chute boss attempted to aim the animal's head forward. Hap glanced at Laramie in the heeler's box, but his partner's eyes were fixed on the steer.

Hap spurred Luke forward, spun him in a circle, and backed him in the corner again, in hopes of settling him down. In the roping box to the right, Laramie clutched a light green, medium-hard nylon rope, poised on a bit-fighting Tully, waiting for the steer's release.

On the far side of the arena, the rodeo clown entertained the crowd with a joke about a mouse and a mule as the 2,259 paying customers at the Del Rio, Texas, Summer Classic Rodeo waited for one stubborn steer to play the game right.

"These Wyoming cowboys need a 6.9 to take the lead," the announcer boomed.

The steer kept his eyes on Luke, Hap's horse. The bovine brain knew what was supposed to happen next.

Hap spun two quick loops above his head, then lowered his arm. He realized the steer had been roped a number of times in the previous three days and showed no hurry to leave the safe confines of the squeeze chute. "Just wait, boy, he's got to turn his head sometime."

Luke shuffled his hooves.

Hap's rope idly spun.

The chute boss cussed.

Then, like a miracle dropped out of the sky, the steer turned his head forward.

Hap nodded.

The gate clanged open.

The black horse galloped at the barrier string.

"Don't break it, Luke . . . wait . . . wait . . . now!"

The barrier string snapped aside a split second before Hap crashed through. The steer sprinted straight ahead.

One loop. Two loops. Toss.

Hap's rope circled the short, leather-wrapped horns of the steer. He cut his horse sharp to the left as his white-cotton-gloved hand dallied the rope around the saddle horn. Laramie leaned forward in the stirrups and tossed his rope at the steer's rear legs.

The animal was jerked to the left. Its rear hooves hopped into Laramie's loop.

Hap watched as his partner yanked the rope.

Dallied.

He backed Tully until both ropes were taut.

The black-and-white vested judge's flag dropped.

Above the crowd's applause, he heard the announcer blurt out, "Looks like these Wyoming cowboys will take home some day money and earn a slot in the short go on Sunday."

Hap gave Laramie a quick nod.

A two-mile procession of red taillights marked the exit of the crowd after the last rodeo event concluded. But like backstage after the curtain dropped, there was plenty left to do.

Animals to feed.

Arena to groom.

Litter to bag up.

Cowboys to pay.

Laramie and Hap ambled to the rodeo secretary's office under the empty wooden bleachers and scooted to the back of a short line.

A hulking, 280-pound steer wrestler loafed in front of them. The word *Wrangler* was silkscreened on one sleeve of his western-cut, long-sleeved, bright yellow shirt. He grinned and stuck out his huge, calloused hand. "I'm Brick

Trotter, boys. Nice ropin' tonight. You the ones from Wyoming?"

"Yep," Laramie replied. "Up north of Casper. And you?"

A crisp, white straw cowboy hat framed his round head. "From Checotah, Oklahoma, originally. But I've been livin' with a friend in Stephenville, Texas, of late. That is, when I'm home. I ain't seen you two around before."

"We mainly rodeo up in our Mountain States Circuit, but we don't even do that much anymore. This was a last-minute decision, based on perceived financial need," Hap explained. "We weren't even sure they had team ropin' down here."

"I've been bulldoggin' all over the country. I'm sittin' twenty-one in the world, which ain't too bad. But I've got to win some big rodeos if I'm goin' to crack the top fifteen, come Finals. I've been winnin' the little rodeos and messin' up in the big ones, you know what I mean?"

"We never entered too many big rodeos, except for Cody . . . and Frontier Days in Cheyenne," Laramie said.

"You ever win big up in Cheyenne?"

"We don't want to talk about it," Hap said.

Laramie studied the rope burn on his left thumb. "We won second place one year, but it isn't a good memory."

Brick shuffled closer to the pay window. "Be thankful you got memories. I won first place in Pendleton, Oregon, one time. I woke up broke in my motel room the next mornin' without any recall of the night before. My pals said I won and spent the twelve-hundred-dollar check on drinks for the house. That's when I gave up drinkin' durin' the rodeo season."

Brick's attention drifted to a young girl with a turned-up nose and red hair who left the pay window. "Am I just gettin' old, or are them barrel racers gettin' younger and younger? Say, you boys want to go out to supper? There's a couple girls from Stephenville who I'm sure can find another friend and we'll have some laughs."

Shouts and crashes from the pen of bulls behind them turned their heads.

"Thanks, Brick, but we're not looking for girls tonight," Laramie said. "Well, Hap's looking, but that's a different story."

He pulled off his hat and rumpled his hair. "You got one picked out?"

Hap nodded at several departing barrel racers who waved at him. "Not here."

Laramie followed the line forward. "My partner only likes girls named Juanita."

"No foolin'?" Brick flashed a wide, dimpled grin. "I got this deal about only datin' blondes. Then I up and swore off 'em for a whole year. I thought I was cured. But this little gal named Inga, with a Swedish accent, cornered me at the Holiday Inn in Tucson. So I rationalized, 'Just a little one won't be bad . . . I can quit any time I want.'"

"You got hooked again?" Hap asked.

"A horrible habit. Some days I can fight it better than others."

Two girls in bright-colored halters, shorts, and flip-flops sauntered by. Each wore a diamond stud pierced in her nose. "Hi, Brick," the yellow-haired one called out. "You were awesome tonight."

He pulled off his straw cowboy hat. "Thank you, darlin', you come back and see me in about five years, okay?"

"Okay!" She giggled as they trailed off in the direction of the parking lot.

He flashed a lopsided grin. "This ain't one of the good days. You got your Juanitas and I got my blondes. Maybe goin' cold turkey isn't the right way to do it. Maybe I should just limit my blondes to one name. Only blondes named . . . Tiffany . . . and Kimmie . . . and Heather . . . and Brooke . . . hmmm. Did you say Juanita? Dadgum it, boys . . . one of my friends from Stephenville is a Juanita. Now I know you got to come to supper with me."

Hap smoothed down his thick mustache. "We do have to eat supper someplace. What's this Juanita like?" He prepared for the reply with a mixture of curiosity and dread.

"She's Mexican, or Puerto Rican, or something Latin. Real purdy . . . with big, dark brown eyes and black hair. If I wasn't hung up on blondes, I just might dance with her myself. Shoot, maybe you know her. I think she used to be up in Colorado . . . or South Dakota. I just met her a couple of weeks ago in Arizona. Her name is Juanita Guzman."

Hap's neck tensed. One time when he was ten, he had lifted a hoof of a big gray stallion that belonged to his grandfather. The horse kicked him in the middle of the stomach and flung him against the corral fence. He felt like that now. Kicked in the gut. Fighting to breathe.

"She won slack on Thursday night and is up again tomorrow," Brick was saying. "I seen her around earlier tonight."

"I thought she was in Arizona." Hap spun on his heels. His head swelled with pain inside his hat. "I'm goin' to the truck to look after the horses. Pick up my check for me," he called back to Laramie. When he got through the gate, and away from the lights, he bent over at the waist.

It was a dry heave.

Thirty minutes later, Laramie yanked open the pickup door. Hap sat slumped behind the steering wheel. Sara greeted him with the wag of her stub tail and a woof.

"Hi, sweetie, is your daddy still in a grumpy mood?" Laramie slipped into the passenger's seat and handed Hap an envelope, then scratched the dog's head. "They let me cash your check: $289.45 each. Not bad for the third rodeo we've entered all year. Counting what we made in slack, we've hauled in over five hundred dollars each and still have the short go."

Hap mashed his temple hoping the pressure would alleviate the pain behind his left eye. "We're goin' to turn out of the short go."

"Why are we going to do that?" Laramie rolled his window down and drooped his arm outside. "We haven't made a short go in over a year."

Hap chewed his tongue and forced himself to speak slowly. "You know dang well why. I don't want to see that woman again, ever."

"Six years is a long time to not forgive."

"She ain't ever asked forgiveness. Let's drive to Presidio."

Headlights from a departing truck beamed across them like spotlights at a prison.

"Two reasons we can't do that. First, we got a chance

to make another four to twelve hundred each if we draw a decent steer on Sunday."

Hap's left hand tapped frustration on the steering wheel, but his right petted Sara as she nuzzled against his knee. "Money ain't ever'thin'."

Laramie folded his share of the winnings and shoved them in his shirt pocket. "I thought money was the reason you are mad at Juanita Guzman."

"It ain't just the money, Laramie. She lied to me and deceived me in a way that tore me in two." His teeth locked tight. His mouth felt parched.

"I was there, remember?" Laramie tugged a water bottle from the cup holder in the console. "That $6,120 she took off with was half mine."

"It was the way she done it." Hap started the truck. "I'm goin' to Presidio. How about you?"

Laramie took a swig, then handed him the bottle. "I'm going to the dance at the sale barn. Brick said they serve free barbecued pork, and I'm hungry." He got out of the truck, swung the door shut, then leaned back into the rig. "There's a second reason we can't leave now. It involves another girl."

"What girl?"

"Sara."

Hap peered down at the dog, who now rested her head on his leg. "What about her?"

"Annamarie said she'd come to Del Rio and pick up Sara in a couple of weeks at the most. It's two weeks tomorrow. She'll want her dog back. And I aim to be here when she returns." He turned and ambled toward the lights of the arena.

Hap turned off the diesel truck. He collapsed against

the headrest, then shoved his winnings into his jeans pocket. One time, when Hap was in grade school, a teen-age bully had chased him down the hall. He hid under Mr. Patterson's desk for three hours. It was the last time he had backed away from a fight, but right now, he wished he had another desk.

He scooted way down in the seat to make his presence less pronounced. "Sara, I don't reckon I told you about this Juanita, did I? It was six years ago this month. Hap and I were at 'The Daddy of Them All' rodeo in Cheyenne. Frontier Days is the last full week in July. It thundered and showered ever' afternoon. Not a cold rain, nope. It steamed hot and humid. Anyway, there was this barrel racer named Juanita Guzman."

Hap peered out into the hayfield turned parking lot. Trucks, horse trailers, and campers scattered like disorganized, giant tombstones, a silent witness to what used to be life. Seeing no human activity, he closed his eyes again.

"I'd seen this Juanita around for a couple of years. She wasn't my Juanita, but she ran close. She's the kind of gal you dream about when you're sixteen. I don't know how to translate that to dog years. She's the kind of gal, if you walk into a crowded room with her hangin' on your arm, ever' man in the place is thinkin', *There's one lucky cowboy,* and ever' married woman is clutchin' her husband's arm."

Hap sat up, turned the key, then lowered both windows a couple of inches, letting in the aroma of French fries and old manure.

"Anyway, she cottoned up to me that summer and we had some fun times. She'd laugh and say there wasn't a better Juanita on the face of the earth. And who knows, maybe she was right. I liked the way her hand felt. I liked the way her lips felt. Shoot, little darlin' . . . I liked the way her ever'thin' felt. That's the closest I've got to givin' up this quest."

Voices in the parking lot stopped him. In the shadows, a man held a little boy by the hand and packed a sleeping girl on his shoulder. Hap watched as the man tucked the children into car seats. He wondered if the guy knew how rich a man he was.

Sara rolled on her back. Hap scratched her stomach. It felt soft like a rabbit pelt that's been blow-dried.

"It was so serious with this Juanita that we said if neither of us were married by the age of twenty-eight, we'd get hitched. At the time, I berated myself for making that promise. But there were other nights I couldn't wait five days, let alone five years."

When the drift of wind shifted, he could hear the distant beat of the bass guitar at the dance.

"Well, we was gettin' chummier by the week that summer when me and Laramie brought in the big bucks at Frontier Days. Finishin' second to Speed and Rich was a big deal back then. About three in the mornin', she came beatin' on the side of our rig. Laramie had that old Ford of his and a camper he'd borrowed from Vin Dollarhide. Juanita was cryin' hard when I went out to talk to her."

Sara rolled to her side and sighed.

He continued to massage her.

A white Dodge pickup's engine started, and it pulled out of the parking lot. Diesel fumes lingered in the air.

"She begged me to buy her truck, her trailer, and her two barrel horses. She said she needed cash in a hurry and would take the bus home. She was hysterical. I couldn't get her to stop sobbin'."

A tall cowboy sauntered next to the truck and peered in. "Are you talkin' to your dog?"

Hap looked up, startled. "It helps her go to sleep."

"I know what you mean. My second wife was the same way."

Hap watched the stranger lope away. "Where was I? Oh, yeah . . . sittin' on the front bumper, in the dark, me wearin' nothin' but Wranglers, she told me the story.

"She said she got a phone call from her sister in Jackson. Her mom was in the emergency ward. She said their dad beat their mom up real bad. Juanita told me the reason she and her sister left home early was because he would come home drunk and . . ."

Hap opened his eyes to make sure no one was around.

"Anyway, she said she and her sister left home when her mom denied what they told her. The mom stuck it out, but he got worse after the daughters moved out. He'd go off on a rage and beat on the mother.

"This time it was so bad they figured they had to move her and rent her a place of her own where he couldn't find her. They were desperate for money.

"Sara, a woman that upset . . . that troubled . . . well, I didn't want her to sell her outfit. It was her life, her livelihood. When I got her calmed down, I told her she could take the Cheyenne winnin's and go get her mamma settled. We'd figure out the details later. I told her to go right home and take care of things and we'd meet up at the Caldwell, Idaho, Night Rodeo . . ."

Hap didn't know how long he stared out into the night, but he didn't start talking again until he heard a girl laugh, somewhere toward the bleachers.

"She didn't show up in Caldwell . . . or Ellensburg . . . or

Pendleton . . . in fact, I never saw her after that night. Oh, but I heard plenty."

Hap noticed Sara's eyes were closed.

"Are you asleep? Maybe I'm borin' you."

A loud bang on the side of a rig and a shout caused Hap to scan the parking lot. He surveyed the shadows but didn't see any movement. The slight breeze carried over the smell of thick arena dust, old hay, and fresh manure. He locked his fingers and cracked his knuckles one at a time.

Sara barked.

Hap scratched her head.

"Where was I? Oh, yeah. I hurt my shoulder and we headed home to Wyoming right after Pendleton. I got a phone call a week or so later. It was from Juanita's aunt Becky. She had been trying to reach Juanita for weeks and heard that she and me were a number. Juanita's father was in the hospital and had been asking for her.

"I lit into that poor lady, telling her what I thought of Juanita's daddy, how he treated his daughters and his wife. Aunt Becky got real quiet. Then she told me that the mother had died when Juanita was three years old, that there was no sister . . . no siblings at all . . . and that her father had raised her by himself. He was a teetotaler and Juanita ran off because he wouldn't let her drink and carouse. Over the years, the aunt said, the only time she showed up was when she was short of cash. She ended with the warning that I should never lend Juanita money."

Hap recognized the tall, lanky, hatless cowboy swerving through the parking lot.

"I tracked her down a couple times that next year. She was rodeoin' in Arizona and New Mexico. When I called, she hung up. You can understand why I don't aim to see her now."

Sara jumped up, jammed her front paws on the armrest, and let out two barks.

"Yep, that's Uncle Laramie. Maybe he's bringin' us some barbecue."

Laramie shoved a paper plate of steaming pork at Hap, then slid into the truck seat.

"Did you see her?"

Laramie shook his head. In the shadows of the contestant parking lot, he stabbed a bite of the sauce-coated meat. "Eli Keller said hello."

"Eli's here?"

"Just pulled out for New Mexico. Remember his little sis? She used to go down the road with him when she was a kid?"

"She was a cutie."

"She's still traveling with him, but now she's Miss Rodeo New Mexico."

"Is she ridin' that taupe-colored paint horse? I've never seen that color on another horse."

"Don't know about that. You missed some other visits."

"I didn't miss anything."

"This is good barbecue," Laramie said. "I wouldn't mind eating the same tomorrow night."

Hap wiped his mouth on the back of his hand. "You tryin' to talk me into stayin' for the short go?"

"I think we should. We don't ever turn out, you know that. We committed to this thing and we should see it through. Remember your lecture to E. A. Greene about how we never quit a job? Besides, we can use the money.

Let's stick it out a day and see what happens. Maybe Annamarie will show up looking for her baby."

Hap fed the boxer a French fry. "I'll stay just as long as me and Sara can hang out here at the truck."

⋅→═   ═←⋅

They tied off the horses' lead ropes at the side of the trailer. Both men flopped on top of their sleeping bags stretched out on the packed brown grass pasture/parking lot next to the pickup. Sara slept between them.

"A man cain't go to sleep with a big ol' dang shinin' moon like that," Hap grumbled.

"Close your eyes."

"I did. I think I got thin eyelids."

"Pull a towel over your head."

"That's easy for you to say. You can fall asleep any time you want."

"That's not true. Sometimes people talk so much, a man can't sleep."

Hap rolled over on his side. "I been layin' here tryin' to figure out what I'm goin' to say if I see her."

"Don't say anything. Just ignore her."

"I can't do that. If she smiles and says, 'Hi,' what am I supposed to do?"

"Be polite. Say, 'Hello, Miss Guzman, I trust your life has been going well.' Then tell her where she can spend eternity."

"Yeah, that's kind of what I'm thinkin'."

"Good. That's settled. Go to sleep."

"If she says she wants to try to explain it all to me, should I listen?"

"Geez, Hap, it's after midnight. Let it go for tonight."

"She probably ain't as young and beautiful-lookin' as she used to be."

"That's right. She could be ugly and weigh enough to take on Mike Tyson. Go to sleep, partner."

"I ain't never seen a good barrel racer who was plump, have you?"

"Come on, Hap, give me a break. I'm tired. Real tired." Laramie stood and dragged his sleeping bag to the front of the truck.

"Where you goin'?"

"I'm sleeping on the other side. See you in the morning, partner."

⋆⇒═◉   ◉═⇐⋆

Sara's growl caused Hap to roll over and reach for the dog. Three more panicked yaps and he sat straight up. The morning sky loomed dark slate gray. Ebony silhouettes in the contestant parking area slowly came into focus.

Some of the shadowy forms hulked and glided like alien monsters in a cheap Hollywood thriller.

Sara growled at the two-thousand-pound beast that snorted and pawed hooves only a few feet from Hap.

"Where did that dadgum bull come from?" He scooped up the quivering dog and jumped inside the cab of the truck, then scooted across and pushed open the passenger door. "Laramie, get in here!"

His partner raised up on an elbow, then rubbed his eyes. "What's goin' on?" A one-horned Brahma bull thundered by only inches from Laramie's sleeping bag.

Barefoot and wearing only jeans, Laramie crawled into the truck.

"The buckin' bulls got loose," Hap said.

"Who's rounding them up?"

"I ain't seen no one on horseback."

"Then let's get going."

Laramie and Hap ran for the nervous horses, who strained against their lead ropes. Shouts echoed from the far side of the parking lot campground. Engines gunned. Horns honked.

A huge, brindle shorthorn bull lumbered past Hap. Sara leaped from his arms and barked her way after the bull.

"Sara!"

Hap sailed his hat straight at the bull.

The massive bovine whipped around and ignored the yapping dog. Instead, he glared at Hap, who reached down and scooped up his hat.

"Come on, bull," he shouted as he blustered into a clearing, away from Laramie, who was saddling the horses. "Come on, you snot-faced butcher shop bait!"

The bull snorted.

Sara snarled.

Hap waved his hat. "Come on, your mamma's a cheeseburger at McDonald's!"

The bull lunged at the black, beaver-felt cowboy hat. At the last moment, Hap darted sidewise and slapped the bull in the rear with his hat.

"Come on, is that it? Is that your best shot?"

The boxer ran up behind the bull with a tirade of canine curses.

"Sara . . . no! Get back here."

The bull's swift left hoof caught Sara midsection and

flung the dog twenty feet. She staggered up, then dove under the horse trailer.

Hap peered down to see if the dog was injured. He heard the snort, then felt the huge animal's forehead slam against his backside. He reached around and grabbed the bull's horns and was lifted straight up as the bull tried to toss him off.

Astride the bull's nose and forehead, but facing forward, Hap clamped his jaw and his grip. The bull sprinted toward a camper in back of a black GMC truck.

He jammed his hooves in the dirt, spun left, then spun right. With wild abandon, he shook his head and kicked his rear hooves high at an imaginary foe.

Hap's grip loosened.

With a violent sling of his head to the right, the bull tossed Hap into the air, landing him on his shoulder between Luke and Tully.

Laramie hovered over him. "Sara's safe under the trailer. If you're through playing with that bull, it's time to mount up."

⊷═⊐   ⊏═⊶

The first three bulls, two Brahma crosses and a little black shorthorn, returned to the pen without fuss. Bullfighter Kenny McMillen, wearing cutoff jeans and a tank top, swung open the gate.

"I'll get dressed and come help," he shouted. "Watch out for the one-horned sucker. He'll try to hurt you if he can."

By the time Laramie and Hap had six bulls penned, two

more cowboys rode with them. When they had ten put back, the stock contractor, Will Clausen, joined up.

"Thanks, boys, you're on the payroll this mornin'. Leave Northstar to me."

"Is that the one-horned bull?" Hap asked.

"Yeah; if we can't pen him, I'll shoot him. He's the reason for this. Him and two drunken cowboys who just got fired."

It took thirty more minutes to round up four more. Laramie, Hap, and the others darted between pickups, trailers, and campers to avoid the charging bulls.

Kenney McMillen, now dressed from boots to cap, swung up behind Hap. They rode out to search for Will Clausen and the one-horned bull. Shouts from the back of the south bleachers drew them to the closed concession stands.

When they arrived at the grassy promenade, Clausen and several other mounted cowboys surrounded the teriyaki shish kebab booth. "We've got to coax him out of there, boys."

"I ate there last night. He'll die of food poisoning, if we don't get him out," one of the cowboys quipped.

"I got him to run at the door a time or two, but he won't come out," Clausen said.

Kenny McMillen poked his head in the open doorway. "He's snortin' mad, now. That's the way he looked at Odessa when he knocked out Johnny Chavez on the first buck out of the gate. Come on, you sorry excuse for animal flesh . . . this is your old pal, Kenny . . . remember how many times you wished you could stomp me to death? Well, here's your chance." McMillen pulled off his Colorado Rockies baseball cap and sailed it into the teriyaki stand.

"Ohhhhh, man!" Kenny dove to the left of the open doorway.

Northstar charged, snorted, and pawed, then backed up into the shadows. The bullfighter repeated the routine three times. The bull refused to leave his sanctuary.

Kenny lifted the swinging door that hung over the front counter and glared at the rebellious bull. Then he hiked over to Laramie and Hap, "Someone needs to hop in there when he charges the door and whip his butt with a rope. He'll keep running if we could do that."

Hap handed the reins to Laramie, then dismounted. "I can't believe I'm doin' this." He untied his coiled rope and clutched it in his right hand as he stalked up to the teriyaki stand, peered in, then covered his nose. "What a mess. He ain't exactly been sleepin' in there."

With mounted cowboys in position, Hap crouched outside the front counter.

"You ready, Hap?" Kenny called out.

"Do it quick before it dawns on me what an idiot I am."

Kenny yelled and bounced a quirt off the bull's nose. Northstar pawed the ground.

"Hap?" Like an English phrase spoken in an Italian opera, the voice seemed out of place.

Ready to leap, he turned back. "Juanita?"

"Now, Hap," Laramie hollered. "Now!"

Hap vaulted into the concession stand before he realized that in the split second Juanita had diverted him, Northstar had charged the doorway and stopped.

"Ohhhh . . . no . . ." Hap moaned. He raised the coiled

rope. The bull spun on him and charged. Hap whipped the coiled rope against Northstar's nose. The bull paused for one second. His eyes blazed.

Hap stumbled on a crate of bell peppers, then flung himself out the opening. He hit the ground hard and scampered on his hands and knees toward a row of portable johns.

He reeled to his feet when he heard a crash. Hap turned to see Northstar plow through the plywood on the side of the teriyaki stand, shattering two-by-fours and the corner post. The bull charged at Hap, who ducked behind Royal Throne Portable Toilet Number 16B. Northstar lowered his head and crashed into the john like it was a clown's barrel in the middle of the arena. Hap jumped back as the outhouse slammed on its side.

Laramie and Will Clausen cut off the bull and forced him south. For reasons known only to Northstar and the Almighty, the bull sauntered straight toward the bull pen and rejoined the fraternity of former escapees.

The crowd dispersed. Will and Laramie returned as Kenny and Hap assessed the damage to the teriyaki stand and the bull-sized hole at one end of it.

"You boys want to work a couple days for me?" Will Clausen offered. "I fired my stockmen, who were also my pickup men. If need be, young Bill and me can do the pickup chores for bareback and saddle bronc. Where I've got to have help is with the bullridin'. We have to be at the buckin' chutes. I need you to push the bulls out of the arena, something you proved you can do."

Laramie glanced at Hap. "What do you say, partner?"

"Are they running barrel racing in between the sets of bulls?" Hap asked.

"Yep," Clausen said.

"We'll help you out as long as we don't have to be in the arena during the barrels."

"Thanks, boys. I'll owe you a big one. Hap, would you close up that concession stand awning?" Will Clausen asked. "Even with that big hole in the side, we ought to try to close it."

Hap yanked the support brace out from the heavy wooded shutter. It banged down on the side of the little stand. He jumped back as it gave way. One side collapsed on another until there was a pile of rubble no more than two feet high.

"That does it," Kenny howled. "I definitely ain't eatin' here tonight."

⊷⊜   ⊜⊶

Laramie and Hap drove down the road four miles to an indoor arena that belonged to a friend of Brick Trotter's and spent the morning practicing their roping. Every window and door in the one-hundred-by-three-hundred-foot building was propped open in an attempt to circulate the hot south Texas air. A half-dozen steer wrestlers and two other pairs of team ropers waited their turns at the south entrance.

When they got back to the rodeo grounds, they parked next to a small poplar tree and picketed Luke and Tully behind the horse trailer. Sara plopped down in the small circle of shade, while Laramie trekked over to the Ketch Pen and brought back double cheeseburgers. The two men sat cross-legged between the tree and the truck and tossed tidbits to Sara. The curly fries dripped grease and Hap didn't bother coating them with a packet of catsup. Each bite seemed to clunk in his stomach like a pebble falling to the bottom of a dry well.

"We haven't worked as pickup men for years," Laramie said. "Think I'll go talk to Clausen after lunch and make sure we do what he wants. You want to go along?"

Hap stared across the ground as a Dodge dually pulled a huge horse trailer into the grounds and parked it next to the side gate. Slouching against a small poplar tree, he studied the two gals who piled out of the truck, relieved when they didn't head his way. "What I want to do is get some sleep. Between a full moon and running bulls, I was awake most of the night."

Hap woke up in a full sweat when Sara let out a bark. The sun blasted his face, so he couldn't see who approached.

"Hap, can we talk without you killing me?" It was the voice of the last woman on earth he wanted to talk to.

If the horses had been trailered he'd have jumped into the truck and driven off. He stroked the boxer, then jammed on his hat to block the sun. Finally, he folded his arms across his chest. "Juanita, I don't want to see you. I don't want to talk to you. I don't want you here."

Her jeans rode low on her waist and her pink T-shirt didn't cover her soft brown bellybutton. "Won't you listen to my side?"

Her mirrored sunglasses covered her eyes, and when she turned her head, they blinded him.

"I would have listened six years ago. I would have listened all those times I phoned and you hung up on me. I gave up wanting to listen to you."

"How can I explain all of that if you won't hear me out? You weren't the only one who phoned. I can't count how many times I dialed your number, but could never force myself to stay on the line. Can you imagine what it's like to live down here, lookin' over my shoulder, worried that I'd see your face? Do you know what it's like not to be able to go home because you're too ashamed?"

Hap noticed her thick, wavy black hair hung half-way down her back. "Juanita, you toughened up my heart. Does it really matter what you say? I don't have any desire to listen to excuses."

"I lied to you and played on your affection for me to cheat you out of thousands of dollars. I should have been arrested and served time for that." She jerked off her black-framed sunglasses. "I cannot even mention the subject without being overcome with shame. Does that sound like I'm rationalizing?" Tears slid down her smooth cheek.

"No, I reckon it don't."

She shoved her sunglasses on top of her head. "Then let me stand here and tell you what's been eating at my heart all these years. You don't have to say a word. When I'm through, I'll leave and try never to enter your life again."

Hap tucked his knees under his chin. "You don't have to stand. You can sit down."

She stepped closer, but he motioned to the shade. "Over there."

Juanita Guzman collapsed on the grass near the pickup. She folded her legs under her and pulled her thick black hair behind her head. She brushed off her dusty red roper boots, then cradled her cheeks and began to rock back and forth.

Sara scooted over and stretched out next to Hap.

"When I left you, my life was so incredibly messed up. I couldn't see clear, and I lied about a lot of things. I don't have a sister. My father didn't abuse me. My mother did not get beat up and hospitalized. She died when I was young. How am I doing so far?"

"Depends on where this is leading." Hap marveled that, except for deeper eye creases, she appeared the same as she had six years before. Her head-turning beauty remained, but her eyes looked worn. Her voice sounded weary.

"I was wild, rebellious, and drinking heavy when I met you."

"I don't remember you that way." Hap knew she didn't possess classic beauty like Annamarie, but a raw, sensual beauty like an actress hungry for a part . . . any part.

"You see? The day you took me to that pizza place and treated me like somebody special, it changed me. I had a reason to be different. Someone to be different for. It was the best few months of my life."

"Mine, too, if I were honest." Hap thought about the time they had borrowed a boat to water ski on Boysen Reservoir. He shook his head as if to erase the memory of her bright yellow bikini.

Juanita traced a finger through the dirt. "I was living a lie, but it felt good."

"A lie? About being in love with me?"

"About being a nice girl, with a happy past and an exciting future. The weekend you and Laramie did so well in Cheyenne, it all crashed down on me. Right before we started going out, I had been on a drinking spree over in

South Dakota. I hooked up with a couple of guys who drove a Hummer. I'd never ridden in one and they said, 'Let's go out and have some fun in the Badlands.'"

"I told them, you provide the booze and I'll go. So, we partied for three days out there. At least, I think we did. Hap, this is horrible to say, but I was so wasted most of the time, I don't know what happened.

"When I finally got back to Rapid City and sobered up, I took off for Hot Springs and soaked for several days trying to get clean. I even thought about killing myself. Hap, it's dreadful when you can't get free from your own stupid acts and decisions.

"I was there at the Springs when you and Laramie arrived, looking for your Juanita. I loved your story. I even went to a tattoo place in Sturgis and asked if they could give me a birthmark that looked like a horse's head. They said tattoos look like tattoos and there wasn't much to be done. But I latched on to you and pledged to myself that I would become the girl you thought I already was."

"You surely convinced me with your lies."

"The good times we shared were not lies. But the night we got to Cheyenne that summer, these guys from Rapid City showed up at my room. They said they needed a favor. They had been arrested for holding up a liquor store and shooting a clerk. There was only circumstantial evidence, so they wanted me to testify they were both entertaining me in a motel room."

"They thought you were goin' to do that?"

"This is where it gets awful, Hap. This is the part that I couldn't tell you back then . . . I don't even know if I can now." She breathed deep, and more tears trickled down her brown cheeks. "They had some video of me and them out in the Badlands. It was porno . . . it was sick . . . it was so horrible I still cry about it. I don't remember one thing about any of it, but there it was on tape."

"Did they blackmail you?"

"They didn't want money. They wanted me to testify that they were with me in a hotel room when the crime was committed. They promised to give me the tape, if I went along with it."

"How many copies did they have?"

"They wouldn't tell me. Besides, the tape ran only a half-hour and I know I was out there with them for three days. I had no idea how much they taped."

"So, why didn't you tell me . . . or the police?"

"Hap, at that time I would rather die than let anyone, especially someone as nice as you, know I had done such damnable things. I was appalled. I just wanted to die."

He refused to let his mind wander to what might be on the tape. "If I'm so nice, why take my money?"

"I thought if I had that much, and could give you a story that kept you away from me, that would be better for you. In my mind, if I ran away and disappeared, no one could ever blackmail me again. I knew if I stayed with you, the guys would return and sooner or later, you'd see everything. I was afraid you would hate me."

"I ain't exactly been lovin' you all this time, as it is."

"I always meant to pay you back. I kept saying, 'I'll earn the money in a couple months.' Weeks turned to months, then to years. And here I am, wishing I could die again rather than tell you this. For the past several years I've dreamed of seeing you and handing you the money and explaining it all."

"You got the money now?"

"No . . . and that's why I haven't tried to contact you. I'm living in my truck. It's not been a real good year. I'd go home and apologize to my dad and my family if I had the funds. I don't even know if I have gas money to get to the next rodeo. Not a good way to live, but I have no one to blame but me. I'm not drinkin' or doin' drugs. Just getting by day to day."

"So, that's your story?"

"Hap, I owe you money. Some day, some way, I'll pay you back. I didn't tell you this to have you feel sorry for me. I'm getting exactly what I deserve. I made a bunch of lousy choices and now I have to live with the consequences. I treated you awful even though I've never had anyone in my life treat me better. Thanks for listening and not shooting me. When I saw you here, I thought about drawing out and running or just hiding out hoping we'd not have to see each other. I decided to come over here and talk. Now I'm trusting that was the right choice."

"To tell you the truth, I don't know how much of this to believe. You understand if I'm skeptical. Obviously, I'm quite susceptible to your deceptions. It'll take some time for all this to sink in."

She stood up. "I'm up in tonight's round. If I make the short go, I'll stay until tomorrow. If not . . . I'll pull out tonight."

Hap stood up and gazed into her wide brown eyes. He remembered the first time, in Gillette, when she closed those eyes and puckered her lips. At the time, he had hoped that moment would last forever.

"I'll see you again, cowboy. Next time I hope I'll have money in my hands to repay you."

Hap shoved his hands into the back pockets of his Wranglers. "I'm glad you came to talk to me. Even a lie is more peaceful than having no explanation at all."

She stuck out her hand. "You got the truth this time. You don't have to like me, Hap. Just don't hate me quite so much, okay?"

"I never was comfortable hatin' you, Juanita." As Hap clasped her hand, she squeezed his fingers.

He didn't squeeze back.

⊷══⊷   ⊶══⊷

Hap's legs sprawled out in front of him as he sat on the dirt. Sara limped over to him and he pulled a sticker from her paw as Laramie sauntered up.

"I told Will we'd do all the pickup work, but if it wasn't going right, he could fire us. He's got pickup horses for us to ride, so Tully and Luke get the night off. You just wake up, partner?"

"Yeah, I think so."

"You worried about her?"

"I guess."

"Look, Clausen has a vet over there right now looking at one of his saddle broncs. Why not let him give her the once-over?"

"Who?"

"Sara. Isn't that who you're moping over?"

Hap shoved the boxer out of his lap. "I had a long talk with Juanita Guzman."

"Did you go find her?"

"She found me."

"Did she give us back our money?"

"She's broke and I don't know if I believe anything she told me."

"Are you doin' okay, partner?"

"Yeah, actually it was good. Maybe I can forget it all now."

"You got to let it go, that's for sure, but don't get sucked back in."

"No, but hatin' takes a lot of work. It was wearin' me out."

⊷━▭   ▭━⊶

The arena lights blazed.

The evening sky cleared.

And the Uvalde Mounted Twirlers performed their big routine as Laramie and Hap rode up to the arena gate on Will Clausen's paint pickup horses.

"We look like bull-ridin' rookies with these dang red and white chaps," Hap intoned. "But you look good in a hat."

"Yeah and you can sing opera," Laramie grumbled.

The bleachers filled as the grand entry continued. It was not until the last rodeo princess exited the arena that they announced the stock contractor and introduced the pickup men. The twelve-foot-wide arena gate swung open, and Laramie and Hap rode out into the lights.

Bareback riding led the events. Once the first rider nodded and the gate swung open, the seconds ticked away fast. Of fifteen contestants, seven got bucked off. Two tried flying dismounts. The other six grabbed onto Hap's back without much effort or complaint.

One horse, a bay mare from Calgary, pitched a fit about

clearing the arena, but the delay gave rodeo clown Tennessee Tommy Reynolds a chance to do his routine with a monkey and a can of tomato soup.

Laramie and Hap watched the steer wrestling and the tie-down roping from the sidelines as the Del Rio Rodeo Royalty ushered the steers and calves out of the arena. The contract act of Pecos Flower Trick Riders performed to the gasps of the crowd as they rode Roman style, standing tall and straddling the backs of two galloping paints.

The saddle broncs proved easier to ride than the barebacks. Hap sat down eleven cowboys; the bucking horses dethroned the other four. He studied each of the steers in the team roping event, wondering which they would draw the next day. They rode the pickup horses back out behind the barrelman, as the Clausens, father and son, loaded the first pen of bulls.

Eight cowboys in a row slammed into the dirt after a couple of bucks. All limped out of the arena, but none looked permanently injured. The crowd yelled and groaned as each man lost his grip on the bull rope.

The hornless black bull dropped his head, spun right, bucked his rear to the starry night, then circled with violent jerks to the left. An eighteen-year-old kid named Tater Doogan earned himself a 91-point ride.

After that came a 71.

Then an 80.

Followed by a pair of 82s.

The fourteenth and fifteenth riders hit the ground before the buzzer.

The first pen of bulls finished with five qualified rides. Everyone exited the arena while a tractor harrowed the dirt before barrel racing.

Laramie sauntered to the Lions Club hamburger stand, but Hap stayed by the fence to watch. Brick Trotter found him there. "Keep your eye on that brunette with bobbed hair and turquoise-sequined blouse. She don't have the fastest horse, but she'll make the tightest turns. Juanita Guzman probably runs the fastest horse, but he's been bumpin' barrels a little too hard."

Fifteen girls ran the cloverleaf pattern around the three fifty-five-gallon drums. One Hap scrutinized.

Juanita ran deep in the dirt as the next-to-last contestant. She needed a time of 17.08 seconds or better to make the finals. Her red roan turned tight on the right-hand barrel, then dashed to the left one. That barrel tilted as she made the turn, but plopped back in its upright position as she rocketed to the far end of the arena, the circle a little too wide to the right. When she brought him back close to the barrel, her knee crashed its rim. It tilted. The crowd offered a collective gasp. She reached back and righted the barrel, as her horse bolted to the finish line.

After a long pause, the time of 17.07 seconds flashed on the scoreboard. Juanita sailed her black hat in the air as she rode out of the arena.

The second pen of bulls behaved similarly to the first. Only a third of the cowboys made qualified rides. Most of the bulls trotted out of the arena as fast as the battered and bruised bullriders.

Northstar steamed out last. Leif O'Day rode him two jumps before he overcompensated and lost his seat with his glove hand hung up in the bull rope. For a few frightening seconds he flopped back and forth like a rag doll. The rodeo bullfighter, Kenny McMillen, dove into the spinning bull as the crowd hooted and hollered. He pulled the bull rope loose and Leif tumbled to the dirt. Kenny took a horn to the hip and was flung out toward the middle of the arena.

Hap plunged the pickup horse between Kenny and the bull. Northstar blustered in front of the other chute, causing the cowboys in the arena to scamper up the fence rails. The triumphant bull made a wall run like a victorious general returning from war.

The crowd cheered him on as he demonstrated no inclination to exit the arena. Most in the stands stayed to witness his attemps to jump the gate into the roping boxes. Laramie and Hap couldn't get behind him. Every time they moved in close, he charged.

Will Clausen mounted an extra horse, but even with three riders, they managed only to corner the bull in the far end of the arena. With his rear slammed against the fence, Northstar took on all comers.

"If there wasn't kids in the audience, I'd shoot him right now," Clausen muttered.

From the safety of the clown barrel, Kenny McMillen hollered, "You talk to him, Hap. You and him is pals."

Hap rode slowly toward the bull and mumbled, "There are a lot of things a man regrets after he's done them. This is one I regret even before I do it."

He punched his spurs into the horse's flanks. The bay pickup horse bolted toward the bull, then, as if coming to his senses, wheeled a hard left. Grabbing the saddlehorn, Hap whipped the entire coil of stiff nylon rope into the bull's nose.

Northstar charged him at full speed.

The horse galloped at a panicked gait.

The crowd roared as cowboys and animals thundered across the dirt.

As they neared the livestock exit, the gate flew open. Hap yanked a hard left. Northstar rumbled straight ahead.

The gate slammed.

The crowd stomped their boots so loud the bleachers rumbled.

Laramie and Will Clausen rode up beside Hap. Laramie handed him his hat. "Do you always have to show off like that?"

"That was one of the stupidest things I ever did."

Clausen laughed. "The folks in the stands loved it. I'll pay you extra to do it every night."

⊷═══   ═══⊷

Hap and Laramie scooted through the darkened contestant parking area to the rig. Dim, battery-operated lights illuminated a few of the campers and trailers. On the far side of the field, a Coleman lantern blazed and a sledgehammer striking an anvil echoed through camp. A fully recovered Sara enjoyed the evening freedom by sprinting from one shadow to the next.

Laramie nodded to a figure standing next to the poplar near the back of the rig where Luke and Tully waited. "Looks like you got company. You want me to stick around or shall I exercise the horses?"

"You stretch the horses' legs, I reckon." Hap strolled over to the woman.

"Nice ride, Juanita," Hap murmured.

"Thanks. I thought that third barrel was going down for sure."

The humble tone in her voice caught Hap by surprise. "Looks like you'll stick around another day."

"Yeah, I picked up some day money, too." She handed him a folded piece of paper. Her warm fingers lingered on his hand a moment before she pulled them back.

"What's this?"

"An IOU and a hundred-dollar bill."

Hap shook his head and shoved the money back. "But you'll need . . ."

"What I need is a clearer conscience more than anything. Turn on your headlights and read the note."

He jammed it in his pocket. "I believe you."

"I know one hundred dollars isn't much compared to what I owe you, but it makes me feel like I'm doing something. I won enough to pay the vet, buy some feed, and gas up for the rodeo in Midland."

He tried to study her eyes, but couldn't make out her features. "You got enough to drive all the way home?"

"I wish." Her tone fell somewhere between a plea and despair.

He pulled out the folded paper and bill. "Why don't you keep the hundred dollars?"

"I really need to give you something. If I win tomorrow, I'll pocket nearly eight hundred bucks. That will buy tires on the truck and send me home with a few decent meals and maybe even a motel and shower. I know my horse isn't the best one here, and the chance of winning is remote, but it's the best shot I've had in a long time."

When a truck swung around, the headlights provided temporary illumination. Hap was drawn to the long, black eyelashes that framed her eyes. "And if you don't win?"

"Then there's Midland . . . then Odessa, Big Spring,

Lubbock, and Amarillo. Some place my luck will turn. When it does, I'm going home to settle things with my dad and others."

"What's the turning point, eight hundred bucks? Is that what it takes to get you to go home?"

"Yeah, that's what I figure. The tires are real bad."

Hap shoved the hundred-dollar bill into her hand. "Now you only need seven hundred." She held it, then handed it back, crumpled. "Please, Hap, let me do this."

He slipped the money back into his pocket.

"I want to go home so bad, I can taste it. Seeing you here reminded me of everything I've missed. I have the feeling if I don't do it now, I never will. I've just got to win tomorrow." She clenched his hand. Her grip felt warm, yielding. He didn't turn loose. He remembered a two-hour hike along the rim of Wind River Canyon when they held hands the whole time.

"You were the best thing that ever happened to me and I threw it all away. I don't know how to say this right, but seeing you down here in Texas jolted me out of a rut. I've lived day to day with no goal except the next rodeo. For years, it's been survive one week at a time."

She wove her fingers into his. "But now I can remember the good times. Like when we took that houseboat out on the reservoir at Flaming Gorge. We meant to fish until dark, then stayed out until morning, with that mild summer breeze and ten thousand stars above. Those were real times, Hap. My life seems so unreal now . . . but when I saw you, I began to think of those things. I got homesick for feeling normal. I have to find something real again." She squeezed his fingers. "You understand, don't you?"

He squeezed back. "I know ever'one needs somethin' to

live for . . . some dream or plan or goal that keeps them going. Is that what you mean?"

"I think so. You make it sound so . . . philosophical."

"I reckon."

She leaned into him and brushed her lips against his, then paused for a soft, quick kiss. "That's not philosophical. That's real," she whispered, then pulled back. "I shouldn't have done that. I'm sorry. I was thinking this afternoon . . . what if Hap wasn't looking for that long-lost Juanita? What if that had never happened and we had met back then and I'd known you would stay with me and not keep looking for another Juanita. I keep wondering, would it have all turned out different if we'd driven all night to Nevada like we teased and gotten married?" Her arms swung around his chest; his circled her back. "Hey, we'd have kids by now . . . Little Hap Junior and Teresa."

He rocked her back and forth. "The 'what ifs' of life can haunt a person." He turned her loose. "We are here, Juanita. And a whole lot of stuff has gone on since then."

"I know . . . I know . . . but just for a split second, I forgot. Did it seem like old times, just for a minute?"

"Yeah, I reckon so."

"That's one more moment of contentment than I thought I'd have. Thank you for that, cowboy. And you know what? I do have a goal . . . a dream, something to look forward to."

"What's that?"

"The day when you and me are both living in Wyoming and you stop by to see me and I place all that money in your calloused but tender hand and say, 'I'm sorry, cowboy.' That's a dream worth following, don't you think? Maybe you'll have your very own Juanita by then."

"I promised Laramie if I didn't find her after we get to Colorado, I'm givin' it up."

She threw her arms around his neck and kissed him hard. "Then I really have something to dream about."

Hap tucked his hands in his front jeans pocket. His left hand rested on her note and the hundred-dollar bill. "Sometimes dreams need a little help."

"Do you know Suzanne Pearson? She's originally from Lander."

"No, I don't think so."

"She opened a café in Jackson called the Waxed Turtle. Anyway, she phoned me this spring and begged me to come work for her. I was too proud to admit my condition and turned her down. I'll bet she'll still hire me."

"Next time I'm over that way, I'll stop by."

"Oh, Hap . . . that would be so great to look up and see my cowboy swagger in with that to-die-for grin."

"What about those old boys with the video?"

"They're both in prison in Arkansas. I don't know who owns the tape now. I'm guessing it's in some porn lover's library. But he doesn't know who I am or where I am . . . I hope." She rested her hands on his hips. "I feel incredibly better after getting to talk to you. Maybe we can visit tomorrow in the daylight. And wish me luck. I want to win tomorrow more than I ever wanted anything. Sometimes you don't know what's a life-changing event until it happens. But this one, I know about beforehand. My whole future will be sprinting around those barrels."

Hap pulled out the contents of his right pocket and mashed them firmly into her hand. "Maybe you already won."

"I won't take that money back."

"I didn't give that money back. This is different money. And it will get you where you want to go. Go home, Juanita. Go back to Wyoming."

"You can't do that . . ."

"Go home . . ."

"But . . . you . . ."

He thought he heard Laramie ride up to the back of the trailer.

"Go home right now, Juanita. Get in your truck and leave."

"You are crazy."

"We are both crazy. Are you going home?"

"Yes."

"Right now?"

"Yes."

He kissed her cheek. "I'll see you in Jackson Hole," he whispered.

"I'll expect more than a kiss on the cheek then."

"So will I."

⊷═══   ═══⊷

The sun sprayed through high, scattered clouds as Laramie stomped around the horse trailer. "You did what?"

"I sent her home."

"I heard that part when I rode up last night. That's when I went to sleep, innocent and happy. I figured you told her to get lost. Tell me the eight-hundred-dollar part."

"I gave her eight hundred dollars to buy some tires and get back to Jackson Hole and settle down."

"You gave her more money? This is insane. What part of 'naïve sucker' don't you understand?"

"You don't got to holler about it. It was my money. I can do whatever I want with it."

"You got any left?"

"I got the hundred dollars she left me last night and we'll probably add to the poke today."

Laramie combed his fingers through his short hair. "This is beyond belief."

"Well, thank you." They both spun around.

"Annamarie?" Laramie took a moment to drink in her crisp black jeans, white silk blouse, and the wide, easy smile on her full lips, even as she raised her eyebrows.

Sara, on the other hand, immediately scrambled over. "Hi, baby . . ." She wrestled the boxer by the ears. "What are these cowboys arguing over?"

"An act of kindness . . ." Hap insisted.

"A complete mental breakdown," Laramie argued.

Hap whipped his hands around as if swatting horseflies. "Look, I forgave someone. So I gave her better than she deserved. I tried resentment and bitterness for six years and I didn't like it."

Laramie's neck reddened. "And now you're going to start six years of insanity? Hap, what's going on here? This is beyond idiot obsession. This is like a horrible plague."

"Whoa . . . time out, guys," Annamarie interjected. She slipped her hand in Laramie's, then pecked him on the cheek. "You better fill me in on what I missed. Back me up two weeks ago to when I last saw you in Laredo."

Laramie brushed a kiss across her lips. "We've got to back you up a whole lot farther than that."

⤙═ ═⤚

The Sunday finals burst into the arena, then flooded back out to the parking lot. The most exciting part of the day's activity was the rodeo queen getting bucked off during the grand entry and the 94-point bull ride on Northstar.

Laramie and Hap finished team roping in second place, .38 of a second behind Teddy James and Cash Filer. While they didn't ignite fireworks in the arena, plenty of sparks simmered in the contestant parking lot.

"Annamarie, you talk to him. Facts don't seem to matter. I truly think he's having a mental collapse," Laramie intoned.

"And I don't see why he's overreacting. I know what she's like. I know that was all sweet talk. I didn't believe it. I just truly wanted to help her be different. She acted like she wanted to turn her life around."

Annamarie lounged on the tailgate of the black Dodge pickup as Sara slept in her lap. "Hap, let me review. Your Juanita admitted conning you out of $6,150."

"She's not 'my Juanita.' And she had a good explanation of why she did what she did six years ago."

"Which you don't want to tell us?"

"It's very personal and reflects poorly on her past judgments. I don't reckon I should. It's not the kind of thing I would repeat about any woman."

Annamarie unfastened the collar button on her blouse and rubbed her long, thin neck. "Then, last night, she gave you one hundred dollars and talked you out of another eight hundred dollars?"

"No, ma'am, she didn't twist my arm. I freely surrendered it. She didn't ask for anything but forgiveness."

"And she claimed to be going home. But Brick Trotter told Laramie he heard that Juanita, Cindi, and Lacee drew out of today's barrels to hurry to Las Vegas and play in a poker tournament."

Hap grimaced. "I hear there was two Juanitas here. It might have been the other one."

"One fact I know for sure," Annamarie added. "The Waxed Turtle in Jackson only lasted one summer. They went broke and it's now Teton Espresso. I phoned the Chamber of Commerce myself."

"She might not have known it went belly-up."

Laramie paced around the back of the truck. "So, Judge Annamarie, what's the verdict? Is Hap a certified loony, or what?"

"Guys, I'm not the judge. But I will give you my opinion. With the details at hand, it seems naïve, or foolish, or both for Hap to give this Juanita more money."

"Yes!" Laramie boomed, "that's what I've been saying."

"However," Annamarie continued, "Hap is thirty-one years old. He has the freedom to be naïve or foolish, if he wants to."

"Or both . . ." Hap said.

"So where does that put us? Where do we stand, partner?" Laramie said.

Sara jumped down at the sight of another boxer. They raced neck and neck between the rigs.

Annamarie laced her hand into Laramie's. "That, my dear man, is the exact question I came all the way to Del Rio to find the answer to. Where do we stand?"

"You and me?"

"Yes, what's our relationship? Of course, I also want that supper you promised you'd buy me."

Laramie hugged her. "Let's go eat."

She turned to Hap. "You coming with us?"

"I ain't hungry."

"Would you mind . . ."

"I'll keep Sara."

"We might be late."

"I'm goin' to sleep early. We've got a long drive tomorrow."

⤙⟹   ⟸⤚

Hap watched his father crawl out from under the Mexican family's old Ford station wagon, grab a couple of hand tools and a flashlight, then slide back beneath the rig.

"Did you hear what I said?"

Hap's eyes snapped to the twelve-year-old girl with tiny silver stud earrings beside him. "You bought yourself a bracelet?"

"No, I said I wanted to buy myself a bracelet. It costs two dollars."

"Why didn't you buy it?"

She stared down at dusty flip-flops that pushed out from under her long white dress. Her voice lowered. "I didn't have the money."

Hap picked up a rock and threw it at a cedar fencepost about thirty feet away. He missed it four inches to the left. "Ask your daddy."

"Mother says I should never ask him for money. He works very, very hard and we barely have enough for rent and groceries."

Hap liked the way listening to her made his throat tickle. "Do you ask your mother for money?"

"Mother doesn't have any. She always gives her pay to father."

He stared down at her chipped, red-painted toenails. "You mean, you never have any money?"

"Sometimes my grandmother sends me some for my birthday or Christmas, or my aunt lets me babysit. I have money then. I just don't have any right now."

Hap plucked up another stone and tossed it at the fence post. This time it flew by two inches to the right. "What was the bracelet like?"

She hunted alongside the road and retrieved a small round rock. "It was silver with the word *Wyoming* engraved in it. One charm hung down, a cowboy riding a bucking horse. Now I want it more than ever. If I had that bracelet, it would remind me of you. Hap, I really like visiting with you this afternoon." She rifled the rock at the fence post and clobbered it dead center. "I wish you lived close to us. We could visit every day."

"I would like that."

"Are you going to come see me? Someday, I think you will."

He smeared dirt when he rubbed his hand on his chin. "I'd like to see you tomorrow."

"What?" Her eyes danced on top of her wide smile. "Do you like me?"

Hap felt his face flush. He jammed his hands in his back pockets. "You . . . you aren't suppose to ask me that."

"I like you." She sailed another rock into the fence post. "Do you like me, Hap?"

He fingered another rock. "You're embarrassing me."

"Because I can hit the fence post and you can't? Or because I said I like you and you know you like me?"

"It ain't the throwin' that bothers me."

"If you say that you like me, I'll show you how to hit the post."

"If you show me how to hit the post, then I'll say that I like you."

"Raise your elbow higher. When you throw, your arm drops down too far. Try throwing with your elbow parallel to the ground."

Hap wound up and tossed the rock. It crashed into the post.

"Now say it," she insisted.

"I liked you before you taught me how to hit that ol' post."

"I know. I could see it in your eyes. Some boys think they can hide their eyes with a cowboy hat, but they can't."

This time when Hap's dad crawled out from under the Ford, he signaled Juanita's father to start the station wagon. The engine caught and ran smooth.

Hap strolled with Juanita back to the car. "I reckon you'll be going now."

"We are supposed to stay with my aunt Lupe in Greeley, Colorado, tonight. I wish I could buy that bracelet. It would always remind me of my Hap."

"Your Hap?"

"Yes, I will be your Juanita, okay?"

"Eh . . . sure."

Hap's father and Juanita's shook hands and slapped each other on the back. "Looks like your daddy's happy now."

"He said you and your father were like helping angels. He said he would pray to the saints for you on Sunday."

"We ain't Catholic."

"Well, then you will need his prayers all the more. Do you pray?"

"Eh . . . I guess."

She bowed her head, folded her hands, and closed her eyes. "Our Father who art in heaven, keep my Hap safe so that we can get married when we are old enough. In Jesus' name, Amen."

"Wh . . . why did you pray that?" he stammered.

"So nothing will happen to you until we get married. You do plan on getting married someday, don't you?"

"Yeah . . . I guess."

"Good. That's all settled then."

Juanita hopped in the backseat of the station wagon where her younger sister and brother slept. She rolled down the window. "Hold out your hand and close your eyes," she demanded.

Hap's eyes flipped open when something bounced in his palm. "A rock?"

"For you to save until we see each other again."

"I'll keep it in my pocket."

"I wish I had that bracelet. How am I going to remember you?"

He stuffed his hand into his pocket, paused . . . then pulled out a toothpick. "Here, this was the toothpick I had when we first met two hours ago and you said, 'You shouldn't talk to a girl with something in your mouth.'"

"Yes!" She retrieved the pick. "This will help me think of you." She clamped it between her lips.

As the car pulled onto the blacktop, the girl stuck her head out the window. "Good-bye, my Hap!"

He trotted after the car for a few steps, then hollered, "Good-bye, my Juanita."

Hap tramped back to his father, who waited by their pickup.

"What was that about 'my Juanita'?" his father asked.

"She's a very nice girl."

"And a cute one, too."

Hap stared down at his feet. "Daddy, you know that two-dollar bill you gave me after the feeder steer sale last month?"

"Yes, what about it?"

"I said I was going to save it forever . . . but I was wonderin' . . . you know . . . sometime if I wanted to give it to someone else, would that be okay?"

"It belongs to you. You can do with it whatever you want. Did you give it to your Juanita?"

Hap yanked out the neatly folded bill. "No. My heart wanted to, but my mind made me keep it for myself."

His father's arms slid around Hap's shoulder. "Son, when it comes to ladies, always do what your heart tells you."

⊷═◦　　◦═⊷

When Bob Wills finished "San Antonio Rose," Hap turned off the radio.

Laramie sat up and glanced over. "Is it my turn to drive?"

"No, I was just relivin' that scene with my Juanita nineteen years ago."

"Do you regret it?" Laramie asked.

"No, but I'm sorry for the turmoil it puts between you and me. You ain't said nothin' since Del Rio. How long are you goin' to stay mad at me for givin' that money to Juanita Guzman?"

Laramie stretched his legs as best he could. The Cummins diesel engine on the 2003 Dodge pickup harmonized with the tires on the pavement of the south Texas highway. "I'm not angry. I'm just trying to understand."

"You tryin' to understand me givin' Juanita Guzman that money or Annamarie Buchett?"

Laramie glanced at his watch and wiped the sweat from the back of his neck.

"I've been thinking a lot about Annamarie, that's for sure. I can't believe how good I feel when I'm with her. You know how easy it is for me to be discouraged or depressed. But when I'm with her, everything's different."

"You don't mind if I'm a little jealous."

"You can be jealous if it's a peaceful jealous." Laramie picked up the Texas map and swatted a fly on the dashboard.

"Peaceful jealous?"

"Yeah, ever since the day we met, there's been some kind of crisis brewing all around us."

Hap tapped his finger on the steering wheel. "Yeah, that was quite a deal. I had to save your tail that day, didn't I?"

"Save my tail? You got me into that mess. You didn't even say, 'Hi, Laramie.' You just fed me to the wolves."

"But think of the memories. Shoot, that wasn't the only time I saved your hide."

"Hap, you're the reason my hide needs saving. I never had my life threatened until I started hanging with you. You toss me in the fiery furnace, then pull me out like a hero."

"You got a point to all this?"

"I'd like some calm and quiet for once. Let's just chug along looking for your Juanita and mind our own business."

"Hey, is that Milt Tryor?" Hap applied the brakes and

pulled over to the side of the road behind a long horse trailer hitched to a one-ton dually.

Laramie rolled down his window. "Milt, you need some help?"

The wide-shouldered, tanned man with a drooping handlebar mustache gawked at them, then whooped. "Laramie? Hap? What are you boys doing in south Texas? It's like seein' a pair of armadillos in the Arctic."

"Just working our way along the border, looking for Hap's lost woman," Laramie said. "You need a lift anywhere?"

"No, I got the cell phone. A tow truck's headed this way, but I'm kind of in a bind. I've got to get these ponies to a horse race in El Paso. I'll get towed into Fort Stockton and fix my rig there, but I won't have time to come back."

"Somethin' you need to do down here?" Hap asked.

Milt waited for two semis to pass. He leaned into the window. "My little sis is living in the Chisos Mountains in Big Bend National Park. My family's had a place down there since Sam Houston was governor. She needs some legal papers and other stuff. I told her I'd bring them down; now I can't make it."

Hap surveyed the open hood of Milt's truck. "You want us to run them papers down to your sis?"

"That would be a lifesaver. It's about two hours from here. I know it's out of your way." He pulled out his wallet and opened up a series of photos. "Here's my little sis. She's purdy like our mamma."

"Milt, you ugly old cuss, she's a beautiful lady," Laramie said.

"And stubborn as Mamma, too. She's thirty-one years old and too smart and opinionated to get a husband. So, don't hang around too long. Just leave the box and get on down the road or she'll sign you up on some political action cause. You'll find yourself in a canoe off Alaska protectin' baby seals."

"Spunky, huh?" Hap said.

"Compared to her, spunky's purt'neer comatose."

Hap studied the picture. "Brown eyes, brown hair . . . she surely is purdy."

"She gets that from Mamma, too. Mamma's Mexican, you know."

Hap glanced at Milt's fair complexion and blue eyes. "I never knew that."

"Will you go down there, boys? It would mean a lot to me."

"What's her name, Milt?" Hap inquired.

"Rosa."

"We'll go," Laramie said.

CHAPTER FIVE

Somewhere to the north . . . or the east . . . or on the West Coast . . . zoning commissions battle late into the night to resolve the conflicts of urban sprawl. In those regions, traffic backs up for miles on the freeways. Smog settles over school grounds. Acre after acre of farmland is consumed by asphalt and concrete.

Laramie and Hap were not in that part of the country.

They drove south through Brewster County, Texas, where four million acres house a population of ninety-two hundred. Every man, woman, boy, and girl could own 430 acres of ground. Bare, dry ground. Of those nine thousand plus residents, more than sixty-five hundred lived in Alpine, the county seat.

Laramie and Hap were not in Alpine, either.

They hadn't seen a soul outside of the few vehicles they passed, for over ninety miles.

Hap locked his Dodge pickup on cruise control until

they arrived at the park entrance. There were no trees taller than the squat, scattered buildings.

The uniformed blonde at the Persimmon Gap gate flashed white teeth in a suntanned face. She seemed the typical college student working summers at a national park. Her short-sleeved shirt was starched and pressed. No lipstick. No mascara. No eyeshadow. Small silver feather earrings dangled from her dainty lobes. "Are you going to camp with horses?" she asked.

West Texas dry heat chafed at Hap's already chapped lips. "No, ma'am. We're not spendin' the night. We just wanted to swing through the park and visit a friend of ours who lives here. Then we'll take Highway 170 to Presidio. We're on our way to El Paso."

"You have vet checks on the horses?"

Hap handed her the papers.

She glanced at them, then transferred them back. "You picked a hot time of the year for a visit. Make sure you and your horses have plenty of water."

Perspiration trickled down Hap's neck as he surveyed the peeling paint on the small, rectangular building. "This is our first trip to the park. We thought we'd find trees and shade."

"If you're looking for trees, drive up to Basin in the Chisos Mountains. Here are some maps. Most of the park is in the Chihuahuan Desert. I noticed your license plate. Are you guys from Wyoming?"

Hap glanced at the rearview mirror. The road leading into the park stretched as empty and barren as the land around it. "I was born and raised there, but he's originally from Texas."

"I grew up in Rapid City," she said. "I've spent a lot of

time in Wyoming, especially in the Torrington area. My grandparents live there. They have a saddle shop."

"Claude Hankgrin?" Hap asked.

Her blue eyes brightened. "He's my grandpa."

Laramie leaned forward, his T-shirt sweat glued to the seat back. "He's a good saddlemaker. We haven't seen him in a few years."

"Neither have I. This will be my senior year at the University of Oklahoma."

She flipped her blonde bangs back with a toss of her head. "Did you say you were going to visit someone who lived in the park? I know all of the staff. Who did you come to see?"

When Hap rubbed the back of his neck, dirt rolled under his fingertips. "Rosa Tryor. You know her?"

She jerked her head back to the tall, red-haired man who shared the kiosk. "Did you hear that?"

He nodded and picked up the telephone. "I'll tell him."

"Tell who what?" Hap asked.

She leaned out of the kiosk and lowered her voice. Hap could smell fruity perfume or bubblegum, he couldn't tell which. "Our superintendent, Mr. Davenport, demands to know if anyone asks for Rosa Rodríguez Tryor. He's kind of strange that way. But I have to follow orders."

"What's the deal?" Laramie asked.

The red-haired male attendant scooted up and the blonde stepped back. "Would you please pull over to the open parking place in front of the office?"

The blonde dusted the ledge of her window with her fingers. "Sorry, guys. The superintendent will explain." She nodded toward a brown-haired man with a thin mustache in a park ranger uniform who marched their way, a Colt semiauto 1911 holstered on his hip.

Hap parked the rig. He and Laramie swung out of the truck. "You figure we're slippin' into the quicksand of government micromanaging regulations again?"

"You still ticked about them confiscating our oranges at the Canadian border last year?"

Hap strode up to the uniformed man. "What's this all about?"

The buttoned collar of Davenport's light-green shirt was drenched. Barrel-chested, he stood several inches shorter than either of them. "I hear you intend to visit Rosa Rodríguez Tryor." He spat the words out like a drill sergeant.

"We were in the area and wanted to say hello," Laramie offered.

The man pulled off his glasses and rubbed the bridge of his nose. "Then your purpose is merely a social visit?"

Hap chuckled. "Is there any other way to visit a purdy lady?"

"This is not a humorous situation." Davenport pulled out a small notebook and shoved it toward them. "You may write your salutations on a piece of paper. I will see it gets delivered."

Hap shot a glance at Laramie. "Is she quarantined? Does she have some infectious disease? Is she under house arrest?"

Davenport watched a sedan and minivan roll up to the entrance gate. "You don't know what's going on here?"

"I reckon we don't. We promised a pal that we'd stop and bring greetings to his sis. We're on our way to El Paso. Got jobs waitin' for us there. Like we told . . . uh, the blonde . . ."

"Her name is Erika."

"Like we told Erika, we just want to drive through the park and head on out."

Davenport's face twitched with obvious impatience. "Take my advice and just go back out the way you came. You don't want to get involved in park business."

"What's there to get involved with?" Laramie said. "We just want to visit Rosa."

"Not today, boys."

The man reminded Hap of his algebra teacher in high school, high strung and authoritative, needing to be in charge, but not quite able to pull it off. "Are you saying that, as American citizens who paid our entrance fee, we're denied entry to a national park without an explanation? I don't reckon our congressman will be pleased to hear that."

Davenport paced in front of the black pickup. "There's no reason to start shouting *congressman*. I didn't say you were prohibited. I just said you'd be better off turning around."

Laramie leaned back against the hot hood of the truck and popped his knuckles. "Thank you for the advice, but I think we'll go see Rosa."

The swollen muscles in the man's neck pulsed. "Don't let some fool cowboy pride get you to do something dumb. I'm telling you, don't mess with us."

Hap started back for the pickup. "Fool cowboy pride has kept us alive for years. You ain't tellin' us what it is we aren't supposed to get messed up with, so we'll just keep on our way."

Davenport stomped back to the trailer. "Not with those

horses, you won't. You'll have to leave them in the corral. We'll call a vet for inspection."

"I already showed Erika the vet papers," Hap explained.

"We have reason to be concerned that they might be carrying the West Nile virus. Therefore, I have the legal right to hold them until a new vet check is performed." It sounded like a memorized speech.

"This is a bunch of bull. What are you really up to?" Laramie pressed.

Davenport rested his right hand on the grip of his holstered handgun. "We want you out of the park before dark. This way, you'll have to come back for your horses."

"This is crazy." Hap felt his neck stiffen with frustration that visiting a friend's sister could turn into such a hassle. "How can you get away with treating ordinary citizens like this?"

"We have the legal right."

"The right to harass?"

"Don't get cocky with me." Davenport folded his arms across his chest. "You can leave your trailer here if you want. Some of the roadway is narrow. Just park it over by the corral. Enjoy your day in the park, boys." The man stomped to the office.

After Laramie unloaded the horses, Hap unhitched the trailer. The barren corral was no more than twenty square feet of faded, three-rail board fence, a wide gate, and a small water trough. There was no sign that animals had inhabited it for a long time.

"I'm wonderin' if those papers Milt sent with us have somethin' to do with this squabble," Hap commented.

"I think it's more than a squabble."

"But it's not our squabble. Let's get this stuff to Rosa and mosey on down the road."

Laramie eyed the kiosk. "Here comes your pal Erika."

"Are you going into the park?" she called out. In the bright Texas sun her hair glistened almost white. She had a certain bounce in her step that Hap associated with teen-age girls and kangaroos.

"Yep, but we didn't like the treatment by your boss," Hap said. "He seems pushy and arrogant."

Hap read volumes into the way she rolled her eyes and shrugged. "Hey, I forgot to give you this brochure. It's all about local noxious weeds and poisonous animals. Read it carefully."

Hap took the four-color printed brochure. "Thank you, ma'am."

"I'll keep an eye on your horses," she said, then whispered, "be careful . . . some weird things are going on back there."

Hap frowned as they hopped into the truck and eased back out on the park road. "We are divin' into 'weird things,' partner. Somehow I don't think this will be that borin' day you ordered." Hap tossed the color brochure to Laramie.

"Yeah, with our luck an army of noxious weeds will ambush us." Laramie opened the folder. "Whoa, Erika wrote you a note on the brochure. It says for us to stop at the store at the park headquarters. 'Take as many groceries to Rosa as you can. She has no refrigeration.'"

"Groceries?"

Laramie turned the brochure sideways and continued to read. "She also wrote not to mention she told us this or she'll get fired."

"You get the feelin' ever'one knows what's going on but us?"

"Geez, Hap, here we go again. How do you do this to me?"

"Don't blame me this time, partner. You were the one all fired up to tell Milt we'd come down to see his sister."

"I trusted that a destination without a Juanita would provide a quiet change of pace."

Loaded with two cardboard boxes of assorted food items and a couple of loaves of bread, Laramie and Hap rolled south toward Panther Pass at the junction west of the Visitor Center. The desert landscape of prickly pear cactus, creosote, and sotol soon gave way to evergreen sumac, mountain mahogany, and beebrush. When they reached the pass, they entered a chaparral of juniper, small oak trees, and piñon pines strewn across the rugged, barren mountains.

"It's nicer here than in the desert, but who in the world would want to live here?" Laramie asked.

"Milt's sister, I guess," Hap replied. "Makes you question her intelligence, don't it? Sorta reminds me of the summer in that Owyhee Mountains cowcamp."

"A nice place, except for the constant tourists."

"Tourists? That was the loneliest place on earth. We only saw two vehicles in twelve weeks, and they was both game wardens."

"Yeah, it was a veritable Idaho freeway."

They followed the hand-scribbled map that Milt Tryor had provided. As instructed, they circled behind the ranger station and took a dirt road marked *For Park Personnel Only*. Short cedars and pines walled the horizon, preventing any kind of extended view.

"Milt's note says take every right-hand fork from now on until we reach a gate that says *Keep Out*. Maybe we should have asked him more questions before we signed on to this deal."

Every right turn raised them higher up the mountain. In the north sides of the draws they spied clusters of pine, fir, and aspen.

"It's getting prettier." Laramie stuck his hand out the window and cupped the air. "And cooler. This might be a pleasant visit after all."

"Then again . . ." Hap pointed on up the dirt road. "Looks like company."

Two unmarked trucks bookended the roadway in front of a closed, battered, metal slatted gate.

Hap slowed the pickup to a stop. "Open the gate, Laramie."

"You think they'll let me?"

"Let's find out. This is still America, ain't it . . . home of the brave and land of the free?"

"Where do you cowboys think you're going?" a burly man with a goatee demanded. Beneath the dust, his black boots looked new, synthetic, his accent East Coast. He toted a bag of sour cream and onion pork rinds.

Hap considered the man's challenge and concluded that condescending tones, just like western drawls, must be handed down from one generation to the next. "To visit a friend."

"Time to turn around. You're not going through here."

The shorter one made sure they noticed his hand on a shoulder-holstered revolver.

"You boys been watchin' too many Marlon Brando movies. Your boss already phoned you and told you we were comin'. He must have mentioned that we have a legal right to go in there. Open the gate, Laramie."

"Don't touch that gate, mister," the shorter one warned.

Laramie glanced over his shoulder. "Do they let you pack a loaded gun or do you have to keep your one bullet in your pocket like Barney Fife?"

The taller man stalked Laramie. "Look, we're tryin' to help you. It's not good for your health to proceed. It's like a . . . think of it as an infectious disease. "

"Is that so?" Laramie swung open the wood-and-wire gate with the hand-painted *Keep Out* sign. "Which are you, virus or bacteria?"

Hap eased the pickup forward. He recognized the tight veins on Laramie's neck and knew his partner was getting steamed.

"What's in the boxes?" burly goatee bellowed.

"Enriched plutonium," Hap mumbled.

"What?"

"Everythin' in them boxes was purchased in the park at official stores," Hap explained. "You boys hungry? I didn't buy any Twinkies."

"We want to search this rig."

"Well, I'm sure you do. And I'd like to spend the afternoon in Bill Gates's vault . . . but some things just aren't meant to be. You look at nothin' in this rig without a warrant," Hap challenged.

"A couple of .357s are the only warrant we need." The

short guy jumped in front of the truck, but Hap kept a steady pace forward.

"Do you wear name tags on your shirts so authorities can identify your bodies?" Hap herded the one tagged *Kurt Munkk* along the road.

The other one, labeled *Manuel Ferguson*, yanked his partner back. "Remember what ol' Davenport said."

"We'll be waiting right here for you two," Munkk shouted.

"What a delight." Laramie closed the gate and slipped into the pickup.

"I thought that went well," Hap said.

"Somehow I feel like a bear in a barrel trap. So far, so good. But how in the world do we get out of here?"

A rifle report and the simultaneous shattering of the side-view mirror on the passenger's side made Hap tromp the brakes so fast, the engine died. Laramie slammed against the dash.

Hap pounded the black steering wheel. "Jist what I need, a matched pair of shot-out mirrors."

"Was it one of the good fellas at the gate?" Laramie asked.

"No, it's someone up ahead. Give me that old white T-shirt." Hap crept out of the truck, waving the rag. "Wait a minute . . . don't shoot. We're lookin' for Rosa Tryor."

A woman's voice filtered down from a thick grove of scrub pines. "What do you want?"

"We're friends of your brother, Milt. He sent us here to bring papers and documents."

"Where's Milt?" she asked.

"He had truck trouble and got towed to Fort Stockton," Laramie called out.

"We also brought two boxes of groceries and two loaves of bread," Hap told her.

"White or wheat?"

Hap glanced back at Laramie, who shouted, "Wheat."

"Okay, drive forward. But I'm not putting down the gun until I spot those papers . . . and the bread."

When they drove around the grove of pine trees, they spied a small log cabin and the barrel of a Winchester .30-30 carbine.

Laramie got out of the truck toting the box of papers. Hap carried a loaf of wheat bread.

The brown-skinned woman, with her thick, curly hair pulled back in a bushy ponytail, grabbed the bread, tore it open, folded a piece and chomped on it.

Dressed in dirty jeans, heavy boots, and a white, sleeveless T-shirt, she wore no jewelry, and no makeup. A red bandanna wrapped her neck.

After the second piece of bread, the tension around her large brown eyes eased. She rummaged in the metal box, let out a deep sigh, then laid the gun against the truck's bumper.

"All right! Thank you, Milt!" She glowered at Laramie and Hap. "I didn't know whether to trust you or not. You don't look like much."

Hap tipped his hat. "Always glad to make a good first impression." It seemed to him she swallowed the bread too fast, with little chewing. He studied her thin arms and waist. "How long has it been since you ate anything?"

"I don't remember. Everything gets confusing. I can't sleep, for fear they're going to sneak up on me. I can't leave. They stashed bulldozers, generators, and lights over in that draw. The minute I'm gone, they'll flatten the place and lock me off our property." She glanced down and tried to brush dried purple stains off her T-shirt. "I know I'm a mess, but you don't have to stare like that."

Hap pulled off his cowboy hat. "You look fine, ma'am."

"Fine?"

"Well, a good scrubbin' would help, but that's true for all of us. This dang Texas heat makes us all a little rank."

When she smiled, her full, wide lips revealed straight teeth. "That's what I love about cowboys. They try to charm and be honest at the same time. Most men give up on one or the other." She nodded at the sacks. "Did Milt tell you to bring me groceries?"

"No. Erika, down at the park entrance, slipped us a note," Hap explained.

"She did? I have to admit you came at the right time. I don't think I'd have lasted two more days."

"What's goin' on?" Hap asked. "I'm guessin' the park service wants this land and you don't want them to have it."

"Didn't Milt tell you?"

"We don't know anything other than you are his sister, Rosa," Laramie said.

She dug through the boxes of groceries. "This is better than Christmas. Who are you guys? Don't tell me your names are Butch and Sundance."

"I'm Hap; he's Laramie. We cowboyed several fall gathers up in Wyomin' with Milt. We even worked one spring along the North Platte in Colorado with him."

She grabbed a big box of Frosted Flakes. "It almost makes a gal believe in Divine Providence."

"You'll need more to eat than bread and dry cereal. I'll

fry us all some bacon and eggs," Hap suggested. "They'll spoil on us real soon if we don't cook them."

Laramie and Hap toted the food while Rosa cradled her Winchester.

"Do you need someone to stand vigil on those guys at the gate?" Laramie asked.

"They won't come in during the day. They know they'll be shot for trespassing."

The one-room cabin had a full, covered porch across the front. Inside there was a fireplace, a woodstove, a small table with one chair, and a bedframe of leather straps with a sleeping bag on top. Sheets covered the windows.

"What happened to the panes?" Hap asked.

"They busted them out one night, trying to scare me off."

Hap studied the cobwebs at the peak of the ceiling. "How long have you been back here?"

"Over a year now. But they didn't start harassing me until May."

Hap tucked his sunglasses into his shirt pocket, then rolled up his sleeves. "How have you survived?"

"I had a wonderful garden. The spring supplies all the water I need. In fact, the creek from our spring provides water for the park headquarters as well. But the goons sprayed weed killer on my garden. Everything's ruined."

Laramie peered out the open front door. "Real nice guys. When was that?"

"About a month ago." She dug through the box of papers. "This is so great . . . this is the hard evidence."

Hap built a fire in the woodstove. Rosa sat on the only chair. She kicked off her heavy boots to reveal sockless, dirty toes and long, unpainted toenails.

Laramie lounged in the open doorway. Short juniper scattered the dirt yard. A dusty gray Subaru was parked beside the cabin. "What's the full deal here, Rosa?" he asked.

Rosa swallowed a lump of bread. "Where do I begin?"

"At the Alamo." Hap laughed. "Every Texan I ever met has stories clear back to the Alamo."

Laramie stiffened. "That's not something us Texans joke about."

Rosa held up her hand. "No, no . . . Hap's right. This story has an Alamo connection."

"See?" Hap boasted.

"I believe one of my problems involves a personal vendetta, but I'll need to provide the background. My family . . . the Rodríguez side, anyway . . . lived in Texas before Stephen Austin and all that bunch came here. During the battle for Texas independence, several members of my family died at the Alamo. Some rode with Houston at San Jacinto. That's history and can be proved. It encompasses five generations, but Ernesto Rodríguez gained title for this 160-acre parcel in 1859. The papers were signed by Governor Sam Houston himself."

"It's a harsh piece of land. I wonder why that great-granddaddy of yours wanted it," Laramie asked.

"Family lore claims that he needed a stopping place above the heat of the desert when traveling a trade route between Mexico and central Texas. I'm not sure about that. Some say he smuggled goods back and forth, but in those days it was hard to tell a customs agent from a smuggler. Anyway, it's been in the family since and used as a vacation cabin, whenever anyone wanted to get out of the desert heat."

"We didn't know what kind of geology to expect down here," Laramie said.

"Do you know anything about Big Bend National Park?" she asked.

"It's our first trip," Hap admitted.

"During the Depression, lots of land got forfeited to the state for nonpayment of taxes. Down in this area, it's so rugged and remote, and mostly unfarmable, that people let it go back to the government. Not my great-grandfather. He loved it up here. He somehow always got the taxes paid. By 1933, the state of Texas found they had about 160,000 acres of this rugged land along the big bend of the Rio Grande. So, they formed the Texas Canyons State Park. Private property like ours dotted the park map. The state petitioned President Roosevelt to make it a national park, so the state wouldn't have to pay for the maintenance."

"Is that when it became a national park?" Laramie asked.

While Hap cooked, Rosa snacked on dry cereal, placing one flake at a time on her pointed, pink tongue. "I think the war interrupted the process, but in 1944, seven hundred thousand acres were given to the federal government. That's when the park got established."

Laramie stepped over to the table. "But some parcels remained private?"

"Yes, that's when the park service began a campaign to buy everyone out."

"And your family didn't want to sell?" Laramie reviewed the papers.

"Not sell. But they offered to trade property."

Hap caught himself staring at the slight curves in Rosa's silhouette. "Land swap?"

"Most people didn't mind an exchange for less rugged and remote land."

Laramie picked up a stiff yellow document. "Is that an authentic signature of Sam Houston with all those fancy scrolls?"

"I hope so."

The breeze through the cabin felt pleasant to Hap, like a summer evening in the Bighorns. "So, your family didn't want to swap land?"

"We weren't even asked. Certain people in the park service maintain that great-grandfather was Mexican, not Texan. Therefore, he should never have been given the property in the first place. That's what Davenport informed me."

Hap forked twelve sizzling slices of sweet-smelling bacon onto a paper towel. "So they don't want to pay or trade because they claim it's already theirs."

"That's about it. A year ago, as their perceived gesture of goodwill, they notified us to take anything we wanted from the cabin, because it was going to be demolished."

"So, you've been hugging the ranch, so to speak, ever since?" Laramie said.

"That's about it."

Hap beat the eggs with a large, almost clean wooden spatula. "So what is it you want from them?" He dug through the sack of groceries for paper plates.

"I know we can't keep the park from getting the land," Rosa explained. "This same thing happens around all national parks. I don't mind that others enjoy it, too. We just want a fair price. Or better than that, some type of equitable land exchange and a couple other assurances. I want to be treated with respect, as a rightful landowner."

"You said some of this is personal?" Laramie questioned.

"That's the strange part." Rosa dug a red apple out of the box. She rolled up her T-shirt and wiped the fruit, which revealed her flat, brown stomach.

Hap jerked his gaze back to the frying pan when the eggs started to burn.

He surveyed the littered shelf behind the stove. Most items showed the dust of years of neglect. "Have you got any pepper?"

"Sorry." She chomped on the apple and wiped the dribble off her chin with her shirtsleeve. "Davenport arrived as superintendent and assumed dictatorial command. Most of the veteran, year-round staff have transferred out of here."

"So this jerk, Davenport, marched in and started making trouble?"

"The first thing he did was hit on me. I think he thought he would romance me out of the place. He told me I was the 'girl of his dreams.' Can you imagine any man saying that?"

Hap spun around with a pan full of bubbling, snapping eggs. "I can imagine it."

She stared at Hap as a slow grin broke across her lips.

"Anyway," he muttered, "what did you say to Davenport?"

"I told him where to go and where to stash his inflated ego. He flew into a rage about cleaning out the illegal squatters from the park."

Laramie meandered back to the open doorway. "Some men don't take 'no' well."

"He's also ticked because he can't prove any ancestors

at the Alamo. He can't admit that I'm more Texan than he is."

"The park service won't put up with a personal vendetta, will they? Did you go above his head?" Hap asked.

"I had a chance to send one long email about a month ago, spelling out my grievances, but I can't do much else. I haven't heard back, but to be fair I haven't checked my email in weeks. Davenport will level this place and lock me out if I leave. It would take months to fight in court. By then, no telling what would happen."

Hap divided the scrambled eggs onto three paper plates. "These groceries will sustain your misery for another week or so. What then? What is your plan?"

"I counted on Milt to help me out. Most of my family thinks it's all a lost cause, that there's no reason to fight. But Mamma made sure the taxes were always paid, as did my grandfather. I think for their sake, and for the sake of great-granddaddy, I need to press the case. I wanted to write an account of the facts, backed up by these documents, and ask Milt to take it to the media. I need someone to know what's going on here. I don't even think the other park service people really know what's happening."

"Shoot, we can do that for you. We can carry out some papers for the media, can't we, Laramie?"

"That part seems simple enough."

The wind picked up and blew the sheet curtains straight into the cabin. Dust off the floor swirled around and Hap tried to shield the eggs with his hat. "Better than just sendin' a story, why don't you go out to the newspapers or television yourself? They're always wantin' to hype some controversy. Havin' a purdy gal—an articulate lady such as yourself—will add punch to the complaint."

"My car won't run. I think they dumped something in the gas tank."

Laramie perused the gray Subaru. "They ruined your car? That's a crime, isn't it?"

"Only if I can prove it."

Hap stirred the eggs. "They want to chase you off, and then they sabotage your only way of escape?"

"They aren't too bright."

"When you say 'they,' do you mean the whole staff here?" Laramie asked.

"Davenport and the two at my gate have been the only ones I've known to take an active part. The regular staff seems afraid to even talk to me, but they've never harassed me. I don't think those two guards are even park service guys."

Hap carried over the plates piled with steaming food. The aroma of smoke and sweet fried meat permeated the room. "Hey, listen to this plan . . . one of us will sneak you out. The other will stay to protect the place."

He pulled up an old wooden trunk to use as a chair, then crammed a forkful of steaming eggs in his mouth. "You see," he mumbled, "Davenport expects us out of here by sundown. We have to pick up our trailer and horses. He'll be so happy to see us go, I reckon he won't check real close who's in the truck."

Rosa padded barefoot across the rough wooden floor to retrieve a large bottle of red sauce. Her calloused feet left tracks in the dust. She handed the bottle to Hap.

He took it and grinned. "A gal who likes Tabasco? Will you marry me?"

"No." She plopped back in her chair. "It's a well-known sociological fact that spice-based relationships are doomed to fail. Now, how are you going to sneak me past Davenport?"

Hap swamped his eggs with red Tabasco. "I figure we wait until almost dark and pull a hat down over your eyes. We can drive straight to Fort Stockton or Odessa, arrange an interview, and sneak you back to the cabin by daylight."

"If I get out, I need to get to a computer. There's no electricity here." Rosa chomped a huge bite of steaming Tabasco-drenched eggs.

Laramie strode over to the open doorway, plate of food in hand. "Sounds to me like a bad plan that doesn't have a chance."

"Good." Hap wiped his mouth on the back of his hand. "That's something we're used to." He dug through the grocery sack. "I thought for sure we bought a jar of pickles."

Rosa untied the bandanna from around her neck and wiped her narrow chin. "I had some homemade ones, but that was supper, last week."

Hap jumped up. "Good grief, do you see that, Laramie? Come here, quick."

"What?" Rosa's hand flew to her face. "What are you looking at? What's wrong with me?"

"Absolutely nothing. I'm looking at the birthmark under your right ear."

She covered her neck with her hand. "Technically, it's not a birthmark. I mean, I was born with it . . . lots of women on my mother's side of the family have it. But they say birthmarks are not genetic. We just call it 'the mark.' So what?"

Laramie shook his head and muttered, "I'll be. I never thought we'd see one of those."

"I'm sorry if it looks ugly."

"Just the opposite, it looks wonderful . . . beautiful," Hap exclaimed.

"I've never had anyone say that before. It's always made me self-conscious. That's why the bandanna."

"Did you say other women in your family have a similar mark?" Hap probed.

"Most all. They have different shapes and sizes."

Hap took a deep breath. His eyes glazed over. "Have you got any relatives named . . . Juanita?"

"Half the women on the Rodríguez side of the family are named Juanita. What's this all about?"

Hap shot his arms in the air. "There is a God in heaven!"

"Are you going to preach?"

"I'm going to tell you of a quest so exciting, it will rivet you to the edge of your chair."

"I think I'll go out on the porch and take a nap," Laramie groaned.

⊶══◉   ◉══⊷

The sun blazed, then teetered on the edge of the horizon like a big red ball about to roll off the edge of the table.

"Take care of yourself, partner," Hap called as they climbed into the truck.

"You're the one taking all the chances. I'm just sitting here, waiting. I'm about two days shy of sleep, so I won't mind some peace and quiet. But if you two aren't back by the time the groceries run out, I'm leaving."

"Give us twenty-four hours," Rosa said, adjusting the

cuffs of Laramie's blue denim jacket, which was bulky on her smaller frame. "After that, just hike out of here."

When they drove to the gate, Rosa slumped down in the seat, Hap's black beaver felt hat pulled over her face.

Hap honked, and Ferguson swung open the gate. After they drove through, he signaled for them to stop as he surveyed the truck. "What happened to your buddy?"

"What happened to yours?" Hap challenged.

"He's sleeping. It's my turn for night duty."

"Laramie got sick. That Mexican gal fed us a bunch of strange vegetables. I passed on them, but Laramie chowed down. They didn't sit well with him."

"Vegetables? She tried to kill you. We sprayed them with weed killer."

"That's nice to hear. Then we'll know who to sue."

"You can't sue us. We don't even exist. We aren't on the government record. We're a private security operation. On loan, so to speak."

Rosa groaned in a deep, raspy voice.

"What did he say?" Manny leaned closer.

"I don't know, but I want to reach Fort Stockton to get his stomach pumped before he barfs all over my truck again."

Hap lurched the rig forward. Ferguson closed the gate behind them.

When they broke out of the trees, Hap patted her knee. "Okay, girl, you can breathe easy for a while."

"Not all those groans were phony."

"You gettin' sick?"

"I think I ate too much, too fast."

"You let me know if you want me to stop."

"You haven't done anything yet."

Hap felt his neck and face warm. "No . . . I meant . . ."

"I know what you meant. For a cowboy, you certainly blush easy."

"You ambushed me with that tease."

"It's been a long time since I could relax enough to tease."

⊷══◯   ◯══⊶

Hap turned right at Basin Junction. The sun dropped. The air bristled with a tinge of chill.

Rosa pulled off the hat. "I'm not used to wearing this. No one can see me in here now anyway." She twirled the hat in her hand. "I can't believe you two would do all of this for me."

"Chalk it up to the cowboy code. You're Milt's sister and he couldn't be here. I'd appreciate some cowboy pal of mine lookin' after my sis, if she needed the help."

"Yes, Milt is that way. But I still say, you don't know much about me."

"That's not true. Milt told us lots."

"Like what?"

"He said you were a really smart, stubborn, opinionated woman who was too forceful and driven to get married."

"Milt blabbed all that?"

"Yeah, is it true?"

She drummed her fingers on her leg. "Yes, but I don't like hearing it."

"Rosa . . . win or lose, this land conflict will be over someday. What then? Where is your life headed?"

"Geez, Hap . . . what is this? I want to get out, hold a press conference, and get back to the cabin. I want to make a scene over the government grabbing private property. I don't have any more plans than that. Just out of the blue, you decide to go philosophical on me? Don't ask such personal questions. You're beginning to sound like Dr. Phil."

"Okay, I'll change the subject. No more brain-numbing discussions of life goals. No politics. No social causes. Let's relax and talk about something generic."

Rosa let out a deep sigh. "Good."

Hap scratched his forehead. "Why don't you wear a bra?"

Rosa burst out laughing. "I love it. Now, that's a nice, neutral, nonphilosophical question. It's a no-brainer and not a feminist statement. I left some clothes drying on a short clothesline stretched between the trees behind the cabin. The jerks came in and stole them one night."

"Kind of like Tom Hanks in *The Terminal*. They're tryin' to make it so miserable that you'll leave. It's a wonder they didn't poison the spring."

"They don't dare. A couple years ago, before this harassment began, the University of Texas conducted a study on natural springs all over the state. The Rodríguez Ranch on Panther Mountain rated the purest natural water in west Texas. I think even Davenport is afraid to contaminate it. Besides, it supplies most of the park residences as well."

"We're close to the entrance. Put my hat back on and play sick. I'll hook up the trailer and load the horses."

Under the dim glow of streetlights, Hap backed up to the horse trailer. When he led the horses from the corrals, Erika waited for him.

Hap nodded. "Thanks for lookin' in on the horses. I didn't figure you'd still be on duty."

"I'm not. This is my own time." She peered across the pickup at the office entrance.

"Is Davenport still here?"

"Yeah, I expect him to barrel out any minute. I probably shouldn't be talking to you. But you need to know something before he does. Then I need to know something."

Hap handed her Tully's lead rope, then walked Luke up into the trailer. "What do I need to know?"

"Those two guys at the gate of her place are not park service employees. They work for Davenport. The two trucks they drive are registered to 'Out West Development Corporation, East Orange, New Jersey.' This is not a park service dispute, but everyone's afraid to investigate further. Most of us are just summer employees and we need the work. Official complaints have been filed, but everything takes a long time to process. We think Davenport's about to be transferred or fired. It isn't the first time he's gone on a vendetta. If Rosa can hang on a while, this could be settled."

"Thanks for the info."

"Now, there is one thing you have to explain to me."

"What's that?"

"Why in the world is Rosa Rodríguez Tryor slouched in the front seat of your pickup with your cowboy hat pulled down over her face?"

"Obvious, huh? We're headed out to the newspapers to tell her story. I'm going to get her back before daylight."

"Your partner is at the Rodríguez Ranch?"

"Yep."

"If Davenport finds out she's gone, he'll go ballistic and bulldoze the place tonight."

Hap looped his thumbs into his jeans pockets. "I'm hopin' a Rapid City cowgirl like you will keep it to herself."

"I won't say a thing. What newspaper are you going to talk to?"

"Probably the one in Fort Stockton, but we're hopin' for broader coverage."

"My college roommate works for a newspaper in Odessa. She's not a reporter or anything, but let me call her. Do you know where Tiny's Café is in Fort Stockton?"

"We'll find it."

"I'll see if I can get someone to meet you there for a story. If no one's there, I didn't have any luck. Go on, now. Here comes Davenport."

Hap slipped into the pickup.

"What are you doing out here?" Davenport called out to Erika.

"You told us to make sure they got out by dark. I thought that meant supervising the loading of the horses." Erika strolled off toward staff housing.

Davenport marched over to the pickup. "I could have you arrested right now."

Hap closed the door, but rolled down his window. "For taking groceries to a hungry woman? Are bread and eggs contraband in a national park?"

"The illegal transportation of firearms is."

"What firearms?"

"You've got two Winchester carbines in the saddle compartment of the horse trailer."

"We didn't transport them anywhere. We left them at the entrance."

"You came 150 feet within the park. I have the legal right to arrest you."

"I just followed your instructions."

"You could be jailed."

"Not without a court fight."

"Don't threaten me with judicial blackmail."

"No threat. A court case might be nice. Then you could explain by what authority you searched our trailer by busting a padlock without permission. In fact, it provides the perfect platform for me to describe the emaciated and wretched condition we found Rosa Rodríguez Tryor in as you tried to starve her out of her own legal property. What do you think, partner? Let's get arrested."

"No . . . wait," Davenport cautioned. "I didn't say I was going to arrest you. I merely mentioned I had sufficient grounds. Now, if you two drive off and I never see you again, I'll get so busy with other duties, I won't even remember your names."

"You don't know our names now. But we're leaving anyway." Hap drove the truck up on the blacktop and headed out of the park.

Rosa sat up and handed Hap his hat. She tossed Laramie's denim jacket behind the seat. "Do you think we can trust Erika?"

"We'll find out at Tiny's Café in Fort Stockton. But this whole deal sounded much more logical in your cabin."

⤙═⊃   ⊂═⤚

When they reached the junction of Highway 90, Rosa pointed to the *For Sale* signs on the southeast corner.

"This is barren, godforsaken country. Who would be crazy enough to buy out here?" Hap said.

"You want to hear something bizarre? A few months

ago, when I had more freedom to come and go, that property sold. So, out of curiosity, I called the county recorder to see who purchased it. It was an outfit called Out West Development Corporation . . ."

"Of East Orange, New Jersey?" Hap replied.

"Have you heard of them?"

"When Erika and me were visitin' by the horse trailer, she said those two pickups at your gate were registered to that same company."

"Wait a minute." Rosa slapped her hand down on Hap's knee. "There's a connection between this barren five acres on the crossroads to nowhere and those thugs at my gate?"

He studied her hand on his knee. "Kind of leaves my head spinnin'. It's got to be oil wells or somethin' dealin' with a lot of money. Maybe you're sittin' on a gold mine."

"Sure, a west Texas gold rush. That sandstone on the ranch is as far away from gold as you can get."

"Diamonds, maybe?"

She let out a smooth, easy laugh that tickled Hap's throat, then pulled her hand off his knee. "You're getting delusional."

"Yeah . . ." he let out a long, slow sigh. "But I know an old guy in the Ruby Mountains of Nevada who claims to have a platinum mine."

"I wish I knew what Out West Development Company really developed."

"It gives us somethin' to ponder, don't it, Rosa?"

⋆⇒══   ══⇐⋆

The blacktop never bobbed all the way to Fort Stockton. The diesel engine roared, the radial tires hummed, and

Hap and Rosa talked nonstop for almost two hours. In the pitch black of night, Texas resembled New Mexico . . . or Oklahoma . . . or even parts of Wyoming. No buildings. No lights. Little traffic. Empty land lay dormant for another century, or millennium, before development.

"Do you realize we haven't seen a town for a hundred miles?" Rosa said.

"But it wasn't a dull trip. I enjoyed our visit. I can't believe all the places you've been. The canopy walks along the Amazon . . . living in a tent all winter in Alaska . . . savin' those little white birds from extinction along the Great Wall of China. You make my life sound monotonous."

"I don't think so. You know what I like about your stories, Hap? It's like all your exploits come to you. You just get up in the morning and adventures happen. Me, on the other hand, I travel all round the world to discover a cause, a challenge, a daring summons. And if they aren't readily available, I have to create one."

"Like the stand for the Rodríguez Ranch?"

"Yes . . ."

"Rosa, I asked you this once before. I really would like to know. What's next on your list of things to do?"

She was quiet a moment. "I think I'd like to go back to the university, get my doctorate, and teach at the college level."

"Why don't you do it?"

"You know the old adage . . . if you can't do it, teach it?"

"That ain't necessarily true."

"Yes, but right now, I can do it. I can get involved. I can work for a cause. I can deliver results. At least, I could until this family deal." She flopped her head against the back of the seat. "Do you know I haven't talked personal to a man for two straight hours since I was eighteen?"

"Why's that?"

"I don't think I've had a captive audience. Most times guys just walk away. They get tired of my rantings. Some think I'm too bossy and controlling. Some believe I have a messiah complex, that I'm out to save the world. What do you think? How would you describe me?"

Hap rolled down his window halfway and siphoned the night air into his lungs. "You want my honest opinion?"

"I don't want you to lie."

"Don't change your strengths, but soften up once in a while. You don't need biting rebuttals all the time."

"Soften up?"

"Do you have a soft voice? Do you ever giggle? Do you do anything crazy like get your toenails painted and lay out on the beach in a bikini just to make the men act like dadgum fools?"

"Is that all you're really interested in?" she snapped.

"You weren't listenin' to me, Rosa. I said, don't change the strong parts. If I ever needed a gal to work alongside of me to make a project go, you'd be the one. After hearin' about your causes and campaigns, I can't imagine any goal you can't achieve, if someone don't shoot you first. But my point is, sometimes I need to crash. To unwind. To forget about my troubles . . . the world's troubles . . . and just enjoy being a man. Don't you ever have those kinds of days when you just want to enjoy bein' a woman?"

"Are you talking about sex?"

"Forget it. This ain't comin' out right. All I'm sayin' is

that you're way too smart and too beautiful a gal to wake up one day an old lady who's all worn out and lonely."

"I might be tired and alone, but I'll have a list of accomplishments that mean something to this world."

"That's true, but a list don't keep your feet warm on a cold night. All the accolades on earth can't whisper in your ear, 'You're beautiful,' on a day when you feel ugly. And a letter of commendation won't comfort you for hours in the middle of the night when you're depressed."

She glanced at her watch. Her voice mellowed. "I know. I know, Hap. You're right. But all of that is a luxury I won't allow myself."

"Why?"

"Because of my mother."

Hap tried to read her eyes in the rearview mirror. "Was she hard-drivin' and goal-oriented, too?"

"No, the opposite. Family was everything. She treated Daddy like a king. She adored the man. She turned down a career so she could stay home and raise us kids. She once told me she couldn't bear the thought of him coming home from work and her not being there to hug him and welcome him. She fixed her hair the way he liked it best. She wore the clothes he admired. Mamma's goal in life was to make that man happy."

"Did she achieve her goal?"

"Apparently not. Dear Daddy left Mamma with six kids when she was thirty-four. He ran off with a 'Budweiser girl' less than half his age. But that was four wives ago. Mamma survived ten years after that, but I never saw her smile again. She soured into a bitter lady who looked twenty years older than she should when she died."

"So you've said to yourself, *There has to be more in life than adorin' a man*?"

Her reply was quiet. "I don't have the courage to invest that much in a relationship. It's too scary."

"That's about as honest a reply as I ever heard. In that case, let's go find Tiny's Café and challenge the tactics of the National Park Service."

"You know what, Hap, standing up against the government is much, much easier than attempting to love someone."

Neither said anything until they rounded the corner on Fourth Street.

"Tiny's Café must be the best spot in town. Look at that crowd," Hap said. "Maybe we should have agreed to meet someplace a little more private. I don't think there's any room in the parkin' lot."

"Drive around the block," she motioned.

"I wonder who we're lookin' for?"

"If Erika didn't reach anyone, I'll make some phone calls. I know a guy in Odessa who covered a story about me one time, though we might have to drive up there."

"What was your cause that time?" Hap slowed the rig.

"Brine flies."

"Did you win?"

She grinned. "What do you think?"

"I think that's the first candid smile I've seen since you spied the loaf of bread. Rosa, you got one awesome smile."

"Well, it wasn't this beautiful smile that saved the brine flies from extinction."

"Yes, but it might save Rosa Rodríguez Tryor from extinction."

"Good point, cowboy. Park by that vacant lot." Rosa glanced in the mirror before getting out. "I should never look. I need to comb my hair."

"Go ahead. We can take a few minutes."

"It's a mess, isn't it?"

"I've always been attracted to thick black hair."

"I know, I know, you told me . . . like your Juanita." She stabbed a comb through her hair. "Wish I had a clean blouse. And I was told I need a bra."

"I can't help you with underwear, but I think there're some clean shirts in that duffel bag."

Rosa sorted through the shirts. "Hey, can I wear this one with the big loud flowers? I like yellow."

"Isn't that about the ugliest . . ."

"I like it."

"So did my sis when she sent it to me. It might be huge on you."

"I'll tie it around my waist. Turn around and don't look."

Hap stared out the window.

"Can I wear your horsehair belt with the silver buckle?"

"Help yourself."

"I know how to braid horsehair," she said. "I learned from a ninety-year-old man when I was in prison in Cuba. Does that surprise you?"

"No, neither your braidin' horsehair nor bein' in a Cuban prison surprises me."

"I suppose it would be too much to ask if you had any lipstick?"

"Actually, I do. Look in the glove compartment."

"In this little leather box with the rock? This Wyoming

bracelet looks a little small for you. Is there a story behind that?"

"A long story."

"Oh, here it is. I can't believe you have lipstick. I won't ask you why."

"And I'm not going to tell you."

"You can look now."

Hap spun around. "Whoa . . . my shirt never looked that good."

She glanced at the rearview mirror again, licked her fingers, and mashed down her bangs.

"Okay, now I look decent enough to interview."

"You look good enough for most anythin'."

"Come on, cowboy, I'll try to ignore that sexist remark. Let's just hope they didn't bring a camera." She stepped out of the truck and slammed the door.

They crossed the crowded parking lot. A dark gray side door flung open. A boy about sixteen scurried out with a large, red "hot bag."

"Is this the entrance?" Hap asked.

"This is the carry-out and delivery door. But go ahead and use it. Just hug the south wall until you get out front."

"Do you always have a big crowd like this?" Rosa asked.

"We never do. It's crazy." The delivery boy jogged out to an old red Mustang convertible, then ripped out of the parking lot.

The take-out entrance brought them into the kitchen. Employees darted around like a frantic last dance. The dining room tables were full. A large group of noisy men and women crowded the front door.

Hap took Rosa's arm as they shoved toward an opening

by the front window. "How are we ever going to tell if there's a reporter here?"

"Ask the first person with a camera or a clipboard. No one comes to a café with a clipboard but the health inspector or a reporter."

Hap tipped his hat at a woman with short blonde hair and a tape recorder fastened to her belt. "Ma'am, are you a reporter?"

"Watch out, comin' through!" a man boomed. As his video camera case swung toward them, Rosa squeezed against Hap's chest to avoid getting hit.

The blonde looked them over. "Cute couple. Yeah, I'm a reporter, but I don't do the society stuff. I'm really kind of busy right now. A potentially big story's about to break."

More people herded into the room and the noise level raised so high that Rosa clutched Hap as they both leaned closer to each other. "I haven't been this crammed into a crowd since my cousin's wedding."

"Was her name Juanita?"

"No, LaDonna." Rosa turned to the blonde reporter. "We were hoping to talk to you about . . ."

The woman's high-pitched voice pierced into a shout. "Did I hear wedding? You two getting married? Hey, that's sweet. Call or email the paper and ask for Gretchen Mourey. She'll take care of the announcement."

Hap pointed to the television camera. "Is this story a secret or can you tell us?"

The lady gawked into the jammed parking lot as a white van with satellite receiver pulled in. "Oh, not KTVT Channel 11. What are they doing way over here?"

"That's bad?" Rosa asked.

"CBS affiliate out of Dallas. Everyone in America will

know about this story before the morning papers hit the front porches."

"What kind of story?" Hap asked.

The lady leaned close enough for him to smell the pepperoni on her breath. "There's a rumor of a Waco or Ruby Ridge kind of uprising at some remote place in west Texas called the Rodríguez Ranch. Almost a civil war, but no one can find out where it is. The state and federal governments deny everything. We received emails circulating from inside the compound that several of the combatants risked their lives to storm past government agents. They're going to meet us here within the hour and give proof of what's going on."

Hap stared at Rosa. "Now, that ain't exactly . . ."

"Geraldo's here!" someone shouted.

Rosa tugged on Hap's arm. "We've got to go. I have a bunch of bride books to look at."

"What?" he stammered.

"Come on, sweetie." Rosa tugged him through the kitchen to the delivery entrance and into the parking lot.

Hap stopped her in the parking lot with his hands on her shoulders. "What are you doin', runnin' away? The place is crammed with reporters. Isn't that what you want?"

She rested her hands on his. "No. I don't want this. They aren't looking for the truth, they're looking for sensationalism."

He began to rub her shoulders. "Erika must be majorin' in public relations to round up this many."

"I think she's more into creative writing. Never underestimate the power of a good internet lie."

He dropped his hands to his side. "What are we goin' to do?"

"I don't know, Hap." She wove her hand into his. "I wanted to talk to one or two people in private. This is a feature story, not a tabloid front page. I'm still in shock about this mob."

"Chalk it up to instant messaging, twenty-four-hour news radio and TV, and a slow news day. Let's give them what they want."

She wound her arm around his waist. "I'm not going to lie."

"No lies. Put your old shirt on. Pull your hair back. Wipe off the lipstick. Mess your bangs. Smear a little dirt on your face. I'll bounce this rig right into the parking lot. Then jump up in the bed of the truck and tell the absolute truth. No embellishments. You don't need to please them all. Just get one or two to take the story and run with it."

"You're not going to feed me to the wolves and leave, are you? I might need a fast exit."

"I'll keep the truck runnin'."

While Rosa slipped back into her grubby shirt, Hap unhitched the trailer. Her hair mussed up and cheeks smudged, she motioned to him. "What do you think?"

"That should do it. But there's a certain kind of beauty that cain't be hid. Are you sure your name is Rosa?"

"You confusing me with a boyhood dream?"

"Do you mind?"

She leaned over and kissed his ear. "No."

Hap steered the truck around the block, then roared into the parking lot with squealing brakes. Dozens of reporters and cameras converged on them. Hap ushered Rosa to the

back of the truck. He straddled the side rail while she tried
to calm the media frenzy and answer questions.

"How many people have been killed?"

"None."

"Is the FBI involved?"

"No."

"Are children being abused in the compound?"

"Of course not. There aren't any children. There is just
a cabin. No compound. Why would you even think to ask
that?"

"Is it true all of you agreed to a suicide pact, if the government decides to move in?"

"Pact? I'm the only one there."

"Is it true your surface-to-air rockets brought down an
army helicopter?"

"That's absurd."

"What about the rumor that a Colombian drug cartel
uses the Rodríguez Ranch for a drop zone?"

"Look, give me a chance to explain . . ."

"Then, it is true?"

"NO!" she shouted.

"What about the charge that you're one of the wives of
a radical Mormon fundamentalist?"

Hap stood up and raised his hands. "Quiet," he shouted.
"Rosa came here to make a statement. Give her a chance.
Then you can ask questions."

"Are you her husband?"

"Her brother?"

"Her lover?"

Hap reached over the side of the truck, grabbed the man
by the tie and yanked him straight up. "I will turn this

man loose when you remain silent long enough to listen to Rosa."

          ◄═══◐   ◑═══►

Twenty-two minutes later, everyone had dispersed except Hap and Rosa. The only vehicles in the parking lot were his pickup and the delivery kid's red Mustang.

Rosa plopped down on the rail next to Hap. "That went well. Normally, it takes me an hour to chase off reporters."

"They were lookin' for somethin' else."

"You said to tell them the truth. Didn't they believe me?"

"Oh, they believe you. That's the problem."

"What do you mean?"

"The truth bored them."

"Did you hear what that one idiot said?"

"You mean, 'As soon as someone gets shot and dies, then it will become a story'?"

Rosa sighed. "A rather cynical view of people's interest levels."

"They didn't seem impressed with a sabotaged vegetable garden and broken windows." Hap pulled off his hat. "Papers want to sell copies. Stations need increased ratings. Reporters seek fame. Ever'one wants somethin'."

"They didn't even care about my documents."

"When they got word of the president's dog barfing on the prime minister of Japan's lap, they all raced off to Crawford."

"Hey, we got an unclaimed Canadian bacon and pineapple," the kid shouted from the front door. "The boss says you can have it for free."

Hap shoved on his hat. "That's good. The trip's not a complete waste. Come on . . . we need pizza and a truck stop."

"You need fuel?"

"That and a few other things. Did you know most truck stops now offer an internet café, so truckers can check their email?"

"Do you need to check email?"

"Nope . . . but you do. You told me so. How many groups have you been active in over the past five years?"

"Hundreds."

"Email them and call in your chips."

"What?"

"Ask them for a favor."

"What favor?"

"Tell them to email everyone on their list with a simple message, 'Ponder Rosa. What are they doing to Rosa Rodríguez Tryor at Big Bend National Park, Texas?'"

"That's it?"

"That's the rally cry," Hap declared. "Ponder Rosa."

"It's silly . . . and simple."

"So is 'Just Do It.' But it works."

"But Erika already did the internet thing," Rosa said.

"No, she contacted the media, who expected a melodrama or violence or ratings or glory. Now it's time to stir up the average person, the internet activist . . . we want them to 'Ponder Rosa.'"

⊷═ ═⊷

Rosa hunkered down in the smoky drivers' lounge at the 4-Corners Truck Stop. She hammered computer keys with a message to fifty-three activist groups and all 106 individual email addresses on her personal Hotmail account.

When she finally wandered back outside, she found Hap sorting through several cardboard boxes. "What did you buy?"

"I found an all-night grocery. Besides more food, I bought a staple gun and all the plastic signs they had in stock."

"What kind of signs?"

"*For Sale. For Rent. Garage Sale. Keep Out* . . . you know, those kinds of signs."

"That's a mixed message."

"The backs are all blank. We're making our own signs. I've got some big marking pens and on every one we'll write *PONDER ROSA*. We'll plaster them all over Fort Stockton and on telephone poles all the way down to the park. We'll start a grass-roots movement. Isn't this the way you do it?"

"I suppose. Hap, why are you doing this?"

"You think it's just because you're a beautiful, desirable woman."

"I never once thought you were doing it for that reason. I do not consider myself to have either of those qualities."

"I'm doin' this because I think you're gettin' a raw deal. And . . . I'm doin' it because you remind me of someone."

"Your Juanita?"

"Funny, ain't it? All these years I've tried to imagine what she would be like at twenty . . . or twenty-five . . . or thirty. When I find her, I'm sure she will be exactly like you."

By nine the next morning, they had stapled the last of the signs at a Highway 385 rest stop. "Now, back to the park," Hap declared.

"Do you think a few small signs will generate interest?"

"Two-hundred-forty-one signs add up to more than a few. Besides, it's the repetition, not the size. Just ask Wall Drug in South Dakota."

"Perhaps we should have advertised free drinks of spring water."

"Now you're thinkin'," he said.

"How are you going to smuggle me back in? There's too much daylight."

"No smugglin'. This time we drive right through."

"But if Davenport sees me, he'll radio for them to bull-doze the cabin before we reach it."

"Were you determined to save the cabin, no matter what?"

"Not really. As you saw, it's about to collapse from old age."

"Then let them tear it up. That will make a good photo op for the blogs. It will demonstrate Davenport's evil intent."

"But where will I stay?"

"In the truck. Me and Laramie can sleep outside. Let's force them to do somethin'. Survivin' is reactionary. It al-lows others to control the scene."

"Are you sure this will work?"

"No, but it's not what they expect. When you fight giants, you have to catch them off guard." He reached over and touched her knee.

Rosa stared at his fingers. "You know what, cowboy? You've made me think of things I haven't thought about in years."

"It feels good, don't it?"

"Yes, very good," she murmured.

⊷═◍   ◍═⊶

Erika greeted them at the entrance gate.

Hap rolled down his window. "What are you doin' on the mornin' shift? Don't you ever sleep?"

"I switched with Tiff. I wanted to see if you'd come back. I stayed up most of the night checking the net for some splashy story. But all I found was this. About 2:00 A.M., this message popped up everywhere." She handed him a printout.

Hap took the note: "Ponder Rosa. What are they doing to Rosa Rodríguez Tryor at Big Bend National Park, Texas?' Say, that's kind of catchy, ain't it?"

"I also got roundabout word that the regional superintendent is headed down here. That could be revealing."

"Does Davenport know?"

"No one is supposed to know."

"Good. Now, call Davenport . . . tell him one of those cowboys and Rosa Rodríguez just drove through the gate. Tell him you heard them say they're headed back to the Rodríguez Ranch."

"But he might do something dumb."

"We're countin' on it. Then, let the other park service people know what's goin' on, so we can drive straight to the Rodríguez Ranch. We'd appreciate it if they don't try to stop us. We're forcin' Davenport to show his hole cards."

Rosa leaned forward to look at Erika. "Tell the tourists to be sure and visit the historic Rodríguez Ranch on Panther Mountain. I think we might need witnesses."

"What's so historic about it?" Erika quizzed.

"Tell them it's rumored to be one of the places Pancho Villa hid out while on the run from both the Mexican and American authorities."

"Ain't that somethin'. I heard that same rumor myself . . . jist today, in fact," Hap said.

"Oh! So did I," Erika added. "By the way, while I surfed the internet last night, I Googled Out West Development Corporation. They own casinos in Atlantic City and Vegas, plus a riverboat near St. Louis."

"That doesn't make sense," Rosa said. "They aren't going to put a casino up here on Panther Mountain."

Erika shrugged. "All I know is that the names of their board of directors reads like the cast of *The Sopranos*."

⌖⌖⌖ ⌖⌖⌖

When they drove past the information center twenty minutes later, all the employees lined the road and waved. One of them held a hand-scrawled "Ponder Rosa" sign.

"I've been back there for almost a year. I never knew I had this kind of support," Rosa said.

"I don't think Davenport is real popular among the staff. They're hopin' you can do somethin' about him, too."

They circled behind the maintenance sheds and bumped down the dirt road to the ranch.

"What about the gate guards?" Rosa asked.

"That's why I put the carbines up here with us. I still wish I knew what Davenport really wanted." Hap studied the dust fogged up behind them. "Do you reckon they want to build an Indian casino down at the highway junction?"

"I don't think there are any reservations in Texas. Besides, that would be a horrible location. For a big operation, you need people . . . and a draw."

Windows down, carbines out both sides, Hap rolled up to the Rodríguez Ranch gate.

"Well, isn't that nice?" he laughed. "I reckon I jist can't leave Laramie alone."

The gate to the ranch stood ajar. Strapped to the post on one side was Manny Ferguson. Bound to the post on the other side was Kurt Munkk. Both had bandannas tied in their mouths.

Hap stopped the truck. "Well, boys, it surely was nice of you to leave the gate open. Thoughtful of 'em, ain't it, Rosa, darlin'?"

"Very considerate."

"You probably regret all those horrible names you called them."

"No, not at all," she replied.

Hap stepped out of the truck and approached Ferguson. With a poster marker he wrote on the man's brown T-shirt: "Ponder Rosa." He scrawled the same slogan on Munkk. "You know, I'm startin' to see that slogan ever'where."

A phone rang on Ferguson's belt. Hap plucked it up and flipped it open. "Yeah?" he growled.

"This is Davenport. I've been trying to phone you for twenty minutes."

"We've been busy."

"Start the bulldozer. Demolish the cabin right now. Rodríguez is not there. Have Munkk stop her and the cowboy at the gate. Tell him to use force, if necessary."

"What do you want us to do with the bodies?"

"What bodies?"

"The two cowboys and Rodríguez. They tried to ram us a few minutes ago, so we snuffed them," Hap rasped.

"You did what? I didn't say to kill them. Good Lord, what have you done? I told Mr. Logina there could be no killing. I'll be there in five minutes."

Hap squeezed the phone back in the man's pocket.

He tipped his hat to the tied men. "Just think of how happy Davenport will be when he finds out you didn't kill anyone. You boys have a nice day."

Hap cruised up to the cabin. He and Rosa carried groceries to the front porch. The lever on a Winchester checked inside the cabin. "You'd better be a man with a black hat and cheesy mustache with a pretty girl named Rosa or I'll shoot."

Hap strolled inside the cabin. Laramie stretched out in the short bunk, Rosa's carbine in his hand, a wet towel over his face. "You're a little testy, partner. I don't think the boys at the gate appreciated your attitude."

Laramie sat up. The towel dropped. "They kept prowling around the house keeping me awake most all night. I had to do something."

"Yep, a man does need his rest."

"Well, I didn't get it. You two are late. Did the media pick up the story?"

"Not yet. But we started our own campaign. And Davenport's on his way."

Laramie glanced around the musty cabin. "If I'd known you invited company, I would have vacuumed. You going to fill me in what you did in town?"

"As soon as we go to the gate and settle with Davenport."

"I get to take care of him," Rosa demanded.

"You need any help?" Laramie paused. "That was a dumb question."

"You and Hap can hike down there with me, to make sure Munkk and Ferguson stay tied."

"Horseback might be more picturesque," Hap said. "We're expectin' an audience."

◦═══   ═══◦

Laramie and Hap rode to the gate, carbines across their saddles. Rosa tramped down unarmed.

Hap nudged Luke behind the junipers on the left side of the gate. Laramie and Tully staked out in the pines on the right. Rosa took her stance in the gateway, framed by bound men. A light green pickup with government plates pulled up. Davenport hopped out with his semiauto .45-caliber pistol in hand.

"What's going on here? I heard someone was shot."

"Not yet, but that could change," Rosa snarled.

His gun pointed at her, Davenport stalked toward the tied men. He flipped open a knife and reached toward Ferguson.

Laramie and Hap drifted out of the trees. "Don't cut them loose, Davenport."

"Aren't you dead?"

"You know, I get that all the time," Hap drawled.

"This is between you and Rosa," Laramie said. "Lay your gun down."

"I'll do no such thing!"

Hap's shot blasted three feet right of Davenport. Laramie's hit one foot to his left. The gun dropped.

A white Oldsmobile, a dark green van, and a Suburban pulled up as Davenport raised his hands.

"What are these people doing here? This is off-limits," Davenport groused.

An older couple with bright shirts, shorts, and white legs got out of the Olds. Eight Italian tourists climbed out of the van. Four boys, two dogs, and two sunburned adults exited the SUV.

"They came to watch the show." Hap rode over to the open gate. "Scoot right on up here, folks. You get to witness a livin' historical presentation about the early days of west Texas."

One of the Italian visitors held up a sign, "Ponder Rosa."

"Yes, this is the famous play, *Ponder Rosa*. Playin' Rosa will be the lovely and talented Miss Rosa Rodríguez Tryor. And playin' the vile and evil villain will be Superintendent Davenport. The handsome and dashin' hero will be . . . me, Hap Bowman. And his quiet, but thoughtful, partner will be portrayed by that talented star of many a roundup, Laramie Majors."

"What in blazes are you talking about?" Davenport huffed.

"Now, don't say your lines before your turn."

One of the boys held up his hand. "What about those two tied to the gate. Who are they supposed to be?"

"Oak trees," Hap said. "Back in the old days, there were more oak trees. Now, here's the story. Mean superintendent tries to eject sweet and innocent Miss Rodríguez off land that has been in her family for over a century . . ."

"This is absurd," Davenport fumed.

"All I want is a simple agreement," Rosa recited, her hands folded beneath her chin. "I want a fair exchange of land, a guarantee this will always be called the Rodríguez Ranch at Panther Mountain, and a promise the spring will be available free of charge to park visitors. Is that too much to ask?"

Davenport crisscrossed his arms. "Stop this insane charade. You are illegally squatting on government land and should be evicted."

Rosa cocked her head, blinked her eyes, and pleaded, "Oh, please don't throw me out in the cruel world. I have nowhere to go."

Hap waved at the crowd. "Come on, folks, this is supposed to be interactive."

The boys booed.

Davenport hiked toward the yellow bulldozer. "This is no game. I should have done this weeks ago. That cabin is coming down now."

"Oh, what shall I do?" Rosa swooned.

"Never fear," Laramie called out. "Stand back, Superintendent, or face the wrath of El Hap."

"I'm not a part of this circus!" Davenport swooped down to grab up his handgun. Rosa kicked it from his hand. He grabbed her leg and tripped her.

The crowd booed.

Two other cars drove up and parked. More people scooted up to watch.

"Unhand her, you villain!" Hap called out as he rode forward and slapped his coiled nylon rope against Davenport's face. Lines of blood dribbled down.

"That looks real, Dad," one of the boys blurted out. "How do they do that?"

"They're actors, son. It's just a stunt."

Davenport clutched his face. "You are all under arrest, every one of you, for obstructing a park ranger in the line of duty. This is no laughing matter. These men are outlaws."

The crowd booed.

Davenport raced to the bulldozer and hopped up on the tracks. Laramie's rope dropped over the superintendent's shoulders. He yanked it tight.

The crowd cheered.

Davenport's hand came up from his waist with a knife that sliced the rope.

The crowd gasped.

One of the dogs sprinted into the scene, tail wagging, tongue drooping, and jumped up on Rosa. She backed up and stumbled to the ground. Davenport lunged at her, grabbed her shoulders, and thrust the knife in front of her face. "This is not a game. I am not going to let you take away my fortune."

The crowd shouted boos.

"Davenport, are you going to slice her up in front of all these witnesses?" Laramie called out.

"That depends on you."

"We could shoot you right now," Hap suggested.

"How far will the knife pierce before I die?"

Hap gawked over at Laramie, then back at Rosa.

"Oh, for petey's sake, you two have forgotten your lines," Rosa scolded. "This is where you lower your guns and I turn like this . . ."

Rosa spun as her knee slammed up and the palms of her

hands jammed down, meeting like a vise on Davenport's groin. His knife tumbled to the dirt. The man crumpled in tears and agonized moans.

The crowd applauded.

"Rosa is a trained professional," Laramie called out. "Don't try that move at home."

"It's a simple trick I learned from a street girl in Cairo," Rosa said.

"This is a dumb skit," one of the boys griped.

"When do we get to go swimming?" another said.

A little old lady shuffled up. "Could you teach me that move, young lady?"

"Which one of you is Rosa Rodríguez Tryor?" A gray-haired man in full-dress park service uniform demanded, pushing through the crowd.

Rosa stepped over a dusty and whimpering Davenport. "That would be me."

"I'm Ed Vines, the regional chief. Our office received over two thousand 'Ponder Rosa' emails by eight this morning. I just received the email you sent a month ago. It got shuffled around while people were on vacation. I want to talk to you about this situation and your allegations."

"I'd be happy to discuss it with you."

"Let's meet in private at the information center in thirty minutes. I need to discuss a few things with Davenport first."

"Can we talk without Davenport present?"

"Yes, that's possible."

"Do you have the authority to negotiate land exchanges?"

"Yes. Is that what this is about?"

"That's all it's ever been about."

Vines caught sight of the two bound men. "Who in blazes are they?"

"Oak trees," a little boy called out.

Laramie and Hap lounged on the tailgate of the black Dodge parked in front of park headquarters. It had been two hours since Rosa entered the office with Regional Superintendent Ed Vines. All of her personal belongings from the cabin were stuffed in a galvanized laundry tub and a wooden Winchester rifle crate in the back of the truck.

Rosa strolled out of the office with papers under her arm and a huge smile.

"I take it you got what you wanted?" Laramie called out.

She waved the papers. "A hundred and sixty acres along the Pecos River, adjacent to a bird refuge. Doesn't that sound wonderful?"

"Noisy, but nice," Hap said.

She slid in the middle of Hap's truck. "Let's get on the road before they run out and change their minds."

"What about the other demands?" Laramie asked.

"They will designate the site as the 'Historic Rodríguez Ranch' on the park map and develop a picnic area at Ernesto Springs."

"Nice name," Hap said.

"I thought so."

"What happens to Davenport and the goon squad?"

"Once I got these concessions, I didn't press charges. I don't want to spend six months down here on court cases.

So, Davenport opted for early retirement and the Out West Development thugs got escorted out of the park."

Hap pulled up to the kiosk where Erika leaned out the window. "Look at this." She held out a light pink T-shirt with rose-colored letters that spelled out *Ponder Rosa.*

"Where did that come from?" Rosa asked.

"Some tourist brought a dozen. She said they're selling them all over." Erika handed the shirt to Hap.

He passed it to Rosa. "You know, it might be easier to start a campaign than stop one. When Oprah phones, we'll have to tell her she's too late."

Erika rubbed her upturned nose. "We're going to miss all the activity. Normally, this is a slow time in the park. But we won't miss Davenport."

"We heard he 'retired,'" Hap said.

"Yeah, but they retained the right to bring embezzlement charges against him later on. That's him in that red Acura. They gave him an hour to pack his things and leave the park."

The Acura roared past them and headed north.

When they crossed the line out of the national park, Rosa raised her clenched fist and shouted, "Yes."

"You won again," Hap said.

"Yep."

"How many victories does that make?" Laramie quizzed.

"One hundred and twenty-two, but who's counting? Of course, my next cause might be the most important of all."

"What's that?" Laramie asked.

"Helping you two find Hap's Juanita. When I get to El Paso, I'll contact my aunt Paula. She sends birthday cards to everyone on the Rodríguez side of the family. She'll track all the Juanitas."

Laramie sighed. "That's the unreal part. I agreed to this whole search thing because I was convinced there was no way to find Hap's phantom Juanita. Now we've stumbled into a whole remuda of under-ear marks."

"Yeah, with any luck, before Christmas, Hap and I could be related." She offered him a sly smile.

"To tell you the truth, this quest has taken on a little less intensity," Hap remarked. "It's not the drivin' force that it's been in the past."

Laramie howled. "Are you saying you want Rosa to change her name?"

"The thought crossed my mind."

"Mine, too," Rosa murmured. "Was that a soft enough reply?"

"Perfect."

"Geez, do you two want me to step outside so you can have some privacy?" Laramie said.

Hap slipped his arm around her shoulder. "No need to do that . . . not until we stop the truck, anyway."

At the junction of Highway 90, Hap pulled over next to the *Sold* signs on the property at the southeast corner. "So, this is the place just bought by Out West Development?"

"Oh, I got so excited about winning, I forgot to tell you," Rosa said. "Davenport admitted that the whole fuss revolves around water."

"I'm not followin' you," Hap said.

"Davenport didn't want the Rodríguez Ranch for the

park. He wanted it for himself. The Out West Development Corporation from New Jersey bought this property at the junction to install a ninety-thousand-square-foot water-bottling plant. After the state listed the water quality ratings, they wanted to exploit the springs at the ranch, haul the water down here, and bottle it. Then they could advertise 'the purest water in the Lone Star State.'"

Laramie surveyed the acreage. "That doesn't make sense. This whole ruckus is over bottled water?"

"It's a big business," Rosa insisted.

"Not compared to casinos." Laramie looked up and down the empty intersection. "And where would they get the employees to work way out here?"

"Look, that's what Davenport claimed. He said he was offered a five-hundred-thousand-dollar bonus and a 15 percent share of the company if he delivered the springs at the Rodríguez Ranch."

"I liked the story better without their ending," Laramie said. "It lacks drama. Will the history books record 'The Bottled Water War of West Texas'?"

"We don't have to mention that part in our memoirs. Wait a minute," Hap shouted. "We'll say we were involved in a classic battle over water rights. Yes!"

Rosa laughed. "I don't think Hap gets any more caffeine today."

"Hey," Laramie said. "Drive around those billboards over there."

When Hap rolled the truck next to the huge, low *For Sale* sign, they spotted a red car.

"It's Davenport's Acura," Laramie said.

"But where's Davenport?" Hap questioned.

"Who cares?" Rosa countered. "I don't ever want to see him again."

Hap piled out of the rig. He circled the Acura, then opened the driver's side. "No one around and the keys tossed on the seat as if to say, 'Steal me.' A lot of his personal things from the office are stacked in the backseat. It's like he jist disappeared. Ain't that somethin'?"

"Maybe he hiked into that barranca to take a leak." Laramie pointed to a deep ravine in the barren desert.

"No one needs that much privacy," Hap insisted. "Besides, after what Rosa did to him, he won't be functional for a week. I say what we've got us here is a legitimate mystery."

"I think we should leave," Rosa said. "This feels weird. Seriously, guys, this is the time to toss the cards in and walk away."

"Remember how you said adventures seem to come to me and you envied that? Well, here's another," Hap reminded her.

"We've had enough exploits for one week, partner." Laramie scrunched around and tried to stretch his legs. "Let's get on to El Paso. I really don't care what Davenport's doing."

Hap prowled toward the ravine. "Then you two set here and twiddle your thumbs. I want some answers."

Laramie crawled out of the truck. "Come on, Rosa, he'll need us to fight off the snakes or something."

"I'm not going down there. I have a lousy feeling about this. Trust me. This is not a good thing to do."

The dirt was soft, yellowish-brown and dry where they hiked down the edge of the steep ravine. They kneeled in the sparse shade of a creosote plant to survey the dry creekbed two hundred feet below them.

Laramie waved at a clump of green bushes.

"He's diggin' a hole."

"He's got one of the cardboard boxes down there."

"Buryin' somethin'?"

"Evidence, perhaps."

"This is gettin' more interestin' by the minute."

"Maybe Rosa's right. Maybe it's time to walk away."

"No way. We're goin' to check this out. Besides, I'm doin' this for you."

"Me? I said we should go on to El Paso."

"Yes, but for the rest of your life you'd regret not findin' out what this is about. You'd lay awake nights, unable to sleep."

"Most nights I'm awake, unable to sleep, now," Laramie said.

They crept along the brush row as they watched a sweat-drenched Davenport dig deeper and deeper into the sandy floor of the steep barranca.

"I think he wants to bury the whole dadgum car," Hap whispered.

Laramie tugged at Hap's sleeve. "No one digs a hole that deep unless he's looking for buried treasure. I just don't care what he's looking for. Let's go back."

Hap pulled loose and strolled out of the shade of the mesquite straight at the laboring Davenport, waist deep in a large rectangular hole. "You plannin' on puttin' in a swimmin' pool?"

Laramie trailed up beside Hap.

Davenport tossed down the shovel. "What are you cowboy idiots doing here?"

"It seems to me you're the one to fit the idiot label," Hap jibed. "You got fired. You lost out on the big-money deal. Now you're diggin' yourself into a heart attack. Maybe we aren't the dumb ones here."

"Oh, but you are the dumbest." A deep voice boomed from the thick brush behind them.

Laramie and Hap spun around. Ferguson and Munkk aimed Smith and Wesson .357 Magnums at their chests.

"I'm killin' the tall one right now," Munkk threatened.

"Not before he digs his own grave," Ferguson said. "No one cheats Out West Development out of a profit. It's too bad you didn't bring that Mexican gal with you. Then we'd have four of a kind."

Hap watched the Smith and Wessons. "All of this over bottled water?"

"Water?" Ferguson hooted.

Davenport tossed his shovel. "You truly are cowboy idiots. The water plant was a front to launder drug money coming out of Mexico. With a plant guaranteed to show a profit, I could be a multimillionaire in a year."

"Now you're going to be freakin' dead in ten minutes," Monkk growled. "Ain't it something how life turns so quick? A couple hours ago we were tied to fenceposts . . . and now we get to bury all of you."

"It's a good thing we called the Texas Rangers before we hiked down here," Hap boasted.

"What kind of morons do you take them for?" Davenport replied. "How could all these plans be ruined by absolute imbeciles? The Texas Rangers? Why didn't you say the cavalry or John Wayne? Or the San Antonio Spurs? Nobody believes that story. This is not the way I envisioned my life's end, between two Mafia hit men and Pancho and Lefty. I'm too savvy for this. I earned a master's degree in forest management. No one is coming to rescue you. You're as dead as I am!" His voice rose higher, like a wounded weasel's.

At the first shot from the cliff behind them, Davenport dove into the hole. Laramie rolled toward rocks to the right, and Hap sprawled behind the fresh dirt pile. Bullets flew off the cliff in rapid succession.

Ferguson and Monkk returned fire. A half-dozen shots blazed.

"There's too many of them," Monkk yelled. "Let's get out of here before they bring in a helicopter."

"They actually called the Rangers?" Davenport shouted. "No one does that but some idiot cowboys!"

Ferguson and Monkk sprinted toward a pickup parked at the north end of the barranca. Bullets from above chased them along.

Davenport raised up to watch the fleeing gunmen.

"Get down," Hap screamed.

The bullet that hit Davenport had already exited the back of his shoulder when the words blurted out. Blood puddled through his shirt, before he crumpled into the sandy hole.

Both Laramie and Hap hunkered flat until the truck roared off across the desert.

"I told you I didn't like the sound of this." Rosa's voice floated down from the rim.

⊷═══   ═══⊶

After Davenport was evacuated by helicopter, it took two hours more for all the police reports to be filled out.

The sun hovered low when they finally got on the road toward El Paso.

Laramie leaned back and closed his eyes. "I'm still due for a quiet, uneventful day."

Hap rolled down the window. Warm air blasted his sweaty face. "Rosa, how did you learn to fire a carbine that fast?"

"It's a little trick I learned from . . ."

"The KGB?"

"No, from my brother, Milt. He's a cowboy-action, quick-shoot guy. But I vote with Laramie. That's enough excitement for a while."

"Oh, great, then we all agree," Hap chided. "Nothin' but lifeless activity for the next few days. We'll eat at the Crunchy Truck Stop Buffet where you can't tell the veal from the tapioca . . . listen to Erma Gluck sing the top ten hits of 1926 . . . and drive forty-five miles an hour all the way to El Paso while we discuss famous land wars in China. We can recite Victorian poetry or debate the lastin' influence of John Stuart Mill's utilitarianism. How's that for borin'? Is that what you two had in mind?"

Laramie turned to Rosa. In unison, they shouted, "Yes!"

CHAPTER SIX

Like a wind waving through tall prairie grass, the cavvy of mares and foals followed the buckskin stallion over every rise that stretched across the west Texas horizon. Laramie and Hap galloped to the top of the treeless hill, then paused to watch the wild horses flee deeper into the heart of the military reserve. When the band stalled at a small muddy spring along the brown prairie, the cowboys waited.

While Hap slipped out of the saddle to check Luke's left rear hoof, Laramie quietly studied the much-creased note Annamarie had slipped into his hand as she kissed him good-bye in Del Rio. His eyes fell on the words, "I need time to understand my feelings. I have to be convinced that I truly can love you with the same depth and intensity that I had for Nate. You deserve nothing less . . ." Laramie knew he would be thrilled with any amount of depth and intensity of affection that Annamarie offered. Whatever she could spare would far exceed anything he had experienced.

Hap swung back up in the saddle. "You studyin' the map?"

Laramie quickly folded the note and stuck it back in his pocket. "We should be getting close to the south fence, but the major didn't seem like he knew exactly what was in here."

Hap surveyed the harsh west Texas desert. "He did know about the bomb fragments. I take it they fly over this military reserve, rather than march across it."

"I noticed he didn't tell us, 'Don't touch anything that looks like a bomb,' until after we signed the contract on this job."

"It was comfortin' to learn they didn't plant land mines in here." Hap yanked out his bandanna and sopped off his face. "But an unexploded bomb is the same as a land mine, ain't it?"

Laramie nodded at the cavvy. "We'll follow them close. If they don't trip explosives, neither will we. That's the theory, anyway."

As soon as the stallion broke for the next rise, the mares and foals thundered after him. Laramie and Hap spurred their horses and cantered down to the muddy spring, then up the other side. At the top of the hill, they spied the band as they dodged in and out of the scattered mesquite trees and creosote bushes. When the horses paused to graze and mill, the stallion positioned himself between the mares and the cowboys.

"He's ready to take us on," Laramie said.

"I don't reckon he feels challenged too often. He's a big boy."

"He's a fine horse and fast. Those mares have to gallop to catch up and it looks like he's at a lope. I'll tell you what,

Hap. After we pen him, I'll buy him from the army and you saddle break him for me."

Hap stood in the stirrups and stretched his legs. "If you want him, you break him."

"I'm not crazy enough to crawl on a horse that mean."

"So you're lookin' for some dumb cowboy to do the hard part?"

"No, I hoped for a brave, reckless bronc buster to consider it a matter of cowboy pride that 'there never was a horse that couldn't be rode.' I surmised he'd view this challenge as a wonderful opportunity to demonstrate his superior horsemanship and mental, not to mention physical, toughness."

"I ain't bustin' my butt breakin' your horses," Hap declared. He swung to the ground and pulled a rag from his saddlebag. He loosened the cinch and wiped down Luke's back. "You know, summer is probably not the best time to be down along the border. Why didn't we do this in the spring or fall?"

"Because we have real jobs in spring and fall."

"This feels like a real job."

"Well, the pay's good and the expectations low. You can't beat that."

Hap tightened the cinch, pulled himself back up in the saddle, and tossed the rag to Laramie. "We get one thousand dollars each and all we have to do is try to round up as many mustangs as possible. If we can't corner any at all, that's okay. They just need us out here so they can take some satellite photos to prove to the public that they tried to save the wild horses before they practiced their bombing. That the way you see it?"

"That's pretty much it." Laramie combed his fingers

through his hatless, curly brown hair. "Don't you love government jobs?"

"I wonder, why didn't the local cowboys jump at this good money?"

Laramie stepped down to the ground, loosened the cinch on his saddle, then wiped his horse with the towel. "I think it has something to do with the other part of the instructions."

"Ahh, when we had to sign the indemnity waiver and then the major said, 'Don't go out there and get your fool head blown off like our last wrangler'?"

"It does somewhat dampen the thrill of it all." Laramie finished toweling his horse, then checked his hooves.

"You don't figure it's your destiny to get Laramie bits scattered across a west Texas desert?"

"I'd rather die an old man surrounded by a loving wife, kids, and grandkids."

"Which, at the moment, don't appear too likely."

"There's a certain nurse who gives me renewed hope." Laramie tightened the cinch, remounted, and handed the towel back to Hap.

"Oh my, Laramie's pinin' after Annamarie Buchett again."

"Some dreams are too sweet to let go."

"Don't I know it? But at some point you try to turn loose of the dream and realize the dream won't turn loose of you."

❖⬗⬗⬗   ⬗⬗⬗❖

Although the clouds stacked up all afternoon, the late August thundershower didn't hit until Laramie and Hap had the remuda penned in the brush corral near the highway. They tried to rub down Luke and Tully in the rain, but finally trailered them grained and unsaddled.

Hap jumped in the truck and started the engine.

Laramie slid into the passenger's side. "We aren't leaving before the major gets here, are we?"

"Nope, but it's raining too hard to roll down the window and way too hot not to have the air-conditioner on."

"After a week of sleepin' on the ground in a bombing range, I didn't know you were that particular."

"I reckon I'm gettin' soft in my old age."

"Well, I won't mind a shower and a motel bed tonight."

"I need to phone Rosa and see what she found out from her aunt Paula."

"Hap, I don't think there are many gals like Rosa who would help you find your Juanita."

"I was ponderin' that this afternoon when we was pushin' that cavvy of wild horses. If a man gets one truly good friend in his life, it's a blessing. That's you, partner. Your loyalty is legendary. And now, Rosa comes along and offers a similar kind of friendship."

"Yeah, but she's cuter than me."

Hap laughed. "That's true, but you're taller. About a foot taller. Anyway, it just seems a privilege to have three good friends I can count on."

"Three?"

"Ol' Lukey, of course. A man's horse is about as close a friend as he can have."

"Luke's a pal . . . but my Tully's an adversary. Every day is a contest to come out on top. But I know what you mean."

As heavy drops of rain slammed the pickup, Laramie thought about the day he had bought Tully for four hundred dollars. He hadn't intended to buy a horse. He stopped by the sale yard to sell six feeder calves for Mr. Averill. But when he witnessed a drunken cowboy bust a two-by-four over the blaze-faced bay's nose, he knew he had to do something. He bought the horse on the spot and shoved the bills in the man's hand before the two-by-four dropped to the dirt. It took him months to gain Tully's confidence and a year to train him to yield to commands. He proved to be a tall, proud, stubborn, independent horse with memories of pain and grief. In some ways, Laramie figured he and Tully were a lot alike.

When the thunderstorm blew over, Hap killed the engine and rolled down the windows. "I reckon that's as long as we can go cooped up with each other without a shower."

"The sun's about down. How long will we sit here waiting for the major?"

"Since we don't get paid until he shows up, I reckon as long as it takes."

With headlight beams on high, neither Laramie nor Hap could tell who occupied the car that pulled up next to them.

"You think that's the major?" Hap asked as he pushed open the door.

"I don't think he drives a white Oldsmobile sedan."

"Hey . . . it's Rosa!"

Wearing jeans, tennies, and a purple T-shirt, Rosa moseyed over to the truck. "Hi, guys . . . I hoped I'd find you here."

"Is somethin' wrong?" Hap asked.

"No, but there's a change in plans." She flipped her wavy black bangs off her forehead.

Hap piled out of the rig. "Did your aunt Paula get back from Lordsburg?"

"She decided to stay there a few more days. I'm at her house with my cousin, but that's what I wanted to talk to you about." She glanced at Laramie and raised her eyebrows.

"Hey, you probably don't need to talk to me," he replied. "I, eh . . . I'm going to go check on the horses. We put them up wet and they might need to be toweled down again."

Rosa squeezed his elbow. "Thanks, Laramie. You're a pal."

"So I hear." Laramie sauntered to the back of the trailer as Hap and Rosa leaned against the hood of the Oldsmobile. He led the two horses out of the trailer and tied the lead ropes to the tall, chainlink fence that surrounded the bombing range. Luke stood quietly, like a trail horse for toddlers, as Laramie wiped off the remnants of sweat and rain.

"Now, Luke, I know I'm not Hap. But your compadre is up there talking about Juanitas with the nicest gal he's ever met. Don't ask me to explain it. Like you, I just came along for the ride. Even Hap doesn't understand why he does what he does. But I can tell you one thing . . . he's the only person on the planet, besides my mother, who would take a bullet for me." He patted the black gelding's neck. "And he'd take one for you, too . . . but I know you'd do the same for him."

Laramie ambled to the back of the trailer and in the evening shadows reached in for a handful of whole oats.

Then he lounged by the fence while Luke's slobbery lips and tongue lapped up each one of the treats.

Tully stretched around and tried to bite his shoulder when he stepped over to towel down the bay horse. Laramie threw both arms around the gelding's neck and hugged him tight until the long-legged horse gave up the protest.

"A little jealous, are you? I know, I know . . . that was a love bite. You're a mess, big boy. If you were human, you'd be on a psychologist's couch three times a week."

Tully shuffled his hooves and snorted.

"Yeah, you're right. If I was a horse, I'd be as neurotic as you. What a team."

When he finished rubbing him down, Laramie retrieved another handful of oats. Tully bit at his fingers and palm until all the oats were consumed or fell to the ground.

In the dark, Laramie could still hear Hap's and Rosa's low voices, even after he loaded the horses. He shuffled over to the brush corral to scan the band of nervous, milling wild mustangs, each apprehensive about what would happen next. The buckskin stallion charged at him, then held up and snorted.

"I know how you feel, big guy . . . that's the way I've started many days . . . penned in, and waiting for something bad to happen."

He was wandering back toward the rigs when he heard the Oldsmobile start up and saw the headlights flip on. The ten-foot chainlink and barbed-wire fence that surrounded the bombing range was supposed to be secure enough to keep people from entering. But Laramie had seen several foot trails across the military reserve and wondered how many illegal aliens had hiked across it to jobs in El Paso. To him, it spoke volumes that for many the dangerous journey merited the risk, considering the rewards up ahead. The thought occurred to him that life itself was like hiking through a mine field. Now, with images of Annamarie Buchett, he felt he had a purpose that made such risks worthwhile. But like the illegals who trekked through the bombing range, he knew there was a good chance he'd never reach that goal.

Laramie had pulled on clean jeans and dried his hair on a white towel before Hap popped back into the motel room. "The front desk said they didn't have the funds to cash these checks. But Rosa's got some relatives that run a dry cleaner's on the other side of town. She figures they might have the cash. We got to go over that direction anyway. There's a Juanita she wants me to meet."

"Give me the plan again. I couldn't hear everything from the shower."

"We're goin' out to supper at some trendy restaurant that a college roommate of Rosa's operates."

"You and me in a trendy club?" Laramie tossed the towel on the white-tiled bathroom floor.

"Yeah, we'll probably be as out of place as a salmon at a grizzly bear convention. You ready to go eat?"

Laramie looped his thumbs in his jeans. "I'm kind of tired tonight. Can you do this without me?"

"You ain't feelin' shoved aside, are you? Hey, we're still in this thing together."

"I'm feeling relieved. You've got someone to meet this Juanita with you and I get a chance to catch up on some sleep."

"You got to have supper."

"I'll call in a pizza."

Hap jammed on his hat. "You realize this will be the first Juanita I've met that has that mark under her ear."

"What does Rosa say she looks like?"

"Like a skinny twelve-year-old girl."

"You checking on kids now?"

"No, but that's how Rosa remembers her. 'Course she hasn't seen her cousin in almost eighteen years." Hap paused at the door. "It don't seem right leavin' you here."

"Geez, Hap, leave. You're actin' like you're afraid to be alone with Rosa."

"You may be closer to the truth than I'm willin' to admit. See you later, partner."

Laramie settled on a preseason football game between the Dallas Cowboys and the Seattle Seahawks on the muted TV and a slice of Canadian bacon, Italian sausage, and El Paso bell pepper pizza. He didn't watch much television, but he stared at the beige telephone while he munched.

He opened the sliding door and scooted onto the tiny motel room balcony that overlooked the swimming pool and a busy El Paso street. The early evening thundershower had cleaned the air. Even in the neon night of a busy city street, he could see bright desert stars.

In the lighted blue pool two little boys with floaties secured around their arms braved the steps of the shallow end, a few feet from their mother's careful gaze. She kept guard between the boys and deeper water in her black, one-piece bathing suit with short ruffled skirt.

She had wide hips, fleshy arms, and a round face, but it was her eyes that caught Laramie's attention. From the balcony he couldn't tell their color or even their expression. But he could see that they followed the boys' every move. While he couldn't discern her words, the tone that filtered upstairs was one of encouragement and love.

Slowly, each of the boys braved another step deeper . . . almost to mother's hand. She slid back gradually so they had to keep venturing out.

A shiny black Hummer rolled into the motel entrance, but Laramie couldn't take his eyes off the mamma and her boys. They reached the step where they could no longer stand with their heads above water. The youngest looked about three. He giggled when he started to float on his own. His older brother, no more than five, followed. Soon both floated, laughed, and splashed their way across the shallow end of the pool, mother within arm's length, but not interfering.

Laramie wondered if the boys would remember twenty-five years from now when their mother taught them not to be afraid of the water. He figured the mother would remember. He knew he would, too. Some images merit saving.

Feeling like an intruder when the mother glanced up at him, he pulled back inside the room and slid the door behind him. It was a nice room. Clean tan carpet. Two queen-size beds. Flowered bedspreads. A recliner, a computer table, large television, closet, double-sink bathroom. It felt cramped.

Pulling the note out of the pocket of his shirt, which had been tossed across the back of the chair, he flopped on the bed and read the words again. Then he plucked up the receiver and punched information. He took a deep breath before he reached the number of Riverview Hospital in Laredo. The front desk transferred him to the emergency room.

"Hi, I'd like to speak to Annamarie Buchett, please."

"She's not here," the female voice replied.

"Could you tell me which shift she's working, so I could phone her?"

"She doesn't work any shifts."

"What do you mean?"

"She's in California."

"No, she was in California visiting relatives. She came back."

"She came back and quit. She moved."

"Moved?"

"Look, this is an emergency room. Do you want to talk to someone else?"

"No . . . if she calls in, tell her Laramie—"

"Wait, you're Annamarie's Laramie?"

"Yes."

"I'm Tina, Annamarie's friend. She said you might call."

"Why didn't she . . ."

"She didn't have any idea how to reach you. She called around, but couldn't track you down."

"We've been rounding up wild horses. What's this about her moving?"

"She said she needed a fresh start somewhere."

"Away from me?"

"Away from Texas. It's been a rough three years for her, Laramie. She's trying to sort everything out in her head. Give her time, okay?"

"Do you think it would be acceptable if I called her out in California?"

"That's up to you."

"What would you do if you were me?"

"I'd elope with her, the first chance I got. She's a great gal, Laramie. But I think you know that. Do you want her mother's phone number?"

"Yes, ma'am."

He jotted down the digits, thanked Tina, then hung up.

Laramie stalked over to the pizza box, plucked up a slice, then tossed it down. He marched back to the phone and dialed the California number.

A man with an accent answered the phone.

"I'd like to speak to Sam, please."

"My name is Sam. Which Sam do you want?"

"Eh . . . the other one," Laramie stammered.

After a pause, a boy's voice said, "Yeah?"

"Is this Sam?"

"Yeah, who are you?"

"I need to speak to a lady named Sam who recently moved there from Laredo, Texas, where she ran a minimart."

"Oh, you want Aunt Ducky."

He plopped back on the bed with the phone still to his ear.

"Hello?"

"Sam, this is Laramie . . ."

"Annamarie's Laramie?"

"Yes, is she there?"

"Sorry, she went to Malibu."

"She went to the beach at night?"

"Not the beach. She enjoys a drive up the Pacific Coast Highway to Malibu, gets a latte and a hot dog for Sara, then drives back. You know how she likes the wind in her hair. Do you want her to call you back?"

"That would be nice."

After giving Sam the motel phone number, he hung up and strolled back out to the balcony. The swimming pool was empty.

Daylight filtered around the heavy flowered curtain as Laramie tried to stretch out his stiff legs. He tugged on his jeans, then opened the curtain. The sun lifted his mood some as he soaked in its soothing rays.

Hap sprawled on top of the bedspread of the other bed, fully clothed, face buried in a pillow. His hat lay, crown down, on top of the TV.

As Laramie trudged toward the bathroom, Hap rolled over. "I ain't asleep."

"You just get in?"

"I was home by midnight, partner. You was sleepin' good for a change. I didn't want to wake you. I sat on the balcony a while, then conked out in that white plastic chair."

"How'd your evening go?" Laramie asked.

"The part with Rosa was nice. Hey, I got our government checks cashed."

"Good. You didn't spend the money yet, did you? Or give it away?"

Hap sat up and grinned. "I deserve that. Nope, it's all right there." He pointed to his wallet, next to keys and a watch.

"No luck with the Juanita?"

"No . . . she was a rail-thin vegetarian with the personality of an eggplant. At least, that's Rosa's description afterward. How about you? Did you miss me?"

"It was a quiet evening, if that's what you mean. I did line us up with some work today."

"Today?" Hap shot back. "I can't work today. I've promised Rosa we'd go visit some more of her relatives."

"More Juanitas?"

"She's not sure of the cousin's name, but she has the mark under her ear."

"Can it wait until tomorrow?"

"No, Rosa wants to drive over to Lordsburg this afternoon. Her Aunt Paula's lookin' after her sick sister. Rosa's going to go get a list of Rodríguez Juanitas from her aunt and meet us up the river someplace. What's this job deal?"

"The major called last night."

"Did the horses break out?"

"No. A real close friend of his, a retired colonel who lived in Florida, passed away. The funeral's today and since the man was an El Paso native, they flew him back here to be buried. The major put together all the military procedure . . . you know . . . twenty-one-gun salute, flyover, folding the flag, Taps . . . everything. When the widow flew in from Florida last night, she was in tears . . . she had forgotten to tell the major that her husband was proud of his west Texas roots. He had made her promise to have a horse and empty saddle at the grave. The major didn't know who else he could call on such a short notice. I promised him we'd be there."

"He'd pay us?"

"Two hundred dollars each."

"What did you say to that?"

"That we'd do it for free or we wouldn't do it at all."

"Good," Hap declared.

"Sorry to ruin your plans with Rosa."

"Listen, one horse has to be riderless, right? So you ride Tully and lead Luke up to the grave. You don't need me. Rosa's got her aunt's car, so you take the truck, pick up the trailer and horses at the stables, and we'll rendezvous back here this afternoon."

As far as Laramie could see, no oaks graced Golden Oaks Cemetery. But there were poplars, elm, box elder, ash, and plenty of shade in the older section of the grounds. The raised tombstones faced east. A canopy spread over a site on the crest of the hill. Artificial flowers marked most graves, with fresh wreaths scattered in a few locations.

The funeral was scheduled for 10:30 A.M., so Laramie arrived at 9:00. The cemetery seemed empty, so he saddled both horses, rode Tully, and led Luke up and down each lane. He parked the rig as far from the site as he could, to stay out of the way.

By 9:45, several cars had entered. At 10:00, a procession of military vehicles parked in the center lane. The major, in full dress uniform, marched over to Laramie.

"Sorry, Major, Hap couldn't make it. But you only need one horse with an empty saddle, right?"

"Yes, I believe so. To tell you the truth, I've never seen this done. I'm just trying to carry out the widow's request."

"The way we do it in Wyoming, one cowboy leads the deceased's horse up behind the casket to the gravesite, then stands there during the service. Is that what she has in mind?"

"Here comes the funeral home limo. I'll ask her."

The major returned in a few minutes. "She said since you brought two horses, she'd appreciate it if you rode one and led the other." He handed Laramie a silverbelly Stetson. "This is his hat. She wondered if you could prop it on the saddlehorn."

"No problem. I'll park the horses by that Humvee. When you signal, I'll ride up, follow your soldiers carrying the casket, then ride over to the other side of the dirt mound during the service. When everything's done, I'll slip out through those trees and back around here."

"Thanks, Laramie. Nice of you to do this for free."

"Major, did you join the service to make a fortune?"

He laughed. "Not hardly. It's in my bones. My wife claims I'd work for nothing."

"I sure didn't choose to be a cowboy to make a fortune either. I lost one friend to machine-gun fire in Afghanistan and another to a car bomb in Baghdad. So, maybe I'm doing this for Lindale and Big T. We all give what we can, Major."

Laramie held Luke and Tully behind the Humvee as the crowd filtered near the gravesite. He watched as the major spoke to the gray-haired lady dressed in black, then hiked his way.

"Eh, Laramie, the widow asked about your cowboy hat. She assumed you would wear one."

"I don't wear a cowboy hat, except in the arena when I rope."

"I'll tell her you don't have one."

"Well, there's one in the trailer, but I just don't . . ." He glanced back across the cemetery. "Hold these lead ropes, I'll go get it."

Mounted on Tully and clutching Luke's lead rope, Laramie adjusted his hat. He couldn't find a comfortable position, so he jammed it on until it hit the top of his ears.

Rifle-packing soldiers stood at attention. The mourners congregated closer to the gravesite. The casket bearers with clusters on their chests and stars on their hats assembled at the back of the hearse.

He patted Tully's neck. "Okay, boy, it's just about time. You stay nice and calm like your pal, Luke."

Instead of signaling, the major jogged back to Laramie. "The widow asked if you would mind riding the black horse and leading the bay. Her husband's horse as a young man was a bay."

"Major, I can't do that. This bay is my horse and the black one is Hap's. Now, old Luke there is bulletproof. He'll stand where you put him, even if fireworks go off under him. But Tully is a jealous cuss. He'll pitch a fit if I ride Luke. He'll buck and kick and bite anyone in sight if he gets ticked off. It won't be a pretty scene getting up there, and worse when the shots are fired and the planes fly over."

"I'll go tell her."

Laramie felt his heart beat faster when the lady in black got up from her chair next to the gravesite and hiked through the crowd toward him. Every eye followed her movement. He stepped down from the saddle and pulled off his hat as she approached.

"Oh, please, leave your hat on. It looks very nice."

He jammed it back on. "Thank you, ma'am. Did the major tell you why I can't ride the black horse?"

"Yes, but it's so important for me to give this one last tribute to Charles. All during our military life, he talked about retiring to west Texas. He loved it here. But I whined and begged that we retire in Florida near my sisters. So he gave up that dream. He had a bay horse when he was young. In his last days, when the pain was great and he was on a lot of medication, he would think he was sixteen and riding that bay horse of his. When I spied that beautiful horse, I deemed it an answer to prayer."

"Ma'am, I would love to accommodate you. But Tully blows up easy. I really am concerned that he will pitch a fit and ruin this memorable occasion."

"That would only make it more memorable . . . and more western. My Charles would love it. Please."

Laramie sighed, then rubbed his beard. "I'll try, ma'am. But please forgive me ahead of time, if Tully acts up."

"Thank you." She pointed her finger at the blaze-faced bay. Laramie panicked that Tully would bite it.

"You behave yourself," she told the horse, then slipped through the crowd back to her chair by the gravesite.

Laramie wrapped Tully's lead rope around his left wrist, transferred the hat, then mounted Luke. "I know this is backward, boys. Just relax."

The solemn procession began. Both horses lumbered along as if in the open prairie, not a crowded cemetery. He rode the horses around the dirt pile covered in green outdoor carpeting and faced the casket. Astride Luke, he pulled his hat off and held it over his heart. As incredible as it was that Tully stood still, he dreaded the flyover and the rifle fire.

A trio sang "Amazing Grace."

The chaplain read from Psalms and Revelation.

A three-star general eulogized the colonel's bravery, leadership, and loyalty.

A man in his early forties who sat next to the widow stepped up to the head of the casket. There was a streak of premature gray in his dark brown hair. His face clean-shaven, his eyes red. Laramie noted his dark suit and polished loafers fit him well. He loosened his tie a little before he spoke.

"I haven't seen a lot of you in years. I'm Andy, the youngest son. I need to say a few things to you . . . to Mom . . . and to my dad, who I hope can hear and see what is going on today. Most all of you in the audience know that military life isn't easy. I lived in twenty-one houses during the first eighteen years of my life. A couple of them, Dad never even saw. Like some military kids, there were times I resented the army taking my father from me. And when he was home there were a number of times, as my mother knows, when I went to bed in tears at being treated like a raw recruit during basic training."

Laramie leaned over and stroked Tully's neck as the man continued.

"But today, I want to say how thankful I am for my dad. I'm thankful for the life of service he gave for our country. But most of all, I'm thankful for the things he taught me. We all get the choice to remember whatever we want about family members who have died. And I choose to remember a dad who was the bravest man on the face of the earth. This man taught me by example about courage and keeping commitments and how to cure a slice in my golf swing."

He paused while the audience chuckled. "He taught me how to face the fears of life . . . and in these last weeks, he demonstrated how to face the fears of death. But, most of all, I want to thank my dad for the heritage of faith he left my brothers and myself. He loved me the very best way he knew how and I will love him with every precious thought and memory. We knew from the day we were born, to the day he died, of his faith and trust in almighty God. There's just one last thing I want to say, Dad." He paused and wiped the corner of his eyes. "You taught it to me when I was a kid . . . and I believe it with all my heart . . . 'Jesus loves me, this I know . . . for the Bible tell me so . . .' Yeah, Daddy, enjoy your rewards in heaven. Your youngest finally got it right."

Laramie meditated on the idea of choosing which memories to hold on to as the final prayer concluded the service. He clutched Tully's lead rope tighter as the jets roared overhead. The one on the right peeled off and soared straight up into the wispy clouds.

Luke raised his left rear hoof as if asleep when volleys of guns fired the twenty-one-gun salute. Then the flag was folded and presented to the widow. A lonesome bugle sounded Taps.

Laramie let out a visible sigh of relief when the service concluded and the crowd encircled the widow. He rode Luke back a few graves, then dismounted. The major marched over to shake his hand.

"That was nice, Laramie, thanks. You sure we can't give you some gas money and buy you lunch?"

"No, sir. It was a privilege to be here. Give my condolences to the widow. I want to get these boys over to the trailer before they plop all over someone's ancestor."

Laramie checked the cinch on Tully. "Okay, big boy, it's

your turn. Enough of riding ol' Lukey. You did wonderful today, and I'm proud of you." He jammed his left foot into the stirrup and swung up into the saddle. His right leg swung over the cantle. He had just found the right stirrup when Tully dropped his head down and kicked his rear hooves toward the west Texas sky.

"Whoa . . . whoa, boy," Laramie shouted as he yanked the rein hard to the right, attempting to get the bay horse to spin.

Instead, Tully jerked his head left and tossed Laramie forward. The saddle horn caught him in the gut and the reins slipped in his fingers. As Tully bucked a trail around the outskirts of the stunned crowd, Laramie fought to regain his balance. With both boots now back in the stirrups, he leaned back and tried to keep his seat. Tully dodged the tombstones as he crashed his way toward the uniformed color guard. The soldiers broke ranks and dove as the bay gelding kicked his rear hooves at phantom enemies.

Laramie reached up and swiped at his hat as it tumbled off his head. One hand gripped the reins, the other now clutched the white straw cowboy hat, then, like a child realizing that the tantrum in the middle of Wal-Mart isn't working, Tully stopped. He snorted, then nibbled on the long grass next to *William T. Gimble, 1892–1959, Beloved Husband*.

The funeral congregation broke out in cheers and applause.

Laramie rubbed his forehead and shoved his hat back on.

Luke remained behind the dirt pile. He hadn't moved since Laramie dropped his lead rope on Tully's first buck. The major led the black gelding over to Laramie.

"Sorry about that," Laramie mumbled. "I'm glad he waited until after the service to blow up."

"They thought it was wonderful."

Laramie gazed over the crowd and noticed the widow wave.

He waved back.

"Most thought it was part of the service." The major handed Luke's lead rope to him, then gave him an informal salute.

Laramie tipped his hat.

The gray-haired lady behind the counter at the motel wore an institutional smile and a crooked name badge. As the dot-matrix printer punched out a copy of the receipt, Laramie glanced around the lobby, with its automatic glass front doors, flowery carpet, and dusty artificial trees. He marveled how all midpriced motel lobbies look the same. Most times he'd rather wake up somewhere out on the prairie next to a campfire.

This was not one of those times.

Hap pulled the truck and loaded horse trailer under the awning. For some places the end of August spelled the end of summer, but the El Paso heat blasted Laramie as he left the air-conditioned retreat of the Star-Lite Motel. He tossed his duffel bag behind the seat and slipped into the passenger seat. "We need to get to a laundry."

"We could just burn our stuff and buy all new clothes," Hap suggested.

"Not until we get to Creede. I figure we can bury them

with this whole obsession of yours. In the meantime, I need something clean to wear."

"Let's do it this afternoon. I take it by the look on your face you got a phone call from a certain nurse in California."

Laramie closed his eyes and thought about Annamarie's wide, easy smile and penetrating hazel eyes. "Hap, did you ever notice how some ladies have a lilt, a tone in their voice that makes you want to listen to them all day long?"

"Why is it those gals never become schoolteachers? My third-grade teacher, Miss Carlton, had a voice that made fingernail scratches on a chalkboard sound like the Boston Symphony. What did the French-Vietnamese Texan tell you?"

"She said that she knows that it's time for changes in her life. She knows what she is changing from, she's just not sure what's up ahead. Those drives along the coast help her think things through."

"Does she mention whether a tall, lanky, sometimes shy and pathetic cowboy figures in those dreams?"

"So far. That's the good news. She said she's fond of me and her heart is trying to convince her brain to love me."

"What's the bad news?"

"I'm not sure when we'll see each other again. Even if we do . . . I can't see how a Wyoming cowboy and a southern California nurse can have much of a life together."

"I feel like it's gettin' time to pass the baton," Hap blurted out.

"What do you mean?"

"We've been chasin' my dream for three months. Now, maybe, it's time to go further west and chase yours."

"We're going to Creede, partner. You know we always finish what we start."

"Yeah, that seems to be a theme, lately. Well, we ain't goin' to Creede right now. We have a birthday party to attend."

"Tell me again. What's the deal?"

"Rosa's cousin's daughter . . ."

"Juanita?"

"No, this one is Heather . . . on the other side of the family. Anyway, before Rosa took off for Lordsburg yesterday she was calling some more family and her cousin mentioned today was Heather's twelfth birthday. She likes to ride her horse, but she has a dozen kids comin' over for the party and they all want to ride. So the plan is that we take our horses over and let them pony around some kids."

"Whose idea was that?"

"Eh . . . mine."

"Hap, you know how snuffy Tully can be at times."

"You said he was a saint at the funeral."

"Then he blew up afterward."

"Well, Lukey can shepherd them. Besides, Heather is just learning to run the barrels and I promised we'd give her a few pointers."

"What do we know about barrel racing?"

"Laramie, we've been studyin' barrel racin' for years."

"If I recall, we've been most impressed by long hair flagging in the wind when they raced to the finish line."

"Well, you tell them how to wear their hair and I'll show 'em how to make a tight turn without flippin' a barrel over. I know it sounds borin', but you like borin'."

"I didn't say boring, I said peaceful. And somehow, a

birthday party for twelve-year-old girls sounds neither peaceful nor routine."

⋆⇒   ⇐⋆

Heather McKay was riding the brown quarterhorse at a lope in the cloverleaf pattern around the three fifty-five-gallon drums when Laramie and Hap pulled up next to Del Norte Arena. A huge white awning stretched over the tables and chairs where several adults attempted to keep paper tablecloths from drifting in the desert breeze.

They had just stepped out of the truck when a lady with short blonde hair and sunglasses scooted up to them. She wore khaki shorts, a crisp yellow short-sleeved blouse, and a very large diamond wedding ring.

She stuck her hand out at Laramie. "I'm Toni McKay, Rosa's cousin. You must be her Hap."

"No, ma'am, I'm Laramie. The cowboy with the cheap black mustache is Rosa's Hap."

She shook both of their hands. "I'm so grateful you came. When we started to plan this, we had no idea everyone would want to ride horses."

Hap grinned. "Kids like horses, all right."

"Well, none will be as thrilled as this group. Say, do either of you know anything about repairing propane barbecue grills? The one we rented doesn't work right."

"Hap's the propane expert," Laramie said. "Would you like me to saddle the horses and take them into the arena?"

"Thank you. We would be happy to pay you, but Rosa said you would refuse."

"Yes, ma'am." Hap tipped his hat. "Seems we do our

best work for free. Now, I'll get my sledgehammer and fix the grill." He sauntered toward the toolbox in the back of the Dodge truck.

"He was joking about the sledgehammer, wasn't he?" Toni asked.

"No, Hap fixes everything with barbed wire, baling string, and a sledgehammer."

Within fifteen minutes Laramie had Luke and Tully saddled. He led them to the one-hundred- by three-hundred-foot open air arena. The four-rail fence boasted a fresh coat of white paint. Two tall cottonwood trees provided shade in the northeast corner near the aluminum stock tank. Heat vibrated from the loose dirt of the arena floor, but a few high clouds defused the sun's piercing glare.

Laramie shut the gate behind him, then dropped Luke's reins to the dirt. The black gelding took that as a sign and closed his eyes as if anticipating a long nap. Laramie swung up in the saddle on Tully and patted the horse's neck.

"I know you'll only tolerate little girls if I tire you out first. You don't get the luxury of pitching a fit today."

The girl on the brown horse rode over to him. She pulled off her riding helmet and shaded her eyes with her hand. "Hi, I'm Heather and today is my birthday."

"Pleased to meet you, Miss Heather. I'm Laramie." He reached over and shook her hand.

Her straight black hair hung just past her ears. Her bangs framed her small, round face. She wore a bright pink T-shirt that read *Rodeo Queen* and black jeans that looked like corduroy.

She turned her head. "Do you like my new earrings?"

Laramie studied the sparkling studs. "Very nice."

"Daddy bought me diamonds."

"They're beautiful, Heather."

"Thank you. Are you the rodeo stars that are friends of my mom's cousin?"

Laramie laughed. "Honey, we're a couple of cowboys from Wyoming who enter roping at rodeos ever' once in a while. But we're not rodeo stars."

"Did you ever win money at a rodeo?"

"Yes, we have."

"Many times?"

"Lots of times."

"That's my goal," Heather said. "I want to win a check at a real rodeo. Just one check. I don't even care how much money."

"That sounds like a reasonable goal. You get a good horse and you keep practicing and you'll do it, I'm sure."

She jammed her hat back on. "That would be so totally cool. Me . . . winning money at a rodeo."

"Sometimes the most important ingredient is having the heart to do it. Sounds to me like you have a heart to win."

"Oh, my heart is fine." Heather grinned. "It's the rest of me that needs improvement."

Loud clanging from the direction of the white awning drew their attention toward the others.

"What's going on over there?" she inquired.

"I believe Hap is fixing the barbecue. How about you and me walking our horses around the barrels. You can tell me what you know about each turn."

"Oh, yes. I do fairly well on the sprints, but the turns kind of scare me."

"If you train your horse good enough, all you have do is hang on and know when to give him his head."

He watched her ride up to the first barrel, tug the reins to the left, and circle the large, dark blue barrel.

"That was good, Heather. Now, watch me. Tully, here, isn't a barrel horse, but he follows orders most of the time."

Laramie dropped the reins around the saddle horn, then rode Tully forward. He circled tight around the barrel and back. Heather clapped when he rode over to her.

"You did all of that without holding the reins."

"When you have your horse at a gallop, you keep ahold of the reins, but I did that to illustrate a point. You want to train your horse to follow knee commands so you aren't tugging on his mouth when you turn him."

"Knee commands?"

"I've got Tully trained that when I put pressure with my knee, he turns. That's the best way to do it."

He saw her neck stiffen, her cheeks swell, her eyes tear. "But I could never learn that," she sobbed.

"Honey, it just takes time. Anyone can learn."

"No, I can't. Don't you understand?"

"Understand what?"

"My legs are paralyzed."

Laramie stared at her jeans. "What?"

"I was in a boat accident five years ago. I'll never walk and I'll never give knee commands," she wailed.

"But . . . but you ride so well. How do you stay in the saddle?"

"Velcro. Mother and Daddy sewed Velcro on my jeans, and Velcro on the stirrup leathers." She patted her black pants. "I can't fall off. It takes two of them to pull me loose."

Laramie straightened and rubbed the back of his neck. "Well, you aren't going to let a little thing like that keep you from winning that rodeo check, are you?"

A wide smile broke across her face as she wiped her tears. "No, I'm not."

"Good, let's do it again. We'll work on head commands."

Laramie and Heather rode the pattern a dozen times before the first guests arrived. Then it was time to give kids rides and demonstrate roping. After an hour in the arena, all the kids and the parents retired to the awning.

At dark, the guests left.

Laramie and Hap sprawled on rented white plastic chairs with Heather's parents, while she rode her horse around the barrels at a trot.

Toni McKay smiled at them. "I can't believe how great you two get along with twelve physically challenged girls."

"They're amazin' little troupers," Hap said.

"You know the most natural horsewoman of the bunch?" Laramie said.

"Seanna?" Toni replied.

Laramie swirled an ice cube in the bottom of his plastic cup. "Her mother said she's been blind since birth. Tully loved her. He pouted when she left."

"Seanna's an inspiration to all the girls," Toni reported. "We love having her come over. They dote on her and forget their own limitations."

"Watching these girls laugh and giggle and act like

ordinary preteen girls gives us perspective," Laramie offered. "I'm sure the rest of us whine and complain way too much."

Brandon McKay's butch haircut and broad shoulders gave him an NFL linebacker look, but his blue-flowered Hawaiian shirt softened his appearance. "Guys, I've got to head to town and return some things to the rental company." He shook both their hands. "Your acts of compassion toward our family will never be forgotten. Today was a huge success due to Toni's planning and your graciousness. But agreeing to the trail ride is a legendary act of kindness."

"Trail ride?" Laramie asked.

"Look, guys, I'm going to pay you five hundred dollars apiece for that. I insist you take the money or it's no deal. You can donate it to charity, or give it away, or go buy new boots, but I have to pay you."

"Trail ride?" Laramie repeated.

Hap cleared his throat. "I forgot to tell you, partner. While you was puttin' up the horses, Toni, Brandon, me, and some of the parents decided it would be a wonderful thing to take this bunch on a trail ride."

"You mean, overnight?"

"Three nights, actually," Brandon added.

"But we will have at least one adult for every child," Toni explained. "We'll need a few days to prepare, so you'll stay with us, of course. We'll take off on Friday and be back by Monday. Hap said you had the time."

"Shoot, partner, it won't be too tough. We just have to wrangle the horse string, supervise things on the trail, and lead singin' around the campfire at night."

"Singing?" Laramie choked. "I don't sing in public, you know that."

"Now, quit worryin'," Hap replied. "We'll do it together. It will be a duet."

CHAPTER SEVEN

When the Pilgrims landed at Plymouth Rock in 1620, Europeans already dwelled in the northern New Mexico town of La Villa Real de Santa Fe. In fact, Santa Fe was the region's second capital. Don Juan de Oñate brought his caballeros to the confluence of the Rio Chama and the Rio Grande on July 11, 1598. There he founded the settlement of San Gabriel de los Españoles that overlooked what was then called Rio del Norte.

There are times when, indeed, the river looks *grande* . . . huge. Other times its most important attribute is the direction of its source . . . in the mountains to the north. Hap figured it was one of those times.

He chewed on a tough breakfast burrito, but kept a hand on the steering wheel. The windows rolled up, his black cowboy hat pushed back, the sleeves on his black shirt rolled halfway to the elbow, his left foot tapped away in time with a phantom tune that floated across the background of his mind. They crossed the border into New

Mexico at Anthony. He glanced at the I-10 freeway sign. "As I was sayin', it was a very emotional experience for me."

Laramie tried to sip on the minimart cup of coffee that was a tad too hot to hold, let alone drink. He brushed breakfast biscuit crumbs off his chin. "Hap, this highway is full of people going through the same thing every day. It's no big deal."

"I know, I know. I can't count how many times I've done it before. But this one was different. Couldn't you tell?"

Laramie repositioned himself in the cab of the truck. "I'll have to be honest. It was pretty much the same as before."

Hap jammed the rest of the burrito in his mouth and felt the hot sauce squirt between his cheek and gum. "You're wrong there, partner. I could feel it in my bones at the very second that I did it. Something in my body, soul, and spirit wanted to shout, 'Yes!'"

Laramie dug in the white paper sack and yanked out a couple of napkins. He shoved them at Hap. "You make it sound like a religious experience."

Hap wiped his chin, then picked at his teeth with his fingernail. "Maybe it was."

"Hap, I'm glad you're feeling good. I'm happy you're headed in the right direction. But to tell you the truth, I don't feel any different than I did before."

"It don't matter how you feel. I'm not leavin' you behind. You've been my partner for over ten years. We've spent day and night together for months on end. You just hold on. Don't lose sight of where I am and I'll take you with me, O ye of little faith."

"But I'm sort of an agnostic in this matter. I just don't have enough evidence to say one way or another."

"Evidence? You want evidence?" Hap shoved the rearview mirror to the right. "Look in that mirror. There's the evidence. Absolute, total proof."

Laramie gaped at his own reflection.

"What do you see?" Hap pressed.

"Eh, besides the fact that I need a haircut and the desert's whipping by in the background?"

"Look on the right-hand sign of the mirror and what do you see?" Hap shouted.

"A tiny neon-green LED letter N."

"Yes! Yes! Yes! You're right. It is the letter N. And do you know what that letter means?"

"I have a vague notion."

"That letter means we have turned north. We are driving north, partner. North! Today it's the Rio del Norte! Do you know what's north of New Mexico? Colorado! And do you know what is north of Colorado? Wyomin'! We are headed home, partner. And we are gettin' closer by the hour. The minute the freeway took a turn north back there I could feel a great relief."

"I still say, it was just a right turn. You've blown it all out of proportion."

Hap pulled around a semi truck, then swung back into the right lane. "It was not merely a right turn as opposed to a left turn. It was a turn north. We are goin' home, after forty years of wanderin' in the wilderness . . ."

"It was more like a hundred days," Laramie corrected.

Hap slapped his hand on the steering wheel. "After one hundred days of wanderin' in the wilderness, we are headed back to the promised land."

"But you said we have a few Juanita stops before we get there."

"That's what Rosa told me on the phone. Her aunt Paula gave her a list of eleven Juanitas, but only a couple seemed worth trackin' down."

"You eliminated all the others?" Laramie shut his eyes and rubbed his forehead as if massaging a migraine.

"Rosa insists they aren't right for me. There's some kind of family reunion this weekend. So, we're going to meet Rosa in Socorro. She'll take us to meet the Juanitas after that."

"Now, tell me, are you feeling good because you're pointed toward Wyoming or because you're headed toward Rosa?"

"I shouldn't be the only one feelin' good. Havin' Annamarie Buchett flyin' in to meet you in Santa Fe ain't somethin' to mope over."

Laramie sat up. "She said she needed to see me before she made some big decisions. But I don't know if I'm auditioning for a part in her life or if she wants to tell me face to face that I didn't make the cut."

"What if it ain't bad news? Laramie, just how big a decision are you prepared to make?"

"A whole lot bigger than when we rode down out of Wyoming three and a half months ago."

"Annamarie changed all of that?"

"Yes . . . and sitting through that funeral service in El Paso. I think I buried a few old memories in that grave. I'm grateful for that. But I'm scared I won't get a chance to make the decisions that I'm now ready for."

"I think we're on a roll. Maybe it's the fresh New Mexico air, but I'm beginnin' to see light at the end of the bridge with my Juanita quest."

"You mean, 'light at the end of the tunnel'?"

"Nah . . . it's a long, covered bridge . . . you knew what I meant. Win or lose, this Juanita thing will be over in a few days. Turn on the radio, partner, I feel like rollin' down the window and singin' at the top of my lungs."

"I'll turn on the radio, but you have to promise not to sing. All those campfire songs with teenage girls wore down my tolerance for Hap Bowman serenades." Laramie spun the dial until a deep bass beat vibrated the speakers.

"I never met ten sharper girls . . ." Hap tapped on the steering wheel.

"Yeah, it's the first time I ever thought about how much fun a daughter could be."

"Laramie Majors ponderin' havin' kids? If the sun don't turn to blood and the stars fall out of the sky today, they never will."

"Aren't you being overdramatic?" Laramie questioned.

"Maybe . . . but it is a great day." Hap smiled. "What song is that?"

"I don't know. I thought a song with the line 'Ain't it funny the turns life puts you through' fit us both right now."

"I like it, but I'm feelin' so good right now even opera would sound like real music. Who are those guys?"

Laramie turned the volume down a little. "The DJ mentioned Tom Boone and Charlie, eh, someone."

"They must be new. But, then, we ain't listened to the radio in months. Turn it up . . . it's a long way before the turnoff and I aim to celebrate."

⇥══ ══⇤

Three hours later they took the Socorro exit marked *New Mexico Institute of Mining and Technology.* Laramie glanced at his watch. "We're late."

Hap studied the tree-lined street. "Road construction zones open for no man."

"Where are we meeting Rosa?" Laramie watched an old man with a cane walk a boxer along the sidewalk. "That looks like Sara."

"Nah," Hap replied. "Sara's cuter. Anyway, Rosa said the reunion's at a park that's hard to find. She's going to meet us at a church and lead us over there."

Laramie scanned the horizon for steeples. "Which church?"

Hap pulled a note from the pocket of his black shirt and studied his pencil scribblings. "Eh . . . St. Somethin'-er-other. It's a Catholic church."

"You don't remember?"

"Maybe it's St. Ignatius. How many Catholic churches can there be in town?"

"In Socorro, New Mexico? There could be a dozen."

Hap pulled off his sunglasses and squinted at the paper. "Shoot, maybe it's St. Stanislaus."

"Let me look." Laramie plucked the note out of his hand. "I can't read any of this."

"Maybe it's upside down."

Laramie turned the note. "This is worse."

"It was dark in the hallway of that truck stop. I'm sure it was a saint. What are some other saints?"

"Hap, I don't know any other except St. Louis, St. Petersburg, and St. Bernard." Laramie tossed the note on the dash.

"Look on the other side of that park. Was I right?" Hap

swung in front of a small church built with used brick and a steep shake roof. Hanging pots of red, white, and almost-blue petunias lined the covered entrance. "St. Andrews. I'm sure that's it."

"It's an Episcopal church, Hap."

"Are we goin' to argue over theological distinctions?"

"Then where's Rosa? Is she driving her aunt Paula's white Oldsmobile?" Laramie gazed at the tree-lined park across from the church. Bright-colored playground equipment stood like horses at the rail, waiting for someone to ride.

Hap still peered at the brick building. "She's not here. But now we can say we went to the wrong church."

"Pull over by the gal in the convertible," Laramie ordered.

"Are you cruisin'?"

"I'm asking directions."

The woman with straight blonde hair and red-framed sunglasses focused on her cell phone conversation when they slowed down next to her.

Laramie rolled down his window. "Excuse me, ma'am . . . we were supposed to meet . . ."

"Never mind, they're here," she said to her phone. She hopped out of the convertible. "Park your pickup and trailer. Quick, you're late."

"Eh, we were lookin' for . . ."

The lady with cherry-red fingernails waved her hand. "She got tied up with logistics, so she sent me to pick you up instead. Now hurry, it's already begun."

Hap pulled in front of the convertible. "I didn't know they were holding up the reunion for us. I figured we could just pop in anytime."

"Maybe your Rosa has a bigger surprise for you than you planned on."

They slipped out of the truck and moseyed toward the convertible.

The blonde stomped up to them as if stalking a naughty dog. "I certainly hope you aren't planning to ride your horses at this late juncture."

Hap tipped his hat. "Eh, no, ma'am."

She pulled off her sunglasses and surveyed them from head to toe. Her blue eyes seemed to be rearranging everything she viewed. "Do you need to change?"

Hap grinned. "No one's perfect. I reckon all of us have some things we should change. But if you're talkin' shirts, we've been on the road a while. This is as good as we have with us that's clean. It's not a formal affair, is it?"

She jammed her glasses back on and spun around. "Of course not. Get in the car."

Laramie and Hap followed her to the convertible.

"Eh, I'll crawl in the backseat," Hap offered. "My legs are a little shorter."

The blonde slid behind the steering wheel. "You will both sit in the back. That will be best." She grabbed her red cell phone. "We're on our way! Stall them." She stepped on the accelerator. The gold Chrysler shot into the street and roared through the intersection. Laramie clutched the seat in front of him. Hap grabbed his hat.

Without looking back, the blonde jabbed her right hand toward them. "My name is Char, but everyone calls me 'Cheery.'"

They shook her hand, a cautious handshake, the kind given when you aren't too sure what germs the contact will bring.

"I'm Hap. This is Laramie."

She peered into the rearview mirror. "I like that. I'm sure in your position you need nicknames for privacy. At least you don't go as Fred Flintstone and Barney Rubble."

Laramie shrugged at Hap. Both cowboys clutched the side of the car when she whipped around the corner.

A crowd of men, women, and kids hovered on the sidewalk at the end of the next block. The majority were women. Most wore shorts, T-shirts, bright-colored flip-flops, and sunglasses.

Hap leaned over to Laramie. "I didn't know this was such a big deal. Rosa must be related to ever'one in New Mexico."

Cheery swerved the car to the sidewalk. Two ladies held what looked like big blank posters.

"They look so much different in person," one lady said. She taped a poster to the door.

"Different than what?" Laramie asked, but Cheery was on the cell phone.

She pivoted around. "Okay, we're all set. It's time for you to sit up on the ragtop."

"Why?" Hap asked.

"For a better view."

The boys crawled up in the back. "Hap, what did you get us roped into? You didn't tell them we were bullriders, did you?"

"You can leave your sunglasses on, but please smile and wave," Cheery called out.

The car lurched into the center of the street to the applause of people stacked deep on both sides.

The boys grinned and waved.

The people cheered. Men held children on their shoulders. Ladies shoved sunglasses to the top of their heads. A plucky teenage girl with red hair and a tiny tube top no wider than a belt ran toward the car and blew kisses. "I love you!" she squealed.

"This is bizarre," Laramie said. "What are we doing in a parade?" The car lurched forward. Cheery jammed on the brakes when a little boy ran across the street in front of them chasing a Frisbee.

Hap faced the crowd on the other side. "There cain't be this many Rodríguezes, even if you count Mexico and South America. And I don't recollect a parade in the details Rosa gave me."

"Did you see that? That lady had *will you* and *marry me?* written right on her . . ."

"I don't want to see it." Hap said. "What's it say on that sign taped to the car?"

When they caught up to a junior high marching band playing "California Dreamin'," they stopped in the middle of the street. Ahead of the band, a big float carried girls in long, formal gowns offering slow waves to the crowd.

Laramie leaned over the edge. "It's some kind of advertising sign, I guess."

When the band, clothed in starched jeans and white shirts, finished their song, they marched forward. The convertible didn't move.

"Cheery, what's the deal here? We don't have a clue . . ."

"Shhh." She pressed her red polished fingernail to her red lipstick. "They're introducing you over the loudspeaker."

"Ladies and gentleman, here they are. On their very first trip to New Mexico. In just two short months, these recording artists have taken country music by storm. Ladies and gentlemen, you've seen them on TV. You've heard them on radio. You have their CD in your rig right now. I present to you . . . Tom Boone and Charlie Crockett . . . of the rocketing duo, Boone and Crockett."

"Stand up, boys," Cheery prodded.

"But we ain't . . ."

"I said, stand up!"

Laramie and Hap stood.

And waved.

"Sing us a song," a teenager with brunette hair down to her waist shouted.

"Folks," the announcer continued, "Boone and Crockett have a contractual agreement with their record company that forbids them from singing here today. So don't ask."

A young girl with a glimmering turquoise blouse and long brown ponytail called out, "What one of your songs is your favorite?"'

Hap glanced at Laramie, then back at the girl. "You cain't beat the one that starts out, 'Ain't it funny the turns life puts you through,' but we love 'em all, darlin'."

The girl screamed . . . then fell flat on her face.

Hap choked. "She fainted?"

The car lurched forward past a crowd three rows deep on both sides. Some clutched balloons, cotton candy, or snow cones. A couple of young ladies raised posters with scrawled phone numbers.

Two blocks later, Laramie grabbed Hap's arm. "How are we going to get out of this?"

"I'd be tempted with a cyanide capsule, but I left mine in my other suit." Hap noticed a familiar face rush toward them. "Rosa?"

"What are you doing in the parade?" she hollered.

"We thought we were comin' to see you."

"I waited and waited for you at St. Mary's." Rosa jogged beside the driver. "Did you know these two are not Boone and Crockett?"

"Yes . . . I suspected so. But they're close enough."

"You knew it?" Laramie asked.

"Not all blondes are naïve and dumb."

"How do we get out of this deal?" Hap asked.

"I'll take care of it." Rosa kept jogging by the car as the boys waved at the cheering fans. "When you get to the end, pull over in front of the fountain at city hall. I'll have an exit plan ready."

⋆⇒   ⇐⋆

Hap slumped behind the steering wheel as they rolled north on Interstate 25 out of Socorro, Rosa next to him. Laramie flopped his arm on the open window.

"That ain't exactly what I call an ideal exit strategy," Hap grumbled.

Rosa patted his knee. "It worked. It snuck you out of the crowd."

"You ever try to put on a two-man donkey costume in the back of a VW van?"

Laramie rubbed on his beard. "Well, it did get us through the horde without being mobbed by our adoring fans."

"Yeah, but you didn't have to be the donkey's tail end."

"They would have stoned you if you told them the truth," Rosa said. "You definitely want to live long enough to meet the other Juanitas."

"Tell me about them," Hap said. "I need to get my mind off this morning."

"Maybe you could wear that donkey suit when you visit these Juanitas. That should impress them," Laramie said.

"I'd toss you out of the truck right now, but I don't know how I'd explain it to Annamarie."

"What time does her plane come in?" Rosa asked.

"Two o'clock tomorrow," Laramie replied.

"I look forward to meeting her."

"She's a lot like you," Hap said. "Only tall, French/Vietnamese/Texan, a nurse, and has a different personality."

"We're practically twins."

"But she doesn't have a mark under her right ear."

"Few women do." Rosa pulled out her notebook. "As far as Aunt Paula could remember, there are three Juanitas left in my family that fit the age range."

"I thought you said only two?"

"Juanita number three lives in Tulare, California, with her chief-of-police husband. She has four boys and runs the YWCA preschool. I didn't think you wanted to go there today."

"You know, three months ago I'd have written down her address and made plans for California. But now, I'm ready for the search to end. Maybe the Juanita in Santa Fe will be the right one."

"She's Juanita Marta Muñoz. She grew up north of Albuquerque along the Rio Grande. Of course, Santa Fe's not on the Rio Grande, but her childhood home was."

"Okay, now we're gettin' there."

"She's an artist. She paints and sculpts . . . mostly pueblo scenes."

"An artist? Didn't I say she might be an artist?"

"Or a lawyer, or nurse, or teacher, or missionary," Laramie added.

"Aunt Paula mentioned this Juanita went to art school in New York and studied for a while in Europe. Her works are featured in galleries in Scottsdale, Arizona; Jackson, Wyoming; Aspen, Colorado; and at her studio in Santa Fe."

"Hmmm, I'm feelin' the attraction already. Do you have a picture of her?"

"No, but I do know she always wears a black hat."

"Are you kiddin' me?" Hap slapped the steering wheel. "A black hat. I've worn a black hat since I was . . . twelve. I had a black hat on the day I met Juanita! Is that a sign from heaven or what?"

"And she has The Mark."

"Sounds like a curse, or somethin'," Hap said.

"Just the opposite. Aunt Paula calls it 'The Mark of God.' She says God was so pleased with his creation that he reached down and touched his finger on each of these special Rodríguez girls."

"She didn't come down to the family reunion?" Laramie asked.

"No, she never attends. She's quite busy with her work, which usually means she doesn't associate with the humbler, poorer side of the family. But I shouldn't say that. What do I know? I've never met her. Aunt Paula hasn't seen her in years, either. She wants me to write a full description."

The rhythm of the highway sang harmony to the rambling conversation of the three in the front seat of Hap's Dodge pickup. They filled the diesel tanks and grabbed ice cream bars in Albuquerque. Back on the freeway, the early September heat faded with the setting sun. When they reached Santa Fe, at more than six thousand feet elevation, they slipped on their jackets.

They left Luke, Tully, and the horse trailer at the home of a friend of Laramie's brother near the rodeo grounds and found a motel on the freeway, just north of town.

Rosa knocked on the boys' half-open door. "Can I come in?"

"Sure," Laramie called out. "Hap's out on the balcony. I'm trying to find football scores."

"Did he phone her yet?"

"No. I think he's fueling the flames and waiting for a head of courage."

Rosa scooted between the double beds, retrieved the telephone, then dragged it to the open sliding patio door.

"Can I join you?" she asked.

Hap jumped up and pulled up the other plastic chair. "Yes, ma'am. I didn't hear you come in."

"Were you sleeping?"

"I was contemplatin' the sunset."

"It's beautiful, even if it is pollution that gives it the red glow."

She plopped down in the chair and set the phone on the floor between them.

"I reckon sunsets are my favorite," Hap mused. "I like mornin's and sunrises, but there is always so much to do ahead of me. It's a time to get body, soul, and spirit wound up tight to meet the challenges. But in the evenin' . . . I start to relax . . . to think through the day . . . you know what I mean?"

"Yes, I do. I enjoy being outside at sunset even in the winter. No matter how cold, even if the sky is cloudy, I like to go outside and watch."

"One thing about ranchin' jobs, I get to enjoy a lot of sunsets."

"I hope you aren't contemplating too much." Rosa reached over and rubbed his shoulder. "I don't want you to hold a grudge for the donkey costume."

Hap patted her hand. "No, I was thinkin' through the whole dadgum summer. The air's startin' to feel like fall. We've got to be back at the ranch by the fifteenth."

"Has it been a good summer?"

"It's been a crazy kind of good. Pushin' cows can be so routine. There are spring chores, summer chores, fall chores, winter chores. Then the cycle repeats itself. You can go for a season—shoot, you can go for a whole year and not have to wrestle much in your mind. That's not to say it's borin'. Ranch work, or rodeo, or horse trainin' has never bored me. But this summer was sort of like sittin' in one of those dunkin' booths at a charity event. You know sooner or later someone will hit the target and you'll plunge into the water."

"Have you taken a lot of plunges?"

"Yes, ma'am, I have."

"Are you going to call Juanita Marta Muñoz?"

"I've been contemplatin' that, too."

"Does it feel like you're about to get dunked into cold water again?"

"Sort of."

Rosa stared down at the phone, then licked her lips. "Would you like me to phone her?"

"I keep wonderin' if I don't have the nerve to phone her,

how can I expect her to be the right one? I got a friend who used to run marathons. He said somewhere about twenty-two or twenty-three miles into it . . . he'd hit the wall. At that moment, he couldn't figure out why he was pushin' himself. He lost all motivation to keep goin'."

"Have you hit the wall? You thinking you want to skip this one?" Rosa asked.

"I can't make myself quit until the job is done, but she seems a little . . . eh . . ."

"Too talented?"

"That's not what I had in mind, but it works."

"I don't think you should skip her. I think you need to finish your quest knowing you gave it your best shot and checked on every prospect. It might make your Wyoming sunsets even more peaceful this winter. Shall I phone?"

"Yeah, thanks, Rosa. You're a pal, that's for sure."

She punched in the numbers, then tucked the phone receiver between her cheek and her shoulder. "Hi, Juanita Marta. This is Rosa Rodríguez Tryor. Aunt Paula gave me your number. I'm in Santa Fe with some friends and we wanted to stop by for a visit. You might remember, I'm the distant cousin you donated that signed print to for the women's safe house in Gallop? You said it should bring five hundred dollars, but it brought in twenty-one hundred. Anyway, if you're in town, I'd appreciate a call back. Thanks."

Rosa left the hotel number and hung up. "If she doesn't phone back, you can drive away without regret."

They gazed over the top of the motel parking lot at flat, tile-roofed houses to the southwest. The shadows blotted out the last streaks of sunlight. With no wind, the leaves of the trees hung motionless like a painting.

"What if this Juanita is the one, Hap? What will you do if you find her?"

He rubbed the back of his neck. "My dream always ends with us livin' happily ever after."

"So, you think your Juanita has been pining for you all these years?"

"One of the signs of the real Juanita is that she will want to be with me as much as I want to be with her."

Rosa reached behind Hap and rubbed his neck. "What are the other signs . . . you know, besides 'The Mark.'"

He dropped his chin to his chest. "I didn't know I'd have to tell you all this."

"We're just visiting, waiting for a return call. What does the right Juanita need to be?"

"She has to allow me to do things for her."

"So, you don't want an independent woman. You like the retiring, compliant type?"

"No. I want her to be independent enough to not need me at all, but then choose to allow me to do things."

"I like that."

When she massaged her pointed elbow into the middle of his back, he squirmed. "And I reckon I'll let her do things for me."

"Really?"

"I need to learn. Cowboy pride and independence can be lonely companions."

"What else?"

"I need her to teach me things she knows that I don't, and learn from me in things I know, but she doesn't."

She continued to stroke his arms, shoulders, neck. "I like listening to you, cowboy. I've never heard you be so serious. But you didn't mention family and all. When you consider your perfect Juanita, do you envision children?"

"Oh, yeah. I want twelve daughters," he declared.

Rosa's hands dropped to her side. "What? You . . ."

The ringing of the telephone interrupted her protest.

"Yes. Bein' with them little darlin's last weekend convinced me to have twelve daughters." Hap grinned. "End of questions. You answer the phone."

"Hello? Eh . . . yes, this is his room. I'm Rosa, a friend of Hap's and . . . oh . . . Annamarie. Laramie talks about you all the time. Yes, he is . . ."

"Hey, partner . . ." Hap called back into the room. "It's the tallest, purdiest nurse in North America and she wants to talk to you about a heart transplant."

Laramie scurried over to the phone, then dragged it into the bathroom.

"Looks like the sun's disappeared," Rosa said. "Now, where were we? Oh, yes, discussing you and Juanita's children. You haven't told me how you will convince the perfect Juanita to have twelve daughters."

"I won't have to convince her of anything. She'll love me so much . . ."

"Hap, you are living in the wrong century. There's no woman in this country who would want to give birth to twelve kids when she's thirty-one years old."

"Eight?"

"Two-point-five, max."

"She's on her way," Laramie called out. "Annamarie caught an earlier flight and just landed in Albuquerque. She'll catch a commuter to Santa Fe. We can pick her up in an hour. I told her she could bunk with Rosa. I need a shower." He pulled off his shirt.

"Then I need a walk," Rosa said. "This is fun having Annamarie come in."

"Laramie, the keys to the truck are on the nightstand. I'm taking a walk with Rosa."

"What if Juanita Marta Muñoz returns my call?" she asked.

"That's another reason to go for a walk."

⊷═╍   ╍═⊷

Laramie paced in front of the baggage carousel, one eye fixed on the ramp leading down from the arrival gates. Clusters of people shuffled and tapped their way across the polished floor. Lights flashed. Buzzers sounded. Baggage circled like prisoners in a tiny exercise yard. In his right hand, green florist paper enclosed twelve long-stemmed red roses.

He scanned the arrival monitor and felt his heart fall when Flight 2106 from Albuquerque showed a ten-minute delay. He circled his arm trying to alleviate the pain in his right shoulder and glanced outside where taxis and hotel shuttles jockeyed for position.

Finally, he slumped between a uniformed sailor asleep with his mouth open and a small gray-haired lady with a lap full of pink crochet. He stretched out his long legs.

"She'll like the flowers," the lady said. Her hands, sprinkled with age spots, never missed a stitch.

"I feel kind of foolish," Laramie admitted.

Her thin lips held only a trace of light pink lipstick. "You look a little foolish."

"You think I shouldn't give them to her?"

"Oh, no, by all means give them. She will know that you

sat here looking like a fool, just to bring her a smile. That means you think more about her than yourself. No woman takes that lightly."

"Thanks. This is not the kind of thing that comes natural to me. I'd rather hide over in the corner and watch things."

She stopped stitching and rocked back and forth. "Are they for your wife?"

"Eh, no."

"Girlfriend?"

"That's what I'm hoping. I've only known her a couple months and she's been gone most of the time."

The lady laid her hand on his arm. "Young man, I was only with Harold for three weeks before we married."

"Is that all?"

"But I wrote to him for two years before that. He was in the war in Italy, then Germany. I signed up for a USO pen pal."

"How long have you and your husband been married?"

"We had fifty-eight years together. He passed on three years ago."

"Congratulations, ma'am, that's wonderful. I'm sorry he's gone. I'm sure you miss him."

"We had some tough years, but you're right . . . it was wonderful. I had no idea how lonely I would be without him. You know, I still have my driver's license. I still live in the same house. I can take care of myself and I certainly don't need my daughters to come over and treat me like a little child. But do you know what I miss most? I miss having someone to take care of. My Harold needed me. Now, I'm not sure anyone needs me. Taking care of someone gives you a delight about getting up each day."

"I reckon it does."

"Are you waiting for me, cowboy?" Annamarie Buchett loomed above him, dark hair perfectly groomed, bright hazel eyes, and wide, easy smile.

He jumped up and shoved the flowers at her. "I thought you were delayed."

She took them and grinned. "I can't believe you bought flowers for me. Nobody does that anymore. In fact, I've never been greeted in public with flowers in my life." She threw her arms around him and kissed his neck.

Out of the corner of his eye, he saw the little lady wink, then go back to her crochet.

Annamarie slipped her hand in his as they hiked over to the baggage carousel. He kept walking, though he considered stopping, closing his eyes, and enjoying the warmth and peace of those fingers laced in his. "How's your mamma doing in southern California?"

"She loves it. She already found a house to buy."

"You figure on moving in with her or do you want a place of your own?"

"I definitely want a place of my own." She led him over to the baggage carousel.

He clutched her hand tightly and stared down at his boots. "Probably a lot of nursing jobs out there."

With her other hand, she rubbed his arm. "Laramie, there are a lot of nursing jobs everywhere. I think I'd like a fresh start. In fact, I happen to know there's an opening for an emergency room nurse in Fort Collins, Colorado. I've been thinking about applying for it."

He looked straight into her eyes. He felt his smile strain his cheeks. "Fort Collins? That's on the other side of Denver, up by . . ."

"By Wyoming, I hope. Meeting you this summer reminded me of some of the things that I've been neglecting. Somewhere in the gloom and depression when my husband was killed, I just gave up on having those things. I'd like to see if I can't revive a few of them."

"What kinds of things would you like to revive?"

She flung her arms around his neck and kissed him full on the lips. "That's one thing."

He towed her roller suitcase and hugged her waist as they strolled out to the parking lot. "When you flew to California, I didn't know if I'd ever see you again. When you said you were flying to meet us in New Mexico, I figured this might be our farewell. Some things have been coming clear to me lately. I know you have issues in the past to release . . . and so do I. In the past couple of weeks I've felt more freedom from all of that."

"Laramie, I like the way you are tender . . . and yet tough . . . the way you're educated and informed about things . . . yet easygoing. I like how you make me feel good to be me."

"Annamarie . . . I just like saying your name, and this might sound kind of immature, but you are the dream I was always afraid to dream. A beautiful woman who could chase away the demons in my mind and the fears in my soul. What I'm trying to say is, I like me when I'm with you. I believe for the first time in my life, I'm able to give my whole heart away . . . but you might have to help teach me how to do that. "

"That could take some time."

He slid her suitcase into the back of the truck. "What are you doing for the next fifty or sixty years?"

She kissed his cheek. "I'll have to check my calendar. Are you in a hurry for an answer?"

Laramie leaned his back against the side of the black Dodge. "No. Just anxious to get to know you better and scared to death for you to get to know me. I have flaws you haven't seen yet."

Annamarie waited for the minivan next to them to back out, then turned to face him. "And you have never heard me scream in the middle of the night."

"You scream?"

"Nightmares."

"I could learn to wake up and take care of you."

She leaned her head on his shoulder. "That's what it's all about, is it?"

"I think so." Laramie stroked his fingers through her silky black hair. "It's having someone to take care of."

"That's what we've got to find out. Do we possess what we need to take care of each other? I thought if I took a job in Fort Collins and you were close by, we'd find time to practice."

"We've got lots of things to practice." He lifted her chin with his fingers.

"What else?" she asked.

When he kissed her lips, Annamarie's arms locked around his neck. This time, she didn't let go. "Oh, no," she sighed. "You don't need to improve that, cowboy. You're as good as they get."

He opened the pickup door for her. "But we'll have to keep at it quite a while, because you can definitely use some practice."

She jabbed her elbow into his side, then slid across the pickup seat to the middle.

When Rosa met Hap in the lobby of the motel the next morning, her thick, black, wavy hair was combed down, framing her wide brown eyes.

He handed her a Styrofoam cup of coffee as they strolled out to the parking lot. "Is your roomie still asleep?" he asked.

"She woke up for a few minutes and we visited, but she conked out again. They were out later than we were. Is Laramie up?"

Hap opened the pickup door for her. "If I didn't know him better, I'd say he was dead. He flopped down on his bed with his clothes still on about three in the mornin' and hasn't moved a muscle since. He don't usually sleep that good."

Rosa hopped in and fastened the seatbelt. "I like Annamarie."

"Yeah, I do, too." Hap pulled the truck out into scattered morning traffic. "Laramie's a pretty easygoin' guy. I mean, it's all internal. He kind of kicks back and observes life. He's always got a good answer and he's always there when you need him, but he don't spend a lot of time doin' things for himself. I truly believe Annamarie is somethin' he wants real bad. I'm hopin' it works out for them." He pulled up to a stop light. "Now, which way?"

"Follow the signs downtown to the Palace of the Governors. Her studio is two streets north of the plaza."

"I jist never figured Laramie would find a gal that tall. They look good together, don't they?"

"I was thinking the same thing. Some couples do look

like they belong together. But what will that mean for you? You and Laramie have been partners so long."

"I reckon we'll stay close friends, no matter what. We've gone through too much together to loosen the ties." Hap tapped the steering wheel.

"Are you nervous about meeting Juanita Marta?"

"Yeah. As long as findin' my Juanita was a vague, unreachable concept, I could enjoy it. But ever' time it gets close to happenin' . . ."

"You aren't sure what to do?"

"Rosa, I have lived and relived the scene of what it will be like when I finally meet her. I know everythin' to say and do. I've practiced my lines for almost twenty years. But it dawns on me, she might have other lines and I only know one script."

"Just relax and wing it."

"I know . . . it just keeps eatin' at me." He glanced in the rearview mirror and noticed the arch in Rosa's thick, black eyebrows.

Rosa tugged at her dangling, silver feather earrings.

"Are those earrings new?"

"Yes, I just bought them in the hotel gift shop. I never wear anything this flashy."

"They look really good on you."

"One dark night on a highway in west Texas, this cowboy stud told me I should have more fun . . . that I ought to do some things for myself. Earrings aren't a big deal, but they are a start."

"Maybe all of us need to do somethin' for ourselves. I think that's what Laramie and Annamarie are doin'. They're gettin' serious and I know that produces changes."

"Are you worried about the changes?"

"That cool air we felt last night signaled that fall is comin'. Seasons come and go . . . each new season has its challenges and its beauty. You can't predict the exact dates and you can't keep it from happenin'. I guess I'll just take what comes and look for the good parts."

"The serious Hap Bowman." She smiled. "I'm seeing more and more of that side of you."

Hap pushed his hat back, then rubbed his clean-shaven chin. "Well, that's about as serious and melancholy as I get. Sorry about that."

"I like it. You know what I've been thinking about this morning?"

Hap turned right at the stoplight, then merged into the left-hand lane. "You've been thinkin' about an Egg McMuffin with extra cheese and tater tots floatin' in catsup like they was a bobber when you're fishin' on the lake?"

"Oh, yuuuuck! Of course not."

"Were you thinkin' of buyin' a black Hummer and drivin' that sucker all the way to Yellowknife, Northwest Territories?"

"Eh, no . . . I was . . ."

"I know, you was thinkin' of strippin' buck naked and jumpin' in the motel pool."

Rosa slugged him. "Hush up, you jerk, and let me talk."

"Yes, ma'am. I can see you and me imagine different daydreams."

"You challenged me last night. Remember when we were strolling through the park and the kids playing that flashlight game got us laughing so much, you asked me again what I did for fun. I think I've eliminated fun from my itinerary for years. Everything became so critical, so important, so urgent. Too many causes, so little time. Fun seemed a distraction." She waved her hand. "Turn left up here."

Hap waited for a green GMC Yukon to pass, then turned. "So you changed your mind about fun and went out and bought those earrings?"

"You have no idea how big a deal it is for me to do that." She leaned back, her hands locked behind her thick black hair. "But, I know I need a break. I need to enjoy what I can. Did I tell you I play the piano?"

"No . . . really?" He slowed down and stopped while a bus took on passengers.

"Mamma stuck me with two years of piano lessons as a kid. I hated it at the time, but wish I'd kept at it now."

A habit-dressed nun marched a group of uniformed children toward the plaza.

"I played with an ensemble during my first couple of years in college. But one cause or another possessed me, so I dropped it."

"You goin' to start back up again?"

"Yes, I am. Hap, do you ski?"

He pulled out at the same time as the bus. "I ain't very good at it, but me and Laramie get out two or three times ever' winter. We usually head down to Steamboat Springs. Laramie, on the other hand, is a great skier."

"I've lived in the Rockies for years and never learned how to ski. I think this is the winter I learn."

He turned right and studied the buildings. "Is this the street?"

"Yes, a few blocks east. I think it's on my side."

One-story residences nestled in the shade of old trees. Most of the homes were painted in various shades of tan stucco, made to look like adobe, and had recessed, flat roofs.

"So, you're goin' to learn to ski and take up piano again. Dadgum it, Rosa, you do have great daydreams. Mine are mighty meager next to those."

"Except you were teasing me with those things." She pointed to a one-story, pale copper stucco building with exposed, round exterior ceiling beams. "There it is."

Hap parked behind a silver Lexus. "Yep, you're right. I was teasin' about my daydreams. Why, shoot, McDonald's don't even serve tater tots."

Rosa hopped out of the truck before he got around to open her door. "I did like one of your daydreams."

They surveyed the cactus and succulent landscaping in front of the studio. "Wow, that's great, darlin'. But I figure we ought to wait until after dark to go skinny dippin', don't you?"

She slugged him again. "Not that one, you dork. I meant the one about going to Yellowknife."

He took a deep breath and let it out slow.

"You nervous?" Rosa asked.

"Yep. Tell me again what she said."

"She has a busy day planned, but she'll give us ten minutes, if we're here by 9:00 A.M. sharp."

"I wonder what Ms. Juanita Marta Muñoz does for fun?" He tugged down the brim of his hat and shoved his sunglasses into the pocket of his long-sleeved black shirt.

The waitress at Emilia's Fine Spanish Restaurant served the sweet iced tea, as the girls returned from the ladies room. Laramie and Hap stood so Annamarie and Rosa could slide into the buckskin-colored booth.

Annamarie squeezed lemon into her drink. "Okay, tell us everything that happened with Juanita, the artist."

"She has a beautiful studio," Hap reported. "It's like a picture out of a New Mexico tourist magazine. Lots of Indian and early Spanish artifacts, red tile floor, potted cactus, ever'thin'."

"Rosa, would you please tell this rambling cowboy I don't give a squat what the room looks like? What happened?"

"Maybe Rosa should tell us," Laramie countered.

"No," Rosa said. "This is Hap's story. I was only there to say, 'Juanita Marta, this is Hap. Hap, this is Juanita Marta.' After that, I perched on a stool shaped like a barrel cactus and listened."

"Okay, you were introduced. What did you say, then?"

"You know, Annamarie," Hap drawled, "for a purdy woman, you sure are pushy."

"Thank you."

"For which . . . purdy or pushy?"

"Both. Get on with it, cowboy."

"Much of it's a blur. I told her who I was. That I had met a girl named Juanita as a twelve-year-old. And how I was interested in finding that Juanita."

"Did you tell her about 'The Mark' and everything?" Annamarie asked.

"Oh, yeah, I gave her the long version of the story and most of the significant events in my life. It must have taken a full ten minutes."

"Nineteen minutes," Rosa said. "I was taking a few notes . . . you know . . . to report to Aunt Paula."

"Then she . . ."

"Wait a minute," Laramie interrupted. "Before you go any further, what did she look like?"

Hap shrugged. "She was attractive . . . a light-complexioned Mexican lady."

"I want a better description than that." He turned to Rosa. "What did you put in your notes?"

Rosa set down her iced tea. "Juanita Marta is five foot six. Weighs 135 pounds. Wears size-ten slacks and had on a rose-red silk blouse that's buttoned at the cuff, but unbuttoned at the collar. Her eyes are dark brown. Her hair, what we could see of it, is thick, black, shoulder-length, straight. She wore a wide, floppy black hat. She had on Italian sandals that probably cost close to five hundred dollars. She wore two rings on each hand. Diamonds and onyx, I believe. She wore thick makeup around her eyes, which probably is meant to cover up crow's-feet. She has had plastic surgery on her nose to make it look thinner than other Rodríguez women. Her earrings were round black onyx stones surrounded by tiny diamonds. At least, I thought they were real diamonds from where I sat. It's hard to say. I had some difficulty picking up the details from that far away."

"Geez, Rosa, I didn't see all that," Hap said.

"Okay, that's better." Laramie gulped down a swig of sweet tea. "Now, what happened after your life's testimonial?"

"She leaned forward, her hand on her chin, and stared for a couple minutes," Hap reported.

"It was only forty-five seconds," Rosa corrected.

"It seemed like twenty years. Then she sat up, turned her head to the side, pointed under her right ear, and said,

'First of all, as you can see, cosmetic surgery can remove some horrid marks.'"

"That's when I blurted out, 'You removed The Mark?'" Rosa admitted.

"She answered with 'I have no intention of going through life as an object of curiosity or derision,'" Hap explained.

"She said that?" Annamarie gasped.

"She said more." Rosa turned to Hap. "Tell them the rest."

Hap cleared his throat. "Well, let me see if I get this straight. She looked me in the eye and said, 'That's the most pathetic story I've ever heard. Get a life.' Then she stood, told Rosa, 'I have work to do. Say hello to Aunt Paula,' and stalked to the back room, closing the door behind her."

"Omigosh," Annamarie exclaimed.

"Did I get it right?"

Rosa nodded. "That's what she said, but you had to be there to catch the full condescending tone. I was embarrassed for the whole Rodríguez family."

"I suppose that eliminates Juanita Marta," Laramie said.

"Some choices are easier than others," Hap admitted. "I was glad Rosa was with me to witness that because it was sort of like a bad dream."

"But you have another Juanita to visit in Colorado," Annamarie reminded him.

"I could use some encouragement about that. Rosa, read to me what your aunt Paula stated about the Colorado Juanita."

The waiter approached with a heavy tray full of steaming food. "Let's wait until after we eat," she replied.

While recorded Spanish guitar music serenaded in the background, Hap leaned back in the booth with a half-filled glass of iced tea. His wide orange pottery plate was slicked clean except for a pile of onions that he had sorted out. He nodded toward Rosa's notebook. "Okay, now tell me about the last Juanita."

"I never thought I'd hear you say that," Laramie said. "Is this really the last Juanita?"

"It's got to end somewhere. I promised you I'd find her this summer or give it up. So, this is it."

"Okay, here's what Aunt Paula said: She's thirty-one years old and has a small place in Wagon Wheel Gap, Colorado, which is just south of Creede, along the Rio Grande. She's fairly light-complected for a Rodríguez. But she looks like Mexico and talks like Chicago."

"That's a nice way of putting it," Annamarie said.

"Looks like Mexico? What does that mean?" Hap asked.

"Aunt Paula says she is 'as cute as she can be.'"

"You know," Laramie mused, "I've always wondered what that meant. Isn't everyone as cute as they can be?"

Rosa squinted at the notebook. "She is not glamorous, but passable when she dresses up."

"That sounds fair enough," Hap murmured.

"She graduated from Colorado State University . . ."

"That's in Fort Collins," Laramie said. "Annamarie's going to nurse up there."

"And she majored in secondary education with a minor in music. She did her student teaching in Loveland."

"She's a high school teacher?" The corners of Hap's mouth arched to his ears. "Now, I like this. No artist . . . no barmaid . . ."

"Is she married?" Annamarie asked.

"Aunt Paula believes she is not married and has never been married."

"Does she have any kids?" Laramie quizzed. Rosa glared at him. "Hey, that's not always the same thing."

"Does she have a dog?" Annamarie asked.

"Aunt Paula didn't mention anything about pets. But, she likes to travel. And has had short-term teaching assignments overseas."

"Sounds very well-rounded in the classroom and the world," Laramie said.

"But what is she like?" Hap asked.

"Here's what I wrote down. She's 'very smart and graduated summa cum laude.'"

"Now, that can be trouble," Hap mused.

"And she is goal-oriented."

Hap leaned forward, elbow on the table, chin resting in the palm of his hand. "Aren't all teachers?"

"She's committed to her family, sensitive to the needs of others, and quite independent."

"I don't know, Hap . . ." Laramie picked his teeth with a blue plastic toothpick.

Hap slapped the table. "Hey, she's brainy and stubborn, just like me."

"Aunt Paula adds that she is spunky."

"Spunky?" Hap said. "I wonder what your aunt means by spunky?"

"Resilient," Annamarie suggested.

"Tenacious," Laramie said.

"Aggressive," Rosa added.

"Wow, this could be the one," Hap replied. "Does she have 'The Mark'?"

"Most certainly."

"I wonder how long the drive to her place is from here," Hap said.

"About 125 miles from here to the Colorado border. Another seventy-five miles to Wagon Wheel Gap," Rosa blurted out.

"You know the exact mileage?" Hap asked.

"I looked it up. I knew you'd want to know."

"That would take about three hours?" Laramie asked.

"More like four," Rosa continued. "Very little of it is on the interstate."

"Then let's leave in the morning in time to be up there by early afternoon," Hap suggested.

"Sounds like a plan," Laramie replied. "Meanwhile, Annamarie and I will go down and check on the horses."

"We can all go," Hap said.

"Well, partner, we'd like to take a little ride out in the hills."

"Oh, sure. Rosa and me will catch the sunset here. I'd better use the washing machine at the motel. Got to look my best tomorrow." Hap leaned back, stared at the ceiling, and sighed. "I don't know if I'm feelin' this way because this whole dadgum Juanita thing is about over . . . or because this one's the right one. But I'm really feelin' that tomorrow will be a very big day."

⊹⊶═⊙   ⊙═⊷⊹

The room was dark.

The pillow soft.

The sleep sweet.

And Laramie's finger was sharp when he jabbed it into Hap's ribs. "Telephone for you, partner." He fell back on his bed.

Hap sat up, fumbled for his hat, but picked up the phone instead. "Yeah?"

"This is Rosa."

"Are you okay? What time is it?" He jammed on his hat.

"I'm okay. It's 4:00 A.M."

"What's the matter?"

"I need to go, Hap."

He stood up holding the phone in one hand, the receiver in the other. "Go where?"

"I can't go with you to Colorado."

"But, why? I'm countin' on you."

"A friend sent me an urgent message. She needs help. She's alone and needs someone on her side. I've got to go, Hap. It's what I do."

"No, no, no . . ." He paced back and forth between the beds. "That's not what I have planned. I need you."

"You have Laramie and Annamarie. My friend has no one."

"You mean you're leavin' right this minute? Can't your friend wait a couple days?"

"No, I've got to go now."

"I'll be right over to your room. We need to talk."

"I'm not at the hotel, Hap. I'm at the car rental."

"No, not like this, Rosa. I . . . I . . . well, you know, don't you?"

"Hap, I know I like being with you, and you know I'm scared to death of getting my heart broken."

"I would never do that."

"I know that you would never do it on purpose. But that doesn't mean my heart won't break."

"Let's forget Colorado. I don't have to go up there."

There was a long pause. "You'd do that?" she said.

"I don't want you to leave."

"I have to go, just like you have to go to Colorado."

"You're wrong, I don't have to . . ."

"Hap, listen to me. You are four hours away from ending a twenty year quest. If you do not go up there, you will always regret it. And someday you'd resent me for keeping you from it."

He plopped down on the bed. "Go with me, please."

"There are two reasons I can't. First, what if she is the perfect Juanita? What if she says, 'Yes, I was in Wyoming, and I've been waiting for you to find me all these years and I want to bear your twelve daughters'? What if you give her a kiss and embrace that lasts a lifetime? I would die if I had to watch that. I don't think I'm strong enough to bear it."

"But . . . but what if she isn't the right Juanita?"

"And what does that tell me? It says that if you can't find the right one, maybe you can get by with me. Hap, I don't want to be the one you just get by with."

"That's not what I meant, Rosa. I need you."

"So do others."

"Rosa, tell me the truth, is there someone who needs you? Or is that your exit strategy?"

"Yes, she needs me, and I must leave now."

"I'm not thinkin' very clear, but this feels wrong."

"It's right for me. I have to do this. Someday you will understand. Good-bye, Hap."

"No, no, no . . . Rosa . . . this is like a lousy movie. Someone edited in the wrong scene."

"Tell me good-bye."

"Good-bye, Rosa . . . thanks . . ."

Thirty minutes later Hap stopped staring at the phone and collapsed facedown in the pillow.

At 10:00 A.M. they turned left at Española and drove north on Highway 84. Sitting in the middle, Annamarie rubbed Hap's arm. "Can you talk about it now?"

"I don't know what to say. She's gone. That's all."

"And you didn't even see her?" Laramie asked.

"She called from the car rental. It was the middle of the night. I couldn't think straight. Why didn't she wait and talk to me face to face?"

"Maybe she thought the pain would be greater if she did that," Annamarie offered.

Hap slammed his fist into his knee. "I don't reckon the pain could be worse than this."

"Did you think she was just going to stand against the wall forever and wait for you to dance with everyone else in the room?" Annamarie challenged.

"Was that what I was doin'?"

"What do you think you were doing?"

"Keeping a promise I made to a twelve-year-old boy."

"No, it was a promise by a twelve-year-old, not to a twelve-year-old. When I was twelve, I promised I would practice six hours a day to become an Olympic gymnast."

"A gymnast?" Laramie asked.

"Yes. I practiced at a local gym for several months, then

had a chance to audition with a famous coach. Within three minutes, he dismissed me: I was way too tall and much too old to begin."

"And your point is?" Hap probed.

"Not every promise a twelve-year-old makes is worth keeping. There are times to let them go."

"Rosa was probably right about one thing. I would regret not making this one last stop."

"Then let's get it over with," Laramie said. "Maybe you can contact Rosa after this quest is completed."

"I don't know where she went."

"Sounds like a job for next summer . . . 'Finding Rosa,'" Annamarie said.

"Oh, no," Laramie protested. "One of these deals is enough for me."

"Yeah, me, too," Hap muttered. "Me, too."

⊶═⊙　⊙═⊶

The San Juan Mountains stretched along the northeast as they left the café at South Fork, Colorado, and zeroed in on Creede and Wagon Wheel Gap. The sky reflected a deep, bright blue. The fast-moving, but scattered puffs of clouds all looked bleached white from the recent long, hot days of summer.

High in the mountains, just below where timber stopped and granite crags began, aspen trees turned yellow. The highway was no more than a blacktop ribbon that followed the mountain contours and paralleled the river, which narrowed to a creek ten to fifteen feet wide. Rio del Norte was now a much more accurate name than Rio Grande. A light-green forest service truck pulled off on a dirt road and emptied the highway of traffic. On the river side of the road, an occasional house or cabin emerged in the trees.

"It's beautiful up here," Annamarie said.

Laramie rolled down his window. The wind blasted his dark glasses and clean-shaven face. "Breathe that air. That's what I've been missing. South Texas in summer doesn't own air like that."

"Makes me want to keep drivin' north and not stop until we see the Bighorns," Hap mused.

"Have you thought about where we go after Wagon Wheel Gap?" Laramie asked.

"I reckon we can find rooms in Creede. But I don't know about tomorrow. We can go over to I-25 and head north to Fort Collins."

"Are you writing this Juanita off before you meet her?" Annamarie asked.

"I've lost heart. For years I've chased my myth. I sought somethin' I couldn't attain. And it feels like I just lost the very thing I was after. Mamma used to say I'd grow out of this Juanita fascination. Maybe it took me this long to grow up. Kind of sad, ain't it? I might have grown out of it one day too late."

"On the other hand, some never grow up," Annamarie said.

Hap slowed the truck and trailer where a dirt road entered the highway. "What's it say on that mailbox?"

"No name," Annamarie said. "What number are you looking for?"

"It's 4440."

"This is it!"

"There's a cabin behind the trees toward the river," Laramie said.

Hap pulled into the drive. He stopped the rig where an old abandoned barn blocked his view of the cabin. He fingered Rosa's notes. "She's thirty-one years old, has a small place in Wagon Wheel Gap, Colorado, which is south of Creede along the Rio Grande. She's light-complected for a Rodríguez. Looks like Mexico, talks like Chicago. As cute as she can be. Not glamorous, but passable when she dresses up," he recited.

"She graduated from Colorado State University . . . majored in secondary education with a minor in music. She did her student teaching in Loveland. She is not married and has never been married. She likes to travel and has had short-term teaching assignments overseas," Annamarie added.

Laramie cleared his throat "She graduated summa cum laude, is goal-oriented and committed to family. She's sensitive to the needs of others and quite independent."

"And spunky," Hap added. "Which means resilient, tenacious, aggressive."

"Don't forget, she also has 'The Mark,'" Annamarie said.

"We got the description so memorized, we almost know her," Laramie said.

"Are you nervous?" Annamarie asked.

"Not as much as I thought. To tell you the truth, I've got sort of an empty feeling. I'm in a hurry to get this over."

"Maybe you'll be surprised. She sounds like a great gal," Annamarie encouraged.

"She sounds perfect," Hap said. "And if she's as smart as I've been told, she'll tell me, 'Get a life.'"

"If Annamarie is willing to try to put up with the likes of me," Laramie offered, "all things are possible."

Hap pondered the narrow, dirt driveway. "I don't know if there's room to turn the trailer around. I guess we can hike up from here."

"We're not going with you. You're on your own this time, partner," Laramie insisted.

"No, seriously, don't you think it would be better to approach the house together? Wouldn't that be less threatening?"

Annamarie shook her head. "This is your mountain to climb. You've struggled up its steep slope for twenty years. You're about to reach the summit. Time to scale the heights, plant the flag. We'll watch from down here."

"I reckon that's the only way to escape more cheesy analogies," Hap mumbled.

"When all the cowboys hear that final buzzer and are summoned to the great roundup in the sky . . ." Laramie droned.

Hap shoved open the door. "That did it. Nothing could be worse than this drivel."

"Have fun. Enjoy the visit, Hap. I believe a nice person lives there, whether or not she's your Juanita," Annamarie called out.

"Hand me the little black leather box in the glove compartment."

Laramie dug it out. "Are you giving these to this Juanita?"

"If she ain't the one, I'm goin' to hike back there and bury them near the Rio Grande. This is the end of it. Right here. Today."

"Take your time," Laramie said.

"What are you two goin' to do?"

Laramie pasted on a grin. "We're going to sit here and make out."

"Yeah, right. Seriously, I could be tied up a while. It could be two minutes or two hours, I just don't know. What are you really goin' to do?"

Annamarie slipped her hand into Laramie's. "I've been told I need practice at kissing. Laramie has agreed to give me a few lessons. I do wish you would run along."

Hap set his hat, then folded his dark glasses and stuck them in his shirt pocket. He rolled down the sleeves of his black shirt and snapped the cuffs, tugged on his silver belt buckle, and wiped the toes of his brown boots on the back of his black jeans.

He let out a deep sigh, but didn't look back at the truck.

The driveway around the old barn was strewn with pine needles and large granite gravel that crunched beneath his steps. He cleared the barn and a row of spruce trees before he spied the log cabin. The front yard was no more than dirt scattered with pine needles and freshly mowed weeds. Two large windows covered with lace curtains prevented his seeing in. White smoke drifted out of the river rock chimney. The steep, green metal roof told a story of deep snow and cold winters.

Hap couldn't spot any trees behind the dwelling, just green weeds and brush sloping off toward the creeklike Rio Grande, which he could see but not hear. Someone inside played a piano. It sounded soft, contemplative, not loud enough for him to distinguish the tune, but familiar enough to make him feel welcome.

The little front porch had a door to the mud room. A small, hand-scrawled sign was thumbtacked to the door: "Step inside and knock on the inner door."

Hap entered to a musty scent, like that of a room seldom used. Dried-out rubber boots perched on a milk crate. A heavy, wool-trimmed parka hung on a peg. The stained-glass oval window in the door glowed with bright colors, but blocked any images from inside the room. The bass notes on the piano sounded melancholy, but the treble ones reflected a hint of joy.

He tugged on his ear.

Scratched his neck.

Pushed his hat back.

Rocked on his heels.

Took a deep breath.

And knocked.

The music stopped. From somewhere deep in the house a feminine voice rang out, "Yes . . . who is it?"

Hap waited for the door to open. When it didn't, he leaned forward. "Ma'am, my name's Hap Bowman, I'm from Wyomin'. Your aunt Paula from El Paso gave me your address and said I should stop by and visit you if I got up your way."

He heard floorboards creak, but the voice was still muffled. "What do you want?"

"Ma'am, I'd really like to tell you in person. If you aren't comfortable with my comin' in, can we talk out in the yard?"

The voice was still indistinct. "What do you want to talk about?"

"A silly dream of mine that has already cost me ever'thin'. I'm hopin' you can put it to rest."

The door swung open.

A woman in her early thirties, with, black, wavy hair, thick eyebrows, and black jeans stood barefoot in front of him. Her trimmed toenails were polished bright red. She wore a scooped-neck pink T-shirt with burgundy-colored words emblazoned on the front: *Ponder Rosa*.

Hap gaped. He moved his lips but it took a moment before any words came out. "Rosa? Wha . . . what are you doin' here?"

"This is my house. This is where I live when I'm not traipsing around the world."

"But . . . where's that other Juanita?"

"All of those things I told you about her are true, except for one. Her name isn't Juanita. It's Rosa. That was all about me, Hap."

He waved his arms like a drowning man. "But, what about that person who needed your help?"

"It was me, too. I needed to do something for Rosa Rodríguez Tryor."

"Why the pretense? Why go through all of this?"

Rosa bit her lip. "Because I wanted so bad to be your Juanita. I wanted to be the one you were so crazy to find."

He stepped forward and circled his arms around her. She leaned on his chest and cried. "I'm sorry, Hap. I'm sorry. I just have a difficult time believing that I'm not the one for you."

He kissed her neck, her cheek, her forehead. "Somethin' inside me died last night when you phoned. All day today, I've been in agony."

"What do you think died?"

"This idiot obsession about findin' a girl I met when I was twelve. I realized it doesn't matter anymore. Your words in the night purged my heart. I didn't even want to come up here. All I wanted was you back. Annamarie made me come up here. I reckon you know that I love you."

She cradled his cheeks and gazed into his eyes. She brushed a kiss across his lips. "Hap, I am not your dream girl. I am not perfect. But I do love you, too. And I know I can learn to love you better. But, listen to me. I will never be able to change the fact that I am not Juanita."

He kissed her firmly on the lips. When he leaned back, a wide, easy grin filled his leather-tough, tanned face. He handed her the small leather box. "These are for you."

"Your rock and the little girl's bracelet? Hap . . . let me be your Juanita."

"No, darlin' . . . I lost that dream last night when you phoned and I never want it back. I don't need a Juanita. I don't want that girl I met when I was twelve. I need you. You will now and forever be my Rosa."